Tailspinner

Frank Bennett Adirondack Mountain Mystery Series, Volume 5

S.W. Hubbard

Published by S.W. Hubbard, 2018.

TAILSPINNER

First edition. December 8, 2018.

Written by S.W. Hubbard.

Chapter 1

Police Chief Frank Bennett vaulted up the steps of the Trout Run Town office powered by a flash of inspiration that had struck in the middle of the night. Eager to share it with his second in command, he dashed past Doris, as ever, on the phone, and flung open the door to the office he shared with Earl.

Empty.

Frank glanced at the clock. 8:15. Very unusual for Earl not to already be at his desk scanning any reports that had come in overnight from the State Police. The patrol vehicle was parked out front, so he wasn't out on a call.

Frank returned to the outer office and stood in front of Doris until she acknowledged his presence with her gaze even as she continued her conversation about the best way to get a grease stain off a tablecloth. "Where's Earl?"

Doris shrugged while writing on a scratch pad. She held up the paper for Frank to read: Not in yet.

Frank sighed and returned to his desk. He was restless to launch his plan. The summer concerts on the green were due to start next week, and Frank thought he'd finally figured out a way to control the traffic flow in the center of town. If this plan worked, directing traffic wouldn't be a two-man job, so one of them could keep an eye on the crowd of concert-goers. And, as an additional benefit, listen to the performance. But the plan required a series of signs, and he wanted to map them out with Earl.

Where was he?

Frank looked at the clock on the wall for the third time in five minutes. He was positive his plan would work. Maybe he'd just call the road department to order the signs right now. His hand hesitated on the phone.

What about that third turn? Earl would have some ideas. He'd better wait. Frank busied himself looking through the state police reports that Earl usually reviewed.

When he reassured himself that no dangerous criminal activity had occurred anywhere near his turf yesterday, he glanced at the clock again. 8:35.

Had Earl told him that he'd be late? Had he forgotten? Or was there a problem? Just as he picked up his phone to call Earl, the familiar Ford pickup rolled into the parking lot.

Seconds later, Earl walked through the door.

"Hey! Where've you been?"

Earl slid into his chair with his eyes downcast and fired up his computer. "Sorry I'm late. I overslept."

Overslept? Earl always rose with the birds. No matter. Frank launched into his road sign plan as he dug through a filing cabinet looking for last year's concert parking diagram.

"Whattaya think? Will it work?" Frank slammed the drawer and spun around.

Earl winced.

For the first time that morning, Frank looked closely at his assistant. "You look kinda pale. Are you feeling okay?"

"Just a headache," Earl said. "Do we have any Tylenol?"

Frank tossed him the plastic bottle. Earl raised his hand a moment too late, and the bottle ricocheted into the middle of the room.

Frank picked it up on his way to show Earl a comparison of the two diagrams. "I think if we keep the cars flowing in one direction around the green, and then block off Chestnut Street, we can create a parking area with one entrance and one exit, instead of the free-for-all we had last year. Except I'm worried about this turn. Do you think people will peel off and try to go in the other direction?"

"Huh?" Earl massaged his temples.

Frank tapped the diagram. "Right here. Do you think—"

Just then Doris entered bearing a Tupperware container. "Look what I brought you, Earl. My sister Gloria made her famous venison sausage casserole. I told her I hafta take some in to Earl. He just loves it."

The heady scent of onions, game, and fennel wafted through the office.

Earl's eyes widened. He leaped from his chair and tore across the room, nearly knocking Doris down in his sprint toward the men's room.

Frank nudged her back toward her own desk. "Better put that in the fridge and save it for tomorrow."

"But..."

Luckily, the phone rang, saving Frank from further explanation.

He now knew what was wrong but saw no need to share with their gossipy secretary.

For the first time in the five years they'd worked together, Earl was hungover.

On a Wednesday?

THE STORY EMERGED AFTER Earl returned, shaky and gray-faced.

"I ran into Billy Flynn at the Stop 'n' Buy last night after work."

Frank knew the guys Earl usually hung around with. Billy Flynn didn't ring a bell. "Do I know him?"

Earl shook his head. "He's been in the Marines since before you moved to Trout Run. I hadn't seen him since high school graduation. He enlisted right after, and he's been all over—Iraq, Afghanistan. Now he's out and back home in Trout Run. He asked me to go to the Mountainside for a beer."

"Looks like you had more than one." Frank was more amused than shocked. He'd never known Earl to drink more than a couple beers.

Earl massaged his temples. "It was the tequila that did me in."

"Tequila? I didn't know the Mountainside even stocked tequila." The nectar of the agave seemed pretty exotic for Trout Run's grittiest tavern.

"Billy learned to drink it in the Marines. He kept buying more rounds."

"How did you get home?" Earl was a stickler. He'd write a DUI citation to ladies who'd had two glasses of wine at book club.

"Walter drove us."

Frank laughed. "Damn good thing you're a cop. I've never known any of the Mountainside's bartenders to offer chauffeur service to drunks."

"Then I had to go back over there this morning to get my truck. Billy's truck was still there. He's only been home a week or so, so he doesn't have a job yet." Earl took a long drink of water. "He kept saying how he dreamed of Trout Run every day he was over there fighting. He was so glad to be back. It was hard to say 'Gotta go. Catch you later', you know?"

"I understand." Frank clapped him on the shoulder. "Go on home. Take a long nap. You'll be fine tomorrow."

Earl looked at the pile of work on his desk. "But I should—"

"Go. It'll be waiting for you when you get back."

Chapter 2

Frank set off on the morning patrol with the windows of the department SUV rolled down. The worst of blackfly season had finally passed, and the cool, late June air didn't require AC. He drove past the old covered bridge which crossed Stony Brook, still high from all the spring rain. The water could put goosebumps on an Eskimo, but with the school year finally over, the rocks below the bridge would soon be filled with swimmers and sunbathers. But at nine-thirty in the morning, the brook surged over the rocks unimpeded by people.

After he climbed the hill on the other side of the brook, Frank saw two men on ladders taking down the sign in front of the defunct Asian Bistro restaurant. The place had opened with great fanfare last year. It wasn't often that a new culinary hotspot disrupted the usual routine of eating at Malone's Diner or the Trail's End, so everyone in a twenty-mile radius had gone to eat there once. But this ill-considered attempt to bring sushi and pad thai to the North Country was doomed to failure. There simply wasn't enough customer traffic to ensure the freshness of the tuna and salmon. And men who worked outdoors all day plowing snow or repairing roofs didn't want a platter of cold raw fish or a bowl of noodles and snow peas for dinner. So the Asian Bistro had closed, and the nice building the investors had built stood empty for months, some forlorn Chinese lanterns over the deck still blowing in the breeze. The sudden activity of workmen indicated another business was taking a stab at finding success in that spot.

Frank drove on, daydreaming about the possibility of a Bar-B-Que restaurant or a good Italian place. He'd have to ask Doris when he got back to the office. As the issuer of building permits, she always knew what was going on. In fact, it was strange that she hadn't already mentioned the coming of a new business to town. Then again, perhaps she had somewhere in the daily tsunami of words that Frank tuned out.

Frank made the next turn in his circuit around the outskirts of Trout Run. Two muddy and grizzled backpackers trudged along the side of the road. They'd probably just come down from hiking Dix Mountain and were heading toward the parking area a quarter mile from the trailhead. When they saw the police car come into view, they suddenly started jumping up and down and waving their hands like bearded cheerleaders without pom-poms.

Frank pulled over.

"What's the problem, guys?"

The two young men crowded around the window of the patrol car. "There's a guy up there on the trail," the taller hiker pointed behind himself. "We think there's something wrong with him."

"He's in trouble," the other hiker chimed in. "He was wandering off the trail with no water. We asked him if he was lost...offered to lead him out. But he ran away from us. He was talking crazy."

"Crazy how?"

The taller hiker grimaced. "We couldn't understand him. I mean, the words were English, but he wasn't answering the questions we were asking. It was like he was having his own conversation with someone who wasn't there."

"Dehydration can do strange things to a person," Frank said. "This early in the morning, he must've been out all night to be in such bad shape. You say he didn't have a backpack?"

"Just a little daypack."

Inexperienced, unprepared hikers were a growing problem in the High Peaks. Vacationers came expecting a stroll in the woods and got rugged terrain and changeable weather they hadn't bargained for. "He must've been out in that cold rain last night."

The hikers nodded. "He was wearing a wet cotton T-shirt and shorts—no fleece, no rain gear."

"Age?"

"Early twenties, thin. He looked fit enough to hike the trail. He just didn't have the right gear."

"I'll call it in to the rangers. How far up the trail did you encounter him?"

They exchanged a glance. "I think we hiked about twenty minutes after we left him before we got to the trailhead."

"Thanks—you did a good deed. We'll take it from here."

Frank squinted at Dix Mountain looming on the horizon. It didn't have to be winter for a person to die of exposure in the Adirondacks.

Chapter 3

When Frank called the Department of Environmental Conservation forest ranger outpost in Keene, he was glad to hear Rusty Magill's voice answer. All the DEC rangers were good, but Rusty was the best: calm, exceptionally fit, and tremendously knowledgeable. He knew the High Peaks Wilderness like a mother knows every inch of her infant's body.

"Not another lost hiker!" Rusty complained. "That's the third extraction this week. We're coming up to a full moon. Brings out all the crazies."

"It'll take you twenty minutes to get here," Frank said. "I'll start up the trail and see if I can locate him."

Frank could sense the objection ready to come through the line. "I'll stay on the trail. No bushwhacking, I promise." He knew Rusty didn't want to be searching for rescuers as well as hikers.

Frank parked the patrol car as close to the trailhead as possible. He always kept a backpack with some emergency gear stowed in the trunk, and now he slung it onto his back and headed up the trail. He wasn't wearing the best boots to navigate the rocks and tree roots disrupting the path, but at least the steepest part of the climb hadn't begun yet. Hopefully he'd find the lost hiker before the real scramble began. He walked steadily upward through the birch and balsam, pausing occasionally to listen. But all he heard was the chattering of a chipmunk and the rush of a small stream.

The scenery here was nothing special. The lookouts with glorious vistas of Elk Lake were several miles in. So there was no reason for a hiker to be tempted off the trail here. Frank assumed the young man had become exhausted and disoriented on the way down the trail. People could get hopelessly lost in the forest even when they were only a mile from civilization.

Frank stumbled over a root and turned his ankle. "Godammit!" he protested. A good, loud shout always soothed an injury.

A weak voice answered him from somewhere further up the trail. "No...don't...I'm trying."

I'm trying? Or did he say, "I'm dying"?

"Hey! Stay where you are. I'm coming to help you." Frank quickened his pace, but the trail grew rougher and he had to watch his step. "Where are you? Shout again."

Silence.

Frank pulled out his binoculars and scanned the dense forest looking for a human amid the trees.

Rocks...leaves...logs...*movement*. Just a flash.

He scanned back, adjusting the focus. A young man came into view. Crouched on his haunches, he held his head in his hands. His mud-caked clothes and limbs provided excellent camouflage.

Frank thrashed through the undergrowth to reach him.

The kid lifted his head, eyes round with fear, and raised his hands as if warding off an attack. "No, no—please. I'm trying."

"Easy, son." Frank slipped off his pack. "Let's get you some water and food." He held out a bottle of water to the hiker, but the young man edged away like a skittish stray dog. Frank unfurled the silver space blanket, and the hiker rose and staggered a few steps further away from the trail. Then he swayed and collapsed in a heap.

Frank rushed to the hiker's side. The kid's lips were blue and his pulse rapid and thready. Frank covered him with the blanket and radioed Rusty. Luckily, the rangers were much faster hikers than Frank and were already just ten minutes down the trail.

Frank watched over the unconscious patient as he awaited their arrival. The kid didn't have any obvious injuries. He looked to be in his mid-twenties, tall and thin with a scruffy, two-day growth of beard, matted auburn hair, and prominent eyebrows.

Soon Frank could hear the rangers on the trail and shouted to direct them to his location. First Rusty appeared, his bright orange hair like a beacon in the green and brown landscape. Two other rangers, a guy in his forties whom Frank had met before, and an attractive young woman who must be new, were right behind him carrying all the rescue gear.

Rusty clapped Frank on the shoulder. "Thanks, man. You made this one easy."

Easily the friendliest, most easy-going man that Frank knew, Rusty looked entirely disgusted as he watched the other two rangers tend to the hiker. "I don't understand what possesses people to go into the wilderness totally unprepared. Look at his shoes. Look at his shirt."

Frank's gaze left the victim's face and took in the rest of his body: a torn Grateful Dead t-shirt, cargo shorts, and Teva water sandals. His feet were filthy, and his toes cracked and crusted with dried blood.

"How did you spot him?" Rusty asked.

"He just passed out a minute ago. Before he went down, he cried out. Good thing, or I would have passed right by." Frank kept talking as the rangers loaded the hiker onto a stretcher. "The weird thing is, when I found him, he tried to run away from me, like he was scared of me."

———◆———

FRANK HAD OFFERED TO help carry the stretcher down the trail, but the young woman ranger took that as a challenge to her competence. She hadn't left the fallen hiker's side and wasn't about to surrender her position now. Given her impressive fitness, Frank reluctantly conceded to himself that she was far less likely to stumble under the load than he was.

As they reached the end of the trail, Frank could see the Trout Run EMS crew standing next to their ambulance. "Do you think they can handle this kid in Saranac, or will we need the chopper to take him to Plattsburgh?" The Adirondack Medical Center in Saranac Lake was the nearest hospital, but it wasn't a trauma center.

"There's not a mark on him," Rusty said. "So he must not have fallen. If he just passed out from dehydration, our boys can fix him up and transport him."

A few moments later, the rescue party entered the clearing at the trailhead. The stretcher-bearers set down their patient and the medics sprang into action. Frank and Rusty watched as they started an IV line to give the young man fluids and checked his vital signs.

"Where's the rest of his gear?" one of the medics asked.

Rusty dropped a small daypack on the ground and kicked it toward the ambulance. "Look at that! I wouldn't send a kid to kindergarten with so little gear."

"No layers, no wind or rain protection, ridiculous shoes—I mean, who hikes the High Peaks in sandals? And we found wrappers for two granola bars in his pack and one empty one-liter water bottle. That's it. No phone. No compass. No map."

"If those other hikers hadn't flagged me down, this guy would be dead from exposure and dehydration by the end of the day," Frank said.

The medics had draped the hiker with a blanket. As the bag of saline solution dripped into his vein, the young man on the stretcher began to stir. One medic dropped to his knees and rubbed the hiker's hand between his own. "Hey, buddy—how you feeling? Can you open your eyes? Can you tell us your name?"

The hiker's eyelids fluttered. He worked to open his mouth, but his lips were so dry they stuck together. The medic lifted the patient's head and held a cup of water to his mouth. He drank eagerly, then coughed and choked.

"Easy there." The medic pulled the cup away. "What's your name?"

"Charlie," he rasped.

"Charlie, good. You're going to be okay, buddy. Can you tell us what day it is?"

Charlie shook his head.

Rusty ran his hand through his wiry red hair. "God knows how long he's been lost."

"Charlie, what month is it?" Frank watched as the medic tried to assess the patient's mental acuity.

The hiker flopped back on the stretcher, his eyes glazed and blank.

The medic tried again. "Charlie, who's the president of the United States?"

"Trump," he whispered.

"That's right. Now Charlie, are you in pain anywhere? Did you hit your head?"

Charlie squirmed on the stretcher. As he slowly came to consciousness, he realized he was strapped down. He struggled against the restraints.

"Easy there, Charlie. We're going to move you onto this gurney and then put you in the ambulance for a trip to the Adirondack Medical Center. Now, can you tell me—"

"No!" The word shot out of him with surprising volume. Charlie twisted and thrashed against the stretcher. "I need to go back." His voice sounded raw and cracked.

"Get me some lorazepam," the medic said to his assistant. "You're not in shape to go anywhere right now, Charlie."

Rusty's forehead creased in concern. "Could he have been with someone else?" Rusty stepped closer to the hiker. "Charlie, were you hiking alone, or with a friend?"

Now the hiker's eyes focused. He looked at all the people gazing down at him and his eyes widened in panic. "I need to go back. Let me go."

"Charlie, did you get separated from a friend? Let us know and we'll go back and search for him. Or her."

"No! I need to go alone. I was so close. So close. Now it's ruined."

"What's ruined?" Frank asked the group at large.

"Maybe he was on one of those Outward Bound type trips, where you're supposed to survive in the woods using your own skills," one of the rangers suggested. "Maybe he doesn't want to admit that he flunked the test."

"Dressed like that?" Rusty snorted. "Outward Bound teaches self-reliance, not recklessness."

The medic got down on his knees to soothe his patient. "Easy, Charlie. Talk to me. What's troubling you?"

"Trying...blue...can't fail." His head lolled on the stretcher as if this speech had exhausted him.

"He must've been trying to get back to the blue trail. Maybe that's why he wouldn't follow the white trail markers when those hikers tried to lead him out." Frank offered this theory.

"He's delirious. Dehydration and hunger can make a person talk crazy." The medic rose. "C'mon guys. Let's get him loaded in the bus."

Frank stood next to Rusty and watched the ambulance roar off. "What do you think that was all about?"

Rusty heaved the heavy rescue pack onto his shoulder and glanced up at the morning sky where the pale outline of the almost-full moon was still visible. "I'm telling you—the full moon brings out all the nut jobs."

Chapter 4

Frank charged through the open area of the town office preoccupied with how to handle the day's work without Earl. He paused and turned back to Doris's desk. "Hey, I meant to ask you—what's going on at the old Asian Bistro? Is there a new restaurant going in there?"

Doris made a face that looked remarkably like the "yucky" emoji on a smartphone. "Not a restaurant. Some kind of new church. The Tabernacle of Living Light, whatever *that* means."

"A church? So it's non-profit—not bringing in any tax revenue. What does Reid have to say about that?" The chairman of the Town Council struggled endlessly to balance the municipal books without raising taxes.

"Fit to be tied. But their paperwork is in order, even if they're not a real church."

Doris was Catholic, and Frank suspected she didn't consider Trout Run Presbyterian to be a "real" church either. But her news about the new church had piqued his interest. "So does the church own the building, or are they renting it from the Asian Bistro owners? I never saw a For Sale sign on the property."

"I haven't processed a title transfer, so I guess the church is just renting." Doris swiveled in her desk chair to face Frank. "But that isn't the *big* real estate news in town." She sat silently with a smug smile on her face.

Although he found her behavior galling, Frank had no choice but to play along. "What is?"

"You know that organic cafe and market in Keene that everyone's so crazy about?"

"Yeah, the Hungry Loon. Penny loves the place." Even though his wife couldn't persuade him to eat their quinoa or their kale salad, he had to admit their marinated chicken and their homemade soup were quite delicious.

Doris sat beaming at him, demanding that he beg some more.

Frank swallowed his ire. "What about it?"

"They're opening a branch here in Trout Run in the old Murdoch house right off the green. The house sold months ago."

"Wow! I was thinking that the Hungry Loon could've moved into the Asian Bistro building. But to have it located right off the green would be even better." Frank walked to the front door and peered out. From this angle, he could only see a corner of the Murdoch house and the back of a pick-up truck parked on the street in front of it. He returned to Doris's desk. "I've noticed some remodeling work going on there, but I thought it was a new family moving in."

"We all did, but you know that house is awful close to the street if you've got kids. Today I decided to go over there and ask if they needed any help painting. Because my nephew does house-painting on the side."

So far as Frank knew, Doris's nephew didn't have a real job for painting to be on the side of, but he let it pass. He was pretty sure if there was work to be had, someone more enterprising than Doris's nephew had already snatched it up.

"I didn't see anyone around, but the front door was open, so I went in. And I saw a newly built display case and counter in what used to be old man Murdoch's living room. Then one of the workers came back and he about jumped up to the ceiling, I startled him so bad. He wanted to get back to work, but I was bound and determined to find out what he was building. 'Cause obviously a business was moving in."

Frank grinned as he imagined some poor unsuspecting carpenter on the receiving end of Doris's verbal onslaught.

"So while he was hammering, I asked him questions and I found out the Hungry Loon is coming, and the grand opening is next week."

Much as he hated to reward Doris by showing too much interest, Frank found himself hooked. "Next week! So soon? Why hasn't there been any news about it?"

Doris gave an elaborate shrug. "Those people who run the Hungry Loon in Keene are real hippy-dippy."

Ponytails and Birkenstocks notwithstanding, the owners of the Hungry Loon had made a smashing success of their first store, so clearly they knew something about marketing and promotion. "Just seems strange that they'd keep it so quiet. Why not spread the word as much as possible?"

Doris swiveled back to her filing. "Maybe they weren't sure how long the remodeling would take, and they didn't want people to be dropping by pestering them all day long."

"Like you?"

"I should've pestered them sooner." Doris heaved a resigned sigh. "No work for my nephew now. They don't need a painter."

Frank left Doris to her work and went back to his desk to call Penny.

"I hope you're sitting down," he warned before hitting her with the news of the Hungry Loon's imminent arrival. Frank got the squeal of delight he had been expecting from his wife, as well as a barrage of who, when and how questions.

"Does Edwin know?" Penny finally asked. "He and Lucy will be over the moon with excitement."

Their best friends, transplanted Manhattanites who owned the Iron Eagle Inn, always complained that what they missed the most about big city life was the 24-hour Korean vegetable market down the street from their apartment. Now fresh produce and gourmet seasonings would be available right in Trout Run.

"I ran into him at The Store yesterday and he didn't mention it."

"Oooo, The Store," Penny murmured. "The Sobels can't be too happy about this."

"Yeah, The Store will finally have some competition."

Penny wasn't a fan of Trout Run's only food market. "Butch and Rita Sobel don't even bother trying to please their customers. If you ask me, a little competition will get them to up their game."

Frank heard a library patron asking Penny a question. "Gotta run," she told him. "I'll call Edwin later."

Frank gazed at the phone, lost in thought. While it was true that the Sobels' maddening mish-mash of useful and bizarre products seemed to fly in the face of the basic rules of merchandizing, The Store had been serving Trout Run for three generations. The town wouldn't be better off if a gourmet emporium closed down the only place a person could buy a ham and cheese sandwich, a quart of milk, and a roll of toilet paper.

Surely Reid Burlingame knew about the arrival of the new business. Frank moved his hand toward the phone to call the chairman of the Town

Council, but the secretary in Reid's one-man law office said he was tied up with a real estate closing. Frank declined to leave a message. State Police reports had piled up on his desk while he was out on the morning patrol. He'd catch up with Reid some other time.

With Earl out, the day passed quickly. A canoe that had been reported stolen from the rental place on Beacon Pond was reported found by a good Samaritan who'd noticed it sitting on the shore for days at the Wilmington boat launch. The State Police arrived to take possession of a stash of oxycontin pills Frank had seized after arresting two punks in a barfight last weekend. Before he'd even drunk his third mug of coffee, it was time for the afternoon patrol. He headed out with a wave to Doris and drove north toward Verona. He hadn't put more than five miles on the patrol car when Doris's agitated voice came over the radio.

"We have a call. Domestic disturbance at 39 Robinson Road. Martha and Gene Flynn."

Frank turned on the flashing lights and made a U-turn toward Robinson Road, talking to Doris as he drove. "We ever had a call from them before?" The name sounded so familiar, but he couldn't recall ever answering a call at that address.

"No. It's not the husband and wife fighting. It's Gene and their son, Billy. Martha called it in."

Flynn. Billy Flynn. Of course—Earl's friend just home from the Marines. Frank accelerated. Domestic disturbances were among the most dangerous calls he had to respond to. Angry people were always unpredictable. Billy had been out drinking and was probably even more hung-over than Earl. Returning veterans could be unstable. There were probably guns in the home.

"What did Martha say? Is she in danger?"

"She was real wound up. There was a lot of screaming and crashing in the background. You better hurry."

Frank sped to Robinson Road. He would arrive in less than ten minutes. But a lot could go wrong in a domestic disturbance in that length of time. Of all days for Earl to be out! He could really use his help here. As he drove, Frank reviewed his de-escalation techniques: separate, distract, get them seated. He turned into a long drive, passing a sign that read Flynn's Wood Services• Woodstoves •Firewood• Cutting & Clearing.

Frank skidded to a stop in a driveway that held five pick-up trucks, three cars, and two ATVs. A small motor boat on a trailer rested in the yard next to a collection of canoes and kayaks. Further back on the property was a barn and the biggest stack of firewood Frank had ever seen. He stepped over a long dog leash on the way to the open front door. Great. Nothing like an angry, defensive mutt to make a bad situation even worse.

Before he made it up the porch steps, the sounds of the argument poured from the house.

"In my house, you'll do as I say!"

"I was smart enough to stay alive killing terrorists for four years. I don't need advice from you."

A crash, as if someone had thrown something.

"Stop! Both of you." A woman's high-pitched wail.

The dog barked ferociously. Of course, the Flynns wouldn't own some powderpuff.

Frank bounded up the steps and positioned himself to the right of the door. In a town where just about everyone owned a gun and absolutely no one appreciated outside interference in personal problems, Frank was acutely aware that the family's anger could be redirected to him in an instant. He pounded loudly on the doorframe. "Trout Run police. What's the trouble here?"

Silence.

"No trouble." The man who must be Gene struggled to keep his tone level. "You can leave. We don't need anything."

"I can't leave until I speak to the person who made the call. Send her to the door, please." Frank peered into the house, but the bright sunlight made it hard to see much in the dim interior.

Frank could hear low, agitated conversation, but could only understand the occasional word. "...why...everyone...our business...rid..."

In a moment, a wiry woman in her late forties appeared at the door. Frank recognized her immediately. She worked behind the counter at the Rock Slide outdoor equipment store, and he'd seen her at the Stop 'N' Buy and the post office. Always pleasant but quiet. Not an outsize personality. He hadn't connected the name and this anxious, weathered face. Her eyebrows tilted up at the center, as if she'd spent her entire adult life gazing heavenward seeking divine intervention.

Martha Flynn mustered a shaky greeting. "I'm sorry we bothered you. Everything's fine. You can go."

Frank offered his most reassuring smile. "Sure. I just need a few details to close out the call." He reached for the door knob and gestured to the porch. "Step out here for a moment, would you?"

Let him get Martha out of the fray. Then he'd focus on separating the men.

Martha cast a nervous glance over her shoulder and an equally nervous glance at the uniformed officer on her porch. Then she slipped out the door, hugging herself as she stood before Frank.

"I hear your son just came home from a tour with the Marines." Frank spoke as if he were chatting at the diner. "We appreciate his service."

Martha smiled shakily. "We're real proud of him. It's just...well, it's an adjustment having him back. He was just a boy when he left."

"It can be hard to remember your kids are grown-ups. Believe me, I know." Frank extended his hands, palms up. "I'd love to meet Billy. I think he left before I started as police chief here. Could you call him out here please? Just to say hello."

"Billy?" Martha's voice quavered. "Could you come here, please? Chief Bennett wants to meet you."

"Get lost," a voice roared from within. Maybe Billy. Probably Gene.

"Does either one of them have a gun?" Frank asked.

Martha's face contorted with worry. She was afraid to answer. She didn't need to.

Separating the two men grew more urgent. Frank's presence as a witness had temporarily silenced the argument. But he could practically feel the men's rage bubbling through the door.

"Billy and Gene have been arguing a lot?" He wanted information he could use to draw one of the men out of the house.

Martha twisted the hem of her shirt. "I'm...we're...so relieved to have him home safe. But...." A door slammed inside the house and Martha flinched. Then she lowered her voice and spoke to Frank in a rush. "Gene thinks Billy should be out looking for a job. My husband has a real strong work ethic."

Frank thought that a man who'd spent several years dodging roadside bombs and sniper's bullets deserved some time to chill out. But maybe Billy had been doing all his unwinding at the Mountainside Tavern. "Has Billy been drinking? Is that why they're arguing?"

Martha chewed her thumbnail and gave a quick nod. "He was out late last night. Gene is irritated that Billy just woke up. I shouldn't have called you, but they were both getting madder and madder." She rubbed her temples. "They've calmed down. I can handle everything myself now. You can go."

"I'd like to go in and have a word with Gene, just to make sure." Frank turned toward the door.

Martha grabbed his sleeve. "No!"

Her command, loud and shrill, prompted a thunder of footsteps from within.

The screen door flew open and crashed against the house. "I'm outta here!" A tall, muscular young man glanced back over his shoulder. Then Billy Flynn charged past his mother and stumbled down the porch steps two at a time.

A middle-aged version of the same powerful man appeared at the door. "Go on back to damn Afghanistan if that's how you want to live. In this house, we wake up in the *morning* and— "

Billy stood on the front walk facing the house, his face purple with rage. "Shut the fuck up!"

Now Gene flung the screen door open and came onto the porch, his hands clenched in fists. "Don't you *ever* talk like that in front of your mother! I'll knock your teeth right out of your head."

Before Frank could move, Martha lunged toward her husband and grabbed at his arm. "Gene, stop. Don't say that. Honey, he didn't mean— "

"Don't defend him!" Gene shook his wife off like a pesky fly. She staggered, and Frank moved to catch her, but she regained her balance just a step away from the porch stairs.

"You care about a curse word but you're willing to push my mother down the stairs?" In three long strides, Billy propelled himself back onto the porch.

Gene lowered his head like a charging bull.

"St-o-o-op!" Martha flung herself between the two men and fell to her knees.

"Gene, Billy—that's enough." Frank stepped forward to pull Martha out of harm's way.

His action was a squirt of lighter fluid on a white-hot barbeque grill.

Both men pivoted toward Frank.

"Get the hell offa my property," Gene screamed. "I can manage my own family."

"Yeah, don't help my mother. He likes to see her beg."

Gene threw the first punch, a powerful roundhouse that could've killed a man.

Nimble Billy danced out of its path and caught only a glancing blow. He spun around and grabbed his father in a headlock.

Now Frank watched 450 pounds of combined muscle and anger stagger in a deadly tango. What good was his gun against two citizens of Trout Run who on any other day loved each other? He pulled out his baton to break Billy's grip on Gene's neck.

As soon as Gene was free, he reached for something in his back pocket.

Martha screamed.

With one deft move, Frank stepped behind the angry father, grabbed his arms, and used his own leg to bring the other man to his knees.

While Gene fought like a hooked bass, Frank panted a command to Billy. "Take a walk. Your dad and I are going to have a conversation."

Billy didn't move. Frank could discern the pleasure in the son's eyes as he saw his father laid low.

"Get outta here, you bastard," Gene spit. "And don't come back. You're no son of mine."

Billy opened his mouth to get in one more dig, but now Martha struggled to her feet and pulled her son off the porch.

Billy had keys in his hand but hesitated as he surveyed the driveway with a bewildered expression. Clearly, he'd forgotten where he'd left his truck.

"Walk," Frank called out, glad that Billy's truck was still in the Mountainside parking lot. The last thing he needed was an angry, hung-over Marine careening around mountain curves.

Billy hunched his shoulders and loped down the driveway.

Gradually, Frank eased his grip on the father.

So much for de-escalation.

Chapter 5

Gene shook off Frank's helping hand and rose to his feet.

"Now, let's go inside and talk," Frank said. "You okay, Martha?"

She hugged the porch rail, keeping a good ten feet between herself and her husband.

Gene had an eternally tanned and wind-burned face. Although his brown hair was thinning, he was still a good-looking man with broad shoulders and powerful arms. He met Frank's gaze, nodded briefly, and walked inside.

Martha let Frank go ahead of her. They followed Gene into the living room, a space with a large sofa and several recliners facing a wide-screen TV. The mounted head of a twelve-point buck hung above the stone fireplace. A large black retriever growled in the doorway that led to the next room.

Gene did not sit down. He faced Frank with his legs spread and his arms folded in front of him. His jaw tilted upwards as he spoke. "This is my house. I built it with my own hands, with money I earned through my own hard work. I've worked every day of my life since I was old enough to swing an ax. I expect every member of this family to do the same."

Frank took a deep breath. This was the point in the domestic violence response when he was supposed to agree and murmur words of understanding, but honestly, it was a struggle. As a father he wanted to say, "give the kid a freakin' break." As a police officer he said, "So, I'm hearing you say you're concerned that Billy hasn't found a job yet."

"If he's not going to look for a real job, he can damn well help me just like he used to when he was in high school. I have a project over near Placid today, trimming some trees that are getting too big near a house. I'm getting too old to climb trees. I rousted him outta bed to help me. I'm feeding him and putting a roof over his head. And he lays around on his ass all day while I'm bustin' my hump."

Frank thought the last thing a hung-over Billy Flynn should be doing today was climbing a tree while carrying a chainsaw, but he kept that opinion to himself.

"I understand. You're a hardworking man and you value that quality in others. I'm just suggesting that you ease off Billy for a while, give him a chance to get adjusted to being back in Trout Run. It's a culture shock. He might even be experiencing some PTSD."

"Don't start with that BS!" Gene's mouth twisted, and he gave a dismissive wave. "My grandfather fought in the Invasion of Normandy. Had to run right into a Nazi firestorm. Came home and started back to logging the next day. This generation is a bunch of wusses."

"You never served at all," Martha murmured.

Gene spun toward his wife. "What'd you say?"

Frank agreed with Martha, but her remark sure didn't advance the cause of getting everyone settled down. Martha must be feeling emboldened by Frank's presence, but she might regret her comment later on. "I tell you what. I'm going to get Billy connected with Trudy Massinay, the county social worker. She can provide some counseling and help him access— "

Gene kicked an overstuffed ottoman and barged toward the door, hollering as he went. "Billy doesn't need any damn shrink. That kid needs a good boot up his butt."

The front door slammed, and Martha perched on the edge of the sofa. She held her wrist up to her forehead as if she'd just finished hauling a load of bricks.

"Is Gene always so angry?"

"It's my fault. I should've woken Billy up this morning."

Frank suppressed a sigh. How often he heard this—women accepting responsibility for the bad behavior of the men in their lives. Martha blamed herself for Billy's drinking and blamed herself for Gene's disgust with Billy's drinking.

"Billy's a grown man. He makes his own choices," Frank reminded Martha.

"Gene doesn't understand that the Marines changed Billy." Martha traced the pattern of the carpet with the toe of her sneaker.

"Changed him how?" Frank asked gently.

"Billy was always such a cheerful kid. He had a million friends. Even though he worked hard alongside Gene, he still found time to play football and go out with the guys. He had a beautiful girlfriend."

"And now?"

"Billy's girlfriend broke up with him a few months after he joined the Marines." Martha bit her lower lip. "She didn't want to wait years for him to come home. She's married to some guy from Schroon Lake now. Some of his friends from the football team are also married, and others went to college and moved away. The only thing that's the same for Billy is that Gene expects him to wake up at the crack of dawn to start cutting trees and chopping wood."

Martha sat staring at her folded hands. Frank waited for a while, but when she didn't speak he prodded. "Something else has changed?"

"Gene has always, uh, set high standards. But Billy always knew how to get on his good side, jolly him along. Now, it's like Billy goes out of his way to provoke his father. He's stubborn, defiant."

"Look at me, Martha."

Obediently, she raised her head.

"Has Gene ever hit you?"

Her eyes focused on a point above Frank's shoulder. "No, Gene would never hit a woman. He doesn't operate that way." Martha grabbed Frank's hand in both of hers. "I only called you because I thought Billy and Gene were going to hurt each other. I shouldn't have called. I should have settled them down myself. In the future, I'm going to try harder to head off trouble."

Martha's denials only served to make Frank more suspicious. In what way did Gene operate? "What happened here today is not your fault, Mrs. Flynn. You did the right thing to call me." Frank nodded toward the gun safe fully stocked with hunting rifles. "Is that kept locked?"

"Yes, always." Martha scampered across the room and tugged on the door to prove it.

"Does Gene keep any handguns?" The man struck Frank as the type who'd sleep with a gun under his pillow to protect his castle.

Martha hesitated, then gave a quick nod. "In our bedroom."

"Does Billy know where it is?"

"Yes...but, you don't think...he wouldn't..."

"Martha, every year, far more people are shot to death in their own homes by family members than by intruders or thieves. All it takes is one moment of impulsive anger."

Martha's response tumbled out in a rush. "I'm going to hide that gun. I'll put it somewhere where neither one of them will ever find it. I'll take care of it."

"Good. Will you be okay here this afternoon?"

"Yes, Gene will come home exhausted and go straight to bed."

"What about Billy? He and his father need some space between them. Can Billy stay somewhere else for a while?"

Martha's eyes welled with tears. "Every day he was gone I prayed for him to come home. I missed him so much. Now he's back, and I can't even enjoy him. I don't know what to do." She gazed at Frank. "What should I do?"

Frank put an awkward arm around her shoulder. "Things will improve." He wasn't at all sure this was true, but what else could he say? All he knew for sure was two powerful, angry men under one roof was one too many. "In the short term, I think you'll all be better off if Billy doesn't live here."

Martha swallowed hard and nodded. "I can send Billy to stay with his sister for a few days. She and her family live in AuSable Forks."

"Good. And I'll get him connected with Trudy Massinay."

Martha's brow furrowed. "He won't like that."

Frank said nothing, just offered another reassuring pat. Billy didn't have to like it. He just had to do it. All Frank had to do was get the kid in the same room with Trudy. She'd do the rest.

Chapter 6

What a day!

By the time Frank finally made it home, he found his wife elbow-deep in dinner preparations. He and Penny had been married less than a year and were still working out the delicate two-step of balancing household responsibilities. They both liked to eat, but neither one particularly enjoyed cooking.

And neither embraced the other's stand-by dishes: pasta with herbs and broccoli and tuna-noodle casserole.

This morning they had agreed to work together on a new recipe for pork tenderloin. But it seemed Penny had launched into it without him.

"Sorry I'm late. Earl went home sick, and I had my hands full all day."

"That's okay." Penny squinted at the recipe on her iPad. "Do you think I can substitute soy sauce for tamari sauce?"

"Do you have a choice? You're not going to find any tamari sauce at 6:30 on a Wednesday in Trout Run."

Penny splashed the dark liquid into a bowl. "I made a list of every ingredient I needed for this recipe last week. Then I left the list at home when I went to Hannaford's."

Not for the first time, Frank smiled at how different the two women he had loved were. His first wife Estelle had kept spreadsheets; Penny stuck Post-It notes everywhere and then couldn't recall the significance of what she'd written. And yet he never doubted that if Estelle and Penny could have known each other, they would have gotten along famously.

Frank read the recipe over Penny's shoulder and began chopping the vegetables for the side-dish. "Caroline emailed me today. She and Eric and the boys want to come for a visit next week. They'd stay at a hotel in Lake Placid. Is that okay with you?"

"Of course. But why don't they stay here?"

Because Caroline can't bear to see her father go into a bedroom with a woman who's not her mother.

"You know Eric is very high-maintenance." Frank worked to vanquish the vee of worry that had appeared between Penny's brows. She tried her best with Caroline but couldn't get past her suspicions that Frank's daughter would never accept her.

His son-in-law was a handy scapegoat. "He needs his own king-sized bed and one of those fancy little coffee makers. They've got both at the Mirror Lake Inn."

The tension drained from Penny's face. "Well, if they'll be more comfortable there, I won't argue."

Frank had asked Penny to bring home from the library a copy of the High Peaks High School yearbook from the year Billy and Earl had graduated. While dinner was in the oven, Frank flipped through the pages. Billy's picture showed a handsome, smiling young man staring at the world with bravado. Under his picture was listed: Varsity football: team captain, Varsity wrestling: team captain, prom king. National Honor Society. Voted Best Smile. Post-graduation plans: Enlist in Marines. Quote: "First to fight. Ooh Rah!"

Earl's picture showed a scrawny kid with too-long bangs and bad skin. The dress shirt he was wearing was too big for him, so his neck looked like a single rose in a giant vase. He stared bug-eyed at the camera as if the photographer had caught him unaware and was too rushed to reshoot the photo. Under his picture was a single activity: 4H. No sports, no accolades from his peers, no plans for the future.

Frank shut the yearbook when the oven timer sounded. Their dinner turned out surprisingly well. After they ate and cleaned up, Frank took the high school yearbook into the living room to study it further. Penny curled up next to him on the sofa and peered over his shoulder. Her finger traced Earl's photo. "Look at that awful tie! And that hair! Earl has changed so much in six years....skin has cleared up and he's filled out. He's really hit his stride. I wouldn't even recognize him if his name weren't printed on the page."

"Do you think Billy and Earl could have possibly been friends back in high school? Billy looks like the kind of kid who would've stuffed Earl in a locker. Why is he suddenly targeting Earl to be his drinking buddy? And why is Earl going along?"

"I can see why Billy is drawn to Earl." Penny stretched her long legs out on the coffee table. "Earl graduated from the police academy and he has a career. He's got what Billy wants." Penny pulled the yearbook onto her lap. "And I understand why Earl wants to be Billy's friend. Even though Earl isn't that forlorn teenager any more, I bet deep down inside, he still sees himself that way. Old self-perceptions die hard. Earl is flattered by Billy's attention."

Frank pursed his lips. "Being flattered by the cool kids' attention is what draws teenagers into trouble."

"Earl's not a teenager, Frank. He's a very sensible young man who has consistently made good decisions. You said Billy needs to be persuaded to meet with Trudy Massinay. Earl's in a much better position to do that than you are. Trust him."

"You're right. Old perceptions do die hard. Even though I trust Earl more and more every day, there's still a part of me that sees him as that goofy kid I inherited as my assistant when I became police chief here." Frank pulled his wife into his arms. "And I still see myself as a cranky old cop who couldn't hope to catch the eye of the beautiful young librarian."

"Wrong on both counts," Penny murmured in his ear.

Frank lost himself in Penny's embrace. The yearbook clunked to the floor.

Eventually, Frank and Penny moved up to their bedroom to finish what they'd started. But long after Penny had fallen asleep in his arms, Frank lay awake thinking of Billy Flynn.

The scene at the Flynn's house troubled him. He didn't think he'd done a very good job defusing the situation. It felt like he'd only succeeded in postponing an inevitable conflagration. Billy Flynn was volatile and unstable. He needed more than a drinking buddy. Earl's natural generosity led him to offer Billy a helping hand.

And Billy deserved help. But Frank didn't want Earl to be harmed in the process. Despite his churning thoughts, he finally drifted off to sleep.

"Frank?" A sharp elbow hit him in the head. He pulled the covers up and rolled over.

"Frank! Wake up. There's someone out on the deck."

Frank raised his head. Through bleary eyes he saw blue numbers glowing on the night stand: 3:50.

"Listen," Penny insisted.

Then he heard it too. The sound of metal scraping against wood, rattling. "Someone's moving the gas grill out there."

Frank jumped out of bed. Everything he wore on his belt when in uniform rested on the dresser. He grabbed his flashlight and moved to the window.

The rattle and clang came again. Whoever was out there wasn't making any effort to be stealthy. Maybe he thought the house was empty.

Frank flattened himself against the wall and peeked out the window. Pitch black, but the almost full moon cast a silvery glow over the deck and the yard.

He debated going downstairs for a closer look but decided to shine the flashlight from where he was even if it gave the intruder time to run off.

The powerful beam sliced through the darkness. Two glowing eyes looked up at him.

Frank laughed. "It's an animal." He should have suspected that from the start, but pre-dawn paranoia clouded his common sense.

Penny rushed over to look. "Is it a raccoon? Maybe he smells grease on the grill."

The animal was about the size of a raccoon, but its fur was all dark. It leaped off the grill and lumbered across the deck.

"I think it's a bear cub. How cute!" Penny headed for the stairs. "I want to see him better."

Frank grabbed her shoulder. "Don't even think of opening the back door. Nothing is more dangerous than a mother bear separated from her cub."

He got in front of his wife and went downstairs first. Together, they peered through the sliding door of the great room. The animal sat on the deck railing, with its long bushy tail hanging down.

"Oh. My. God. A great big cat." Penny clutched his arm in excitement. "Do bobcats come in black?"

Frank laughed. "That's just a standard-issue domestic shorthair, honey. But he sure is the biggest tom I've ever seen." Frank slid open the door and clapped his hands. "Scat! Go on!"

The cat closed his eyes and maintained his pose.

Penny nudged Frank aside. "He's so beautiful. Look, he has a little white tip on his tail, like he dipped it in paint." Her voice rose to a high-pitched wheedle. "Hey, big boy." She rubbed her fingers together. "Come here, fella."

"Don't approach him. He's probably feral."

Penny laughed. "There are no alley cats in the Adirondacks. There are no alleys! And how could he get that fat eating mice? He belongs to someone."

She slipped out onto the deck in her nightgown despite the early morning chill. The cat watched her approach with no concern whatsoever. Frank had to admit that it couldn't be feral. Maybe it was a barn cat who roamed outside but was used to people. Penny stroked the cat's head and scratched behind his ears. He purred so loudly Frank could hear him from the doorway. "C'mon, Penny. Let's go back to bed. That cat will go home on his own."

"Maybe he's lost. He doesn't belong to our neighbors. And he doesn't have a collar."

"Pen-*nee*" Frank warned.

"Okay, Yogi Bear." Penny petted the cat one last time. "If you can't find your way home, you can always come back here."

Frank led his wife back to bed. "Wash your hands. That cat's probably got fleas."

Chapter 7

Frank entered the office on Thursday morning to a whirlwind of activity. Earl sat at his desk, fingers clattering over his keyboard. The incoming state police reports had already been reviewed and filed. And he'd already sent the weekly police blotter report to the *Mountain Echo* before the editor called three times to beg for it.

"I see you're feeling better."

Earl looked up from his typing, his face a study in remorse. "I'm really sorry about yesterday, Frank. It won't happen again. I promise."

"Oh, don't worry about it. You've never missed a day of work except for the time you were in the hospital." Frank still felt queasy at the memory of those dark days Earl had spent in a coma. But his assistant's youth and vigor had protected him from any long-term consequences. Frank poured himself a cup of coffee and headed to his desk where he spied a small white paper bag. "Hey, what's this? Maple cruller! You have been busy this morning." Frank dunked the donut in his coffee and chewed thoughtfully. "I'm glad you're back, though. Yesterday was really busy. I helped rescue a hiker. And then I had to break up a fight at your friend's house. It didn't end so well."

He told Earl about the domestic disturbance at the Flynns', and how he hoped Earl could persuade Billy to meet with Trudy.

Earl gnawed on his lower lip. "I heard. Billy called me and wanted to go to the Mountainside again. I told him he needed to take a night off. Chill and watch a movie with his sister's kids. Said I'd meet him for lunch today at Malone's."

"Think he took your advice?"

Earl shrugged. "Hope so."

Frank spun his desk chair away from Earl and spoke with his nose buried in some paperwork. "How come you're taking such an interest in Billy? Were you close friends back in the day?"

"Not really, but everyone knows everyone at High Peaks High. I just, well, I feel kinda sorry for him. He seemed to have it all when we were kids.

Smart and athletic and popular. He always talked about joining the Marines. Said he would enlist and rise in the ranks and go to Officer Candidate School and become a general."

"So what happened? Why did he leave the military?"

"I'm not sure. At the beginning of the night we went out, he was full of stories about his adventures. The places he'd seen, the missions he'd carried out with his platoon." Earl paused in his typing.

Frank glanced over and saw his assistant gazing into space. Earl had never expressed much interest in seeing the world. Frank wondered if he felt some longing to get away now that he was older. But Earl gave a little shudder and resumed talking. "Then the drunker Billy got, the more he talked about how awful it was. Little kids getting killed, but also kids being used as suicide bombers. How he never knew who to trust. How he thought the whole war was a waste and the Pentagon didn't know what they were doing."

"Sounds pretty disillusioned."

"That's it. He had a dream and it didn't turn out like he expected. Meanwhile, I became a cop and my job is better than I expected. I kinda feel...."

"Guilty for being happy? Don't go there."

The intercom buzzed, and Doris's screech filled the room. "Frank, there's some lady on line two, and I can't figure out what her problem is."

Earl grinned and grabbed the patrol car keys. "I'll go do the morning rounds."

Frank looked at the blinking light on his phone, took a deep breath, and lifted the receiver. "Police Chief Bennett. How may I help you?"

"Uhm. Hello? I don't know if you're the right person...it's my son... we're worried because we haven't heard from him. But maybe it's nothing, but maybe..." Deep, quavery sigh. "I've been texting and calling, and he doesn't answer but he's done this before but still—"

"Ma'am—"

"... And my husband says leave him be, he's a grown man but I worry, you know, because he doesn't always make good choices and—"

"Ma'am, can I have your name please?"

"Oh, right, sorry—Maeve Dunleavey. And so my son told me he was going to Trout Run and we live in Glen Rock—that's in Bergen County...New

Jersey, you know—and I had to look at a map because I never even heard of Trout Run—"

"Ma'am—" Geez, no wonder the kid had gone AWOL. Who wouldn't with a mother like this?

"and it's really far and I'm not clear who he was visiting there, but it's been three days and at first he answered me but now he doesn't, but my husband said if he had crashed the car, we would have been notified but still—"

"Ma'am!" Frank barked into the phone, demanding silence. "Can I have your son's name, please?"

"Oh, didn't I say that? Chip. His name is Chip and he's five foot eleven, and how many pounds? Gee, I don't even know. Isn't that terrible? But maybe let's say one hundred fifty—he's pretty skinny...I tell him he needs to eat better...and he has brown hair, reddish brown, really."

Frank took notes as she finally said something worth recording. "Age?"

"He'll be twenty-two on July 18. I guess that's considered an adult but he isn't really an adult, don't you agree? They're so young and innocent. They just don't know the ways of the world and—"

Frank studied the description he'd jotted down. Twenty-two tall, thin, auburn hair. Chip was a nickname. For what? "What's your son's full legal name, Mrs. Dunleavey?"

"Charles Dunleavey, but I've always called him Chip, but now he doesn't like that, and he calls himself— "

"Charlie?"

"Yes, how did you know?"

"Ma'am, yesterday a hiker that matches your son's description was rescued from the Dix Trail. He didn't have any ID on him, but he said his name was Charlie. He was a little disoriented from dehydration, so the EMTs transported him to the Adirondack Medical Center in Saranac Lake."

"Oh my God! Patrick!" she shouted. "Chip's in the hospital. I told you so!"

Frank held the receiver away from his throbbing ear and waited for her to settle down. Eventually, he was able to reassure her that her son was most likely fine, and probably hadn't wanted to worry her by calling from the hospital. He gave her the phone number of the Medical Center and hung up.

One mystery solved. Frank returned to a report on a rash of car thefts on the east side of the county.

After he'd read a few pages, the intercom buzzed. "Frank, that crazy lady is on the phone again."

Pot...kettle. Gingerly, he lifted the receiver. Maybe she was calling to thank him.

"He's not there." Although the voice was certainly Mrs. Dunleavey, her tone had changed. Gone was the meandering. Now she was trembling on the edge of panic. "They told me he checked out early this morning against doctor's orders. He's still sick, and he left the hospital. Where is he?"

"I don't know, ma'am. What did the doctor say?"

"He wouldn't tell me anything. HIPPA...privacy...blah, blah, blah. I don't care about their rules. This is my child, my baby! I finally got a nurse to talk to me. She was a mother, so she understood. Told me that when she checked on him early this morning, he was gone. IV pulled out. Hospital gown on the floor. Disappeared."

Frank had to admit that was odd. Where would the kid have gone in Saranac? Did he even have any money? Rusty and the rangers had checked his pockets and backpack for ID and found nothing. They'd put the backpack in the ambulance with him. Could Charlie have stashed a few bills in a compartment of the pack? And where could he go without his car, which had to be at a parking area somewhere along Route 73.

"What kind of car does he drive? Do you have the license plate number?"

"It's a Mini Cooper. Stupid little car. Not safe at all." She yelled for her husband to bring her the license plate number.

Frank couldn't remember the precise make and model of the three cars that had been parked at the trailhead where the ambulance picked up Charlie, but he knew none of them was a Mini-Cooper. It wasn't a common car among locals in the mountains or among hikers—not practical for snow or gear. But Charlie could have entered the wilderness from any number of trailheads. Maybe that's why he'd been trying to get to the blue trail—to get back to his car. He apparently had been wandering around lost for days. "I'll put out an alert for his car. And I'll call the Saranac Lake police department and ask them to keep a lookout for him. He didn't have a phone on him when he was found, but you say you did reach him by phone at least once?"

"Yes, on the first day he was gone—Sunday. I asked him if he got there safely and he said yes and that's the last I heard."

"And the friend he was planning to visit in Trout Run?"

Now she began to weep. "He wouldn't tell me. We've had issues about this. The therapist says my husband is too controlling, and I'm too hovering. And Chip reacts by withholding information. But you see—I'm right to hover because look what's happened! Chip is in trouble, and who will help him? Who-o-o?"

BY THE TIME FRANK HAD contacted the ranger station with a description of the car and the Saranac Lake police with a description of Charlie Dunleavey, Earl had returned from the morning patrol.

"Hey, what's going on at the old Asian Bistro," Earl asked as soon as he came in.

"Doris says it's going to be a church, The Tabernacle of Something-some-thing."

Earl raised his eyebrows. "St. Margaret's in Verona is three-quarters empty every Sunday, and Trout Run Presbyterian is even emptier. We don't hardly need another church."

"Yeah, they seem to have hit upon the one thing that would be even less popular in Trout Run than a sushi bar." Earl's question prompted another thought. Frank pointed his pen at Earl. "Hey, did you know the Hungry Loon is opening a branch in the old Murdoch house? I found out yesterday."

Earl's eyebrows shot up. "News to me. Who told you? Marge Malone?"

"No, Doris." Frank scratched his head. As owner of Trout Run's decidedly nongourmet diner, Marge Malone was another person who should've known about the new store, but didn't. Weird.

Earl glanced at the clock on the wall. "I'm meeting Billy Flynn for lunch at Malone's at 12:30."

"So you want me to get my lunch first." Frank rose from his desk. "I'll grab a sandwich from The Store. Be right back. Oh, and if a lady named Mrs. Dunleavey calls, let Doris take a message. Believe me, you don't want to get involved."

Frank crossed the green, waving to the garden club brigade who were weeding the flower beds around the gazebo, getting it ready for the first concert on the green of the summer, still two weeks off.

As he got closer to The Store, he saw the front door of the Presbyterian Church open. A man came out on the landing between the door and the steps and looked up at the sky. A few steps closer and Frank could confirm that the man was Pastor Bob Rush. He waved, and Bob waved back as he descended the steps. Then he turned away from Frank and gazed heavenward again.

What was Bob looking at? Not the sky, which was crystal clear. Curiosity drove Frank to detour on his way to lunch.

He strode up alongside the pastor and joined him in looking up. Then he saw it: a good-sized hole in the base of the steeple where it joined the roof. As they watched, a fat raccoon shot out of the hole and scampered across the shingles.

"Looks like you got a little varmint problem there," Frank said.

"Big problem. There must be a whole colony of them up there. They've eaten through the wiring that lights the sanctuary. And they've caused a leak that's going to damage the organ if we don't get it fixed right away."

"Rollie Fister can find you someone to do the work. It shouldn't take long."

"Finding someone isn't the problem. *Paying* someone is the problem."

"Can't your handyman crew of church members handle it?"

"Norm Ellison is eighty. And Finn Corliss just had a hip replacement. I can't let them go up there."

"I could patch the hole for you," Frank offered. "But I don't like to mess with wiring. Screw that up, and the church will burn to the ground."

Pastor Bob massaged his temples. "If it burned down, would anyone even miss it?"

"Whoa, what's gotten into you?"

"Wallowing in self-pity, I guess." Bob jammed his hands in the pockets of his perpetually saggy khakis. "Donations are down. Attendance is down. Young families don't bring their kids to church anymore. Everyone's too busy—working two jobs, pushing their kids to play hockey or baseball or something so they get a scholarship."

Frank was at a loss to know how to reassure his friend. Bob's lament made the opening of the new church in the Asian Bistro even more perplexing. He wanted to ask if Bob knew about it, but it seemed like a bad time to bring up the fact that more competition for parishioners was on the way.

A call on Bob's phone rescued Frank from further awkwardness. "It's the electrician," Bob told him. "I've gotta take this."

Frank waved good-bye and headed to The Store thinking about the church. Trout Run Presbyterian reigned over the town green, casting a protective shadow over the other shops and houses that circled the park. Its spire graced the postcards tourists mailed home during fall foliage season. Trout Run wouldn't be Trout Run without it. His own attendance had been a little spotty lately. He made a vow to prod Penny out of bed this Sunday or go to church without her.

When Frank opened the door to The Store, a familiar smell engulfed him: fresh coffee, over-ripe bananas, cleaning solution, cheese. The Store sold a little bit of everything and not a lot of anything. Its shelves were stocked following a peculiar logic—vegetables next to greeting cards, condiments alongside bobby pins—that made quick shopping impossible. The line for sandwiches started in front of the deli counter and snaked down the aisle devoted to snacks and automotive supplies. Men started work early at Stevenson's lumberyard and Venable's Hardware, so they were ready for lunch before noon. Frank got behind two guys who worked on the county road crew and resigned himself to a long wait. Oppressed by the nearby temptation of Lay's potato chips and the scent of tree-shaped air-fresheners, he searched for someone to talk to. Behind him he heard a voice that sounded familiar. Frank turned and saw the broad muscular back of a young man with close-cropped hair.

The guy high-fived another man coming toward him down the aisle. "Hey, long time, no see!"

"Billy! How you doin' man? You home for a visit?"

"Nah. I'm done with my tour. Home for good."

"Great! Workin' with your dad?"

"Uh, no—I'm looking around for something else. You know anyone who's hiring?"

"Not off the top of my head, but I'll—"

Crash!

A loud metallic clamor echoed from the stock room, prompting a woman's high-pitched squeal.

"Godammit!" a man's voice shouted.

Frank turned with the crowd and craned to see what was going on.

A second later, Frank found himself splayed into the chip display. A plastic bottle of windshield wiper fluid hit his head. Now the screaming was right in his ear.

"Incoming! Take cover!"

Frank scrambled to his feet. The snack aisle was a shambles. Billy Flynn had pulled down a wire display rack, sending bags of chips and pretzels flying. He hunkered down behind it, his eyes scanning left and right. "Hajis at two o'clock."

Billy lobbed a can of motor oil at the deli case. A large crack split the glass.

Customers screamed and ran to get out of the way.

Billy's breathing was ragged but the hands that held the next can of motor oil aimed steady and true.

"Billy," Frank spoke in a low, calm voice. "I need you to put down the can. There's no problem here. Someone just dropped something in the stock room."

Billy's eyes continued their rapid assessment of the scene. The kid seemed to think he was back in Iraq conducting a house-to-house search for insurgents or something.

The Store had mostly emptied out. But the girl who made sandwiches behind the deli counter stood frozen in place, her eyes as round as the hams in the case. Billy had the oil can aimed right at her head.

"Billy, you're scaring Paula. She didn't do anything. She was just making sandwiches. She made that sound because she was startled by the loud noise." Frank's hand brushed against his own weapon. But he feared that bringing a gun into Billy's field of vision would only serve to convince the veteran that he really was under attack.

Billy's eyes focused now on Paula, a slender young woman with curly hair pulled back in a ponytail. Frank had seen her playing in the park with two cute toddlers. She was a mom, caught in the line of fire because she worked a few hours in the midday rush to help make ends meet. He couldn't let her get hurt in this melee.

"Billy, today is Thursday. You're at The Store in Trout Run. In a few minutes, you're going to meet Earl Davis next door at Malone's. You're going to have lunch with Earl, remember?"

Frank's words seemed to reach the ex-soldier. He blinked his eyes, turned his head a little. The mundane details of his all-American location began to sink in. The liters of orange soda and bags of pretzel twists reassured him. The collapsed pyramid of Pennzoil ceased to be grenades and turned back into automotive products.

He wasn't in Iraq. There were no bombs.

Slowly, Billy's arms sank to his sides. He let the can clatter to the floor.

Frank grabbed Billy's arm and led him out of the Store. A crowd of customers edged away, murmuring and uneasy. A few people shook their heads. No one would meet Billy's gaze. As Frank and Billy walked down the steps, they met Earl coming toward them.

Earl smiled. Then the smile faded as he noticed Billy's glassy stare and the way Frank was steering Billy with a firm grasp on his arm.

"We're all going back to the office." Frank gestured with a nod to get Earl to follow. "No lunch for us until this gets straightened out."

Chapter 8

Once he was seated in the police department office, Billy gradually emerged from his trance. His right foot tapped relentlessly, and the tremor spread to his hands. Earl handed him a glass of water. Half of it spilled onto Billy's shirt.

"Do you have flashbacks often?" Frank asked.

The young Marine sat silently.

Eventually, Billy's voice came from miles away. "We were out on a routine patrol. Everything was going smooth, no problems. Then there was a loud bang and the next thing I knew, three of my buddies were down. We were in a firefight. It came outta nowhere."

Billy put his hands over his ears and rocked back and forth in the chair.

Frank and Earl exchanged a glance. Then Frank saw something click in Earl's understanding.

"Billy, loud noises bother you. Is that why you can't work with your dad?" Earl leaned toward his friend. "The sound of the chainsaws and the wood-chippers would be too much?"

Billy's gaze locked on Earl, but he said nothing.

Frank suspected Earl had given voice to Billy's fear, spoken the words the poor guy couldn't bring himself to say. Maybe Billy hadn't even recognized the problem until now.

"My dad thinks I'm lazy," Billy whispered. "I want to work, just not...."

"Of course you're not lazy," Earl said. "You'll find a job, a different job that's right for you."

But even as Earl worked to reassure his friend, Frank had his doubts. He could imagine word of the episode at the Store ricocheting around town as they sat here talking. Competition for good jobs was always stiff. Why would anyone hire a volatile veteran who might go off the rails at any minute when there were three or four other guys vying for the same position?

"I'll help you," Earl continued. "I know a lotta people."

Earl definitely knew a lot of people, but Frank knew the one person Billy really had to talk to. "Billy, I'm going to call Trudy Massinay, the county social worker. She can get you connected up with—"

Billy jumped out of his seat. "I don't need to talk to no shrinks! There's nothing wrong with me. I just need a little peace and quiet."

"Trudy's not a shrink," Earl said. "She just helps people out. Give her a chance. You'll like her."

Billy spun around to face Earl, his voice a fierce growl. "Don't you tell me what I'll like, what I need to do."

Now Frank could see the shadow of the father in the son. No wonder the two were constantly at loggerheads. Just as Frank was about to speak, loud voices carried in from the outer office.

"I wanna see Frank Bennett right now."

"You can't go in there," Doris insisted.

"That SOB Flynn tore up my whole store. I wanna know what the police are going to do about it."

Clearly, Butch Sobel, owner of the Store, had heard about the commotion and had come to inspect the damage.

"Okay, but you have to—"

Frank opened the door to the outer office, jumping from the frying pan into the fire. He left Billy and Earl behind.

"Hi, Butch." Frank extended a hand to shake. "I understand you're upset. Let's sit and talk about it, okay?"

Sobel gave Frank's hand a reluctant shake, but he declined to sit down. "Have you arrested Billy Flynn? He chased off all my customers and scared poor Paula to death. I want to know who's going to make him pay for all the damage he caused."

A few crushed bags of chips, a couple of dented cans of motor oil that Butch would try to sell anyway—had there really been much damage done? It seemed to Frank that the owner of the Store just needed to blow off some steam. "I know Billy caused a commotion that disrupted your lunch business. But the kid's been through a hard time. He didn't come in intending to make trouble."

"He didn't mean to do it." Butch mocked Frank in a high-pitched voice. "Well, sorry doesn't fix my cracked display case, does it? I'm trying to get the

Store spruced up to face the competition I got comin' from that fancy Loon place. And Billy comes in and tears up my business."

Ah, so Butch knew about the new store and was feeling the heat. And Frank had forgotten about the damaged display case. "I'm sure Billy will repay you for that. Just give him a little time."

"He doesn't even have a job. I can't get blood from a stone. I'll have to put in a claim with my insurance. And for that, I need a copy of the police report. So that's what I'm here for."

Frank pursed his lips. He understood Butch's need, but arresting Billy would only make his situation worse. But then Frank saw a way to use Butch's outrage to his own advantage. "Look, I'll write up a report and we'll charge him with misdemeanor vandalism. That'll do for your insurance. Earl and I are going to work with Trudy Massinay to make sure Billy gets the help he needs. If Billy doesn't cooperate, I'll up the charge to assault."

Butch Sobel left muttering oaths. Frank took a deep breath and prepared to go Round Two with Billy. Clearly, Earl wasn't as influential as he'd hoped to be. Billy probably didn't appreciate getting advice from a kid he'd kicked around in high school.

But when he reentered his office, Billy sat calmly in the chair in front of Earl's desk while Earl spoke on the phone. "Thanks, Trudy. I'll bring him right over."

Earl waved Billy ahead of him as they headed for the door. "I'll be back in an hour."

Frank watched the two young men through the window. Earl held open the truck's passenger door, and Billy hopped in with a smile on his face. He leaned back with his elbow out the window as if they were cruising off to the Mountainside.

Frank had been a cop twenty-five years longer than Earl. There was still plenty the kid could learn from him. But he had to admit, there were things he could learn from Earl, too.

Chapter 9

A loud rumble from his midsection reminded Frank that in all the commotion of the morning, he never had managed to get lunch. With no desire to cross paths with Butch Sobel again, Frank headed to Malone's Diner.

A large mid-day crowd filled the place, but Frank spied Reid Burlingame sitting alone at a table for two. To save time he put in his order at the counter and weaved through the crowd until he reached Reid's table. "Mind if I join you?" Frank sat down before Reid could answer. "I've been meaning to talk to you."

"Oh?" Reid cut his grilled cheese sandwich into perfect squares and ate it with a fork. "Not about spending town money, I hope."

"No worries. I'm curious about the opening of the Hungry Loon. When did the owners decide to open a branch here?"

Reid's eyes lit up. "The project came together very quickly, I think. We're very fortunate. The Hungry Loon will attract many new shoppers to Trout Run—all the other businesses are anticipating an uptick in sales—the Craft Center, the Rock Slide, Malone's, even The Store."

"Really? Rita and Butch Sobel seem pretty worried about the competition." Frank glanced over his shoulder at the large figure of Marge Malone behind the counter. "And Marge can't be thrilled."

Reid dismissed this with a wave of his fork. "A rising tide lifts all boats. People buy some delicacies from the Loon, then pick up the basics at the Store. Having more options here in town means shoppers will make fewer trips to Lake Placid and Plattsburgh." Reid rubbed his hands together. "And real estate transactions are up sharply. I did four closings this week. One is a house that had been sitting on the market for three years."

"You attribute that to the Hungry Loon?"

"No, oddly enough, I think it has to do with that new church, the Tabernacle of Living Light. The pastor and several other church members have bought houses in Trout Run. They're doing.... oh, he had some word for it... church planting. That's it!"

"You've met the pastor?" The waitress sailed by and dropped off Frank's hefty pot roast special. He realized belatedly that Penny had warned him to eat a light lunch because Lucy and Edwin had invited them to dinner at the Iron eagle Inn tonight.

"Yes, Adam Fortway," Reid continued. "Pleasant fellow—mid-forties, very affable."

"Why did he choose Trout Run to plant a new church? Attendance is pretty low at the ones we've got."

"Real estate is much more affordable here than outside of Glens Falls. I think that's where the church started. Pastor Fortway has a lot of energy. I think he aims to attract people who aren't regular churchgoers. And he's also running some sort of spiritual retreat center alongside the church. Meditation. Communing with nature. That sort of thing."

Frank swallowed a bite of pot roast and grimaced. "In Trout Run? This guy thinks he's going to get people here to sit around for hours chanting a mantra and looking at trees?"

Reid's face took on the pained, pitying expression that he reserved for anyone who didn't immediately embrace his vision of Trout Run in the 21st Century. "The full name is Tabernacle of Living Light Community Congregation and Spiritual Retreat Center. The retreat center is targeted at frazzled city people," Reid explained with exaggerated patience. "They can come up here to connect with God and Nature." He gestured out the window at the mountains surrounding the green. "Unplug. Refocus. If the Retreat Center becomes popular, the Tabernacle will need to buy more property."

Frank cocked a skeptical eyebrow. "Possibly." Reid was practically licking his lips over the prospect of closing more real estate transactions. Of course, he made money regardless of whether the sale brought a successful or a failing business to the area. "If this spiritual retreat center charges money for people to come to Trout Run to meditate, shouldn't it be classified as a for-profit, tax-paying business?"

Reid pursed his lips. "The Retreat Center is affiliated with the Tabernacle of Living Light church, and the church is a registered 501c3, nonprofit organization. If the IRS says it's a legitimate church, who am I to argue? Besides, the Catholics have retreat centers all over—Franciscan Retreat Centers, Sisters of Charity Retreat Centers. And the Buddhists!" Reid flung his hands up as if to indicate you couldn't turn around in the North Country without tripping over Buddhists. "They're all tax-exempt."

"But the Asian Bistro changing from a for-profit restaurant to a non-profit church is still a net loss for the Trout Run tax base, no?"

Read heaved a sigh as if he were talking to a stubborn teenager who willfully refused to see reason. "In the short-term, yes. But if the Retreat Center attracts visitors, that will be good for our local businesses. And if people move here to be part of their spiritual community, that's even better for our tax base."

"So the community congregation part of the Tabernacle is what's aimed at local people?"

"Yes. Pastor Fortway hopes to foster a greater sense of community among young adults and young families. I'm sure you've noticed that there's hardly a soul under forty in church to hear Bob Rush's sermons."

What was that supposed to mean? Did Reid perceive Bob Rush as a slacker? Frank felt the need to keep challenging. "But there are a lot fewer people to be members of a church here. How can the people starting this new church afford to buy houses? Do they have jobs outside the church?"

Reid gave an exasperated huff. "I was representing the sellers, not the buyers, Frank. All the paperwork was in order. The money was there. The end result is, three houses that were formerly empty are now occupied. That's a good thing." Reid grabbed his check from the table and left.

Frank finished the rest of his pot roast in solitude. He supposed Penny would agree with Reid's upbeat vision of the new church. She scolded him regularly for always seeing the glass half-empty. But cops were trained—paid—to anticipate problems where others saw nothing but smooth sailing. And he didn't see how this new guy would succeed when Bob Rush worked so hard yet struggled to keep his congregation afloat.

Chapter 10

When Frank and Penny pulled up to the Iron Eagle Inn later that evening, they found an unfamiliar SUV parked in the guest parking area.

"Who does that belong to?" Frank scowled. "I thought the reason we were invited tonight was because the Inn has no guests."

Penny hopped out of the truck. "I guess we'll find out." She laughed at her husband's dour expression. "C'mon, Grouchy. Meeting new people isn't supposed to be a torment."

"For you, it's not." Frank had been looking forward to a nice quiet dinner with friends. He didn't feel like being on his best behavior making chit-chat with Inn guests.

They entered through the back door, as they always did, to find Edwin clattering around the kitchen. "Ah, there you are!" Edwin paused in stirring a pot on the stove to give Penny a kiss.

"Something smells fabulous. Is that farro?" Penny poked around the pots on the stove. "I saw a recipe that called for that, but I had no idea where to buy it."

Frank wrinkled his nose at the bug-like grains in the pot. As far as he was concerned, Edwin could keep the purveyor of farro a state secret.

"Yes, I bought it online," Edwin explained. "But I hope they might carry it at The Hungry Loon. Then I can get it all the time."

"And the marinated tarragon chicken salad—mmmm." Penny pirouetted in joy.

"I love that! I've tried to make it here, but I can't duplicate it. They must have a secret ingredient."

"The Hungry Loon grand opening is coming soon." Penny held up her hand for a high five. "Then you'll be able to go up to the green and get a fix whenever you want it."

"Who else is here?" Frank cared less about the food than the company. "I thought you were empty tonight?"

Edwin shoved a glass of wine into Frank's hand and winced. "Adam Fortway is joining us for dinner. He's in the living room with Lucy."

"The pastor of that new church? Why would you invite him?" Penny raised her hand to her mouth, realizing how rude she sounded. "I'm sorry. I didn't mean it that way. I'm just, er, surprised."

"Not more surprised than I am," Edwin grumbled. "He sort of invited himself. I didn't see a way out of it." Edwin flipped the grain out of the pot and tossed it with some greens and tomatoes and cheese. "I was out in my herb garden when he drove up. Wanted to know what our room availability was like the next few months. Apparently, his spiritual retreats are booked to capacity. He's looking to buy some more houses. Until then, he might need the Inn to hold some overflow...guests...followers...whatever you want to call them."

"That's good for your business, right?" Penny found a clean fork and tasted the salad Edwin was working on.

"I suppose." Edwin's brow furrowed, and he squeezed more lemon over the greens.

Frank couldn't be sure if Edwin's dubious tone was related to Adam Fortway or the strange mix of ingredients in the bowl. "But how did he end up coming to dinner?"

"We started talking, he followed me in here, and the next thing you know, he was staying for dinner. Honestly, I'm still not sure how it happened."

"It's okay," Penny hugged Edwin. "We've both been curious about this new church. Now we'll get the inside scoop."

Frank sighed as he followed his wife out of the kitchen. Weird food and a weird guest were more than he'd bargained for.

But when he got to the living room, he found Lucy chatting animatedly with a perfectly ordinary-looking middle-aged man. A tray of cheese puffs, which Frank knew from experience were quite tasty, sat on the coffee table.

Lucy performed the introductions, and Adam Fortway beamed at them. "How fortunate I am to meet two such important members of the Trout Run community." He leaned toward Penny and put his hand on her arm. "A library is the heart of a community. A repository of knowledge and a gathering place for young and old. I've heard that you were instrumental in establishing the Trout Run library."

Frank grabbed a cheese puff and sat back to watch how this would unfold. Penny loved talking about the library, but he was attuned to the way his wife leaned away as Fortway leaned forward. Penny was an extrovert, but her disastrous first marriage had made her cautious of overly friendly men.

Penny explained in businesslike terms how Clyde Stevenson, the founder of Stevenson's Lumberyard, had provided the initial funding for the library, and that she now served on the Board of Directors in addition to being head librarian. Then she turned the conversation back to Fortway. "So tell me more about these spiritual retreats you run. Are they open to anyone?"

"Anyone who seeks to achieve his or her full potential by releasing inner darkness."

Oh, brother. Here we go. Frank swallowed a slug of wine and reached for another cheese puff.

"I see." Penny offered a half-smile and glanced at Lucy for help.

"Adam was just telling me that the Tabernacle runs retreats for people who are having trouble reaching their full potential because of crippling anxiety and self-doubt. I know so many people back in Manhattan who could benefit from a retreat like that."

Frank didn't doubt that Lucy had a whole posse of high-strung friends. Whether they'd appreciate a week in Trout Run with Fortway remained to be seen. "So people who attend the retreats might stay here at the Inn?" Frank asked. "I heard you bought several houses in town."

Lucy must've felt Frank was being unduly inquisitive. "The Tabernacle has a core group who have chosen to live as a community, and—" she gestured to her guest. "Well, I'll let you explain it."

Fortway straightened up in his chair. He wore a polo shirt, jeans, and boots, so he looked like any guy responding to a "what line of work are you in?" question at a party. But instead of explaining that he sold industrial valves or marketed insurance products, he elaborated on the ins and outs of liberating trapped souls. "People come to us mired in the darkness of self-doubt, fear, and anxiety. We teach them how to let go of that negativity and strive toward their light."

"Uh-*hunh*." Penny extended her leg and brushed the toe of her shoe against Frank's ankle.

"So how long does that take?" Frank asked. "On average."

Fortway paused to consider, as if Frank had asked him a quantifiable question, like how long it took to roast a turkey. "Well, it depends upon how ingrained the negative pathways are and how receptive the person is to receiving the light."

"Ri-i-i-ght." Frank wasn't that interested in Fortway's New Age BS, but he was curious about how the church could afford to buy up houses and send overflow customers to the Inn. "But some people stay with you and others come and go?"

"Yes, as Lucy mentioned, our core community lives in three houses near the Tabernacle. But the retreats are open to people who might only stay for a week or two."

"And you charge a fee for the retreats?" Frank continued.

Fortway extended his hands palms up. "On a sliding scale. Of course, we never turn away anyone who is in pain."

Or anyone with a pocket full of cash. To disguise his eye roll, Frank busied himself pouring everyone more wine. "And the people who moved up here with you—where do they work?"

"Most assist me with the retreats. Some work outside the community." Fortway took a tiny sip from a wine glass that hadn't needed refilling. "All according to their talents and preferences." He sat back in his chair and crossed his legs.

Fortway noticed Frank staring at his extremely clean hiking boots. "I just bought these. I'm told I should wear them around the house for a while to break them in before I take them out on the trail."

"Good advice. You don't want to end up as a statistic on the forest rangers' weekly rescue report," Frank said. "Do you plan to do a lot of hiking with your retreat groups?"

"Oh, yes—I want everyone at the Tabernacle to be in communion with nature."

"What about these free community dinners I hear so much about?" Penny asked. "Are you hoping those people will join the Tabernacle?"

Fortway gave her a patient smile, the way a first-grade teacher might smile at a new reader stumbling over a big word. "The Tabernacle is not something one joins like a country club or a traditional church. It's a community that offers a beacon of light to those who are struggling. If a person chooses to follow that beacon, then he or she might choose to spend more time in our community."

And what if a person just wants to load up on free chicken?

But Frank wasn't destined to find out. Edwin popped his head into the living room. "Dinner is served."

Thank God. Even the weird salad would be a welcome distraction.

Chapter 11

"So what did you think?" Frank asked as they drove home. "Cocktail hour was certainly odd, but he seemed pretty normal during dinner."

Frank had to agree. Edwin and Lucy had made a concerted effort to talk about family, and a class Lucy planned to teach in the fall, and their plan to remodel the barn at the back of their property. When no one asked direct questions about the Tabernacle, Fortway didn't talk about it; he just joined in the general chit-chat. They learned that he wasn't married and didn't have kids, that he'd gone to the University of Connecticut and still followed their basketball team, and that he wasn't handy with home repairs.

"A guy who keeps a March Madness bracket can't be all bad, even if he does spout a lot of New Age claptrap about embracing the light." Frank reached across and squeezed Penny's knee. "I got the impression you didn't like him coming on so strong about the library."

"I don't like it when people who don't even know me start telling me how fabulous I am."

"Do I know you well enough to tell you you're fabulous?" Frank teased.

"You know me too well." Penny stretched out in the passenger seat and let the cool balsam-scented breeze blow into the car. They drove toward home in companionable silence.

As they descended the hill toward the bridge over Stony Brook, the air felt damper. The scent had changed too. Frank's keen nose picked it up first, but then Penny caught a whiff.

She sat up straight. "Whoa!"

Frank pulled onto the shoulder and grabbed the powerful flashlight he always kept in his truck. "Sit tight."

A high-pitched shriek reverberated through the narrow valley, followed by gales of male laughter.

"Frank, be careful."

The powerful, skunky scent of marijuana smoke drifted up to him. On the rocks under the covered bridge he could see the shadowy outlines of four people and a tiny pinprick of light moving as they passed the joint back and forth. Despite Penny's warning, Frank headed toward the group without concern. This was a favorite hang-out for teenagers. He only intended to move them along toward home.

He switched on the flashlight and its bright beam pierced the night. "Trout Run police," he announced.

For a split second, the four of them froze. Then the lit joint sailed into the brook, and three lanky boys took off running, leaving behind the fourth kid. As Frank skidded down the muddy path to the brook, he could see that the kid left behind was a tall, slender girl. She swayed slightly, clearly more stoned than the others. Then she tried to flee, but her foot slipped on the mossy rock and one knee slid into the rushing water.

She screamed.

Frank reached the girl and grabbed her arm to pull her up.

"Leave me alone!" But she clung to him until he pulled her onto dry, level ground.

Although Frank wore civilian clothes, the girl recognized him as a cop. This made the second time in a month that he would be escorting Laurel Caine home after a brush with illegal activity. Two weeks earlier, the Trout Run Crafts Center had called to complain that they'd caught a teenager shoplifting a pair of earrings. By the time Frank arrived, Laurel had already relinquished the earrings, and the store manager had agreed that a ride home in the patrol car was punishment enough. But on the drive to Laurel's house, Frank discovered that parental supervision was in short supply at the Caine home. Her father worked long hours at a job in Plattsburgh. Laurel's mother had died from cancer, and her father had taken up with a younger woman, who had moved in. When they got to the empty house, Frank demanded her father's cell phone number. Laurel gave it up without resistance and sat staring blankly while Frank left a lengthy message outlining her shoplifting escapade.

He'd asked the father to return his call, but he doubted that the man would do so. Laurel had plenty of reasons to be unhappy, and Frank suspected she shared her rage at the world whenever she could.

Now Frank wished he'd been a little more persistent with Mr. Caine. He nudged the teenager toward the path to the road. "C'mon, Laurel—fun's over for the night."

"No." She plopped her butt down on a rock and nearly slid off. "And don't give me that bullshit lecture about talking to my father. He's at the Mountainside getting hammered with that bitch."

Frank figured this was the sad truth. "How about I just give you a ride home."

She didn't budge, and it occurred to him she might be afraid of him. He gentled his tone. "Up you go. My wife's in the truck. We were just on our way home from a friend's house."

Frank boosted her by the elbows and she staggered forward. He didn't know what Laurel had been doing all evening, but she'd definitely had more than just a couple hits from one joint. Finally, he got her loaded into the truck next to Penny, who tried to carry on a chipper conversation with the girl. But the effort soon overwhelmed even Penny's good intentions, and they rode in silence to Laurel's house. The small bungalow hunched dark and unwelcoming amidst a stand of tall white pines.

Frank walked Laurel to the door to make sure she actually went in. The front door had been left unlocked, and when she opened it, a stale gust of cigarette smoke and burnt food greeted them.

"Mr. Caine? Trout Run police!" Frank shouted into the darkness, but the only creature who responded was a big brown and black mutt.

Frank patted the girl's shoulder. He could deliver a stern lecture to Laurel, but he doubted she'd recall a word in the morning. "Get some sleep, Laurel." There was more he wanted to say—*Life gets better.... Hang on 'til you graduate and then move far away....You deserve more.* She disappeared into the dark interior without a word.

Frank climbed back into the truck. The warm glow of an evening spent with good friends had been extinguished. "I'll drop you at home, then I'm going over to the Mountainside to find Laurel's father," he told Penny.

But nearly forty-five minutes had passed by the time he crisscrossed Trout Run and made it to the Mountainside. The bartender confirmed that Matthew Caine had been there but had left. Frank contemplated driving clear back to the Caine house, but let the idea go. The skies had opened, and rain battered his truck. The father was probably too drunk to listen to parenting advice. He'd track him down tomorrow.

When he got home, he found Penny sitting up waiting for him.

"I was worried. Why didn't you call?"

He pulled her into a hug. "I'm sorry. I forget sometimes that I don't live alone anymore."

The rain sluiced down, hammering the roof and flinging itself against the windows. Brilliant bolts of lightning lit the sky moments after the deafening clap of thunder. Penny curled next to Frank on the sofa trying to read, but she couldn't stop flinching after every flash and boom.

In a brief stretch of silence, another sound joined the cacophony.

Meow.

Penny's head jerked up from her book.

Me-e-e-o-ow.

Penny flew to the sliding door before Frank could even get his feet on the ground.

"Oh, Yogi—you poor thing!"

With his fur plastered to his body, the cat shot into the living room. Looking half the size he had in his previous visit, he shook himself, spraying rainwater against the wall, then leapt onto the sofa Frank had just vacated and rolled himself in the afghan Frank had just removed from his own lap.

"Hey!" Frank clapped his hands and tugged the afghan.

The tomcat rolled onto its back and waved its paws in the air.

"O-o-o, you sweet boy. Do you want your tummy rubbed?" Penny sat next to the cat and petted him until he purred like an idling lawnmower.

"Get him off the furniture," Frank said. "He's shedding."

Penny scooped the cat into her arms. "Are you hungry, Yogi? Let's go get you a snack. How about some nice leftover chicken from Edwin's house?"

"I was going to take that for lunch tomorrow," Frank protested.

"You can eat at Malones." The cat wrapped his paws around Penny's neck as she carried him to the kitchen.

As Yogi was borne out of the room, Frank could swear the cat looked back and winked.

Chapter 12

"What do you know about Matthew and Laurel Caine?" The next morning, Frank greeted Earl with the question before the kid even had a chance to pour himself a cup of coffee.

"I know the names, but I can't put faces to them."

Frank feigned falling out of his chair.

"Sorry to let you down." Earl bowed his head. "Every once in a while, there's actually someone in Trout Run I don't know."

Frank gave his assistant a run-down of his encounter with Laurel. "It's not that big a deal, but it's the second time she's been in trouble this month. Seems like her dad is letting her run wild."

Earl smiled. "Shoplifting and weed-smoking are pretty typical teen rebellion. She doesn't exactly sound like a one-girl crime wave to me. You're not worried about the other three kids who out-ran her last night."

"I'm worried because she was so stoned, she couldn't outrun *me*."

The intercom buzzed. "Matthew Caine is on line one," Doris announced.

"Speak of the devil," Earl said. "Maybe Laurel confessed to her father and he's worried."

But when Frank picked up, a different story emerged. "This is Matthew Caine." The voice sounded wary yet tinged with defiance. "Butch, the bartender at the Mountainside said you came in looking for me last night?"

"I did." Pretty early in the morning for the jungle drums to be beating. He suspected the bartender had called Caine as soon as Frank had left the Mountainside last night, which made him wonder why both men were so jittery. Frank recounted Laurel's latest escapade. "You may recall that I left you a phone message about the shoplifting incident."

"I talked to her about that." Now the father sounded defensive and eager to please. "Look, she's a good kid. She's just hanging out with the wrong crowd. I'll talk to her again. I'll tell her she's grounded. We don't want any trouble."

"I don't want trouble either, Mr. Caine. And I don't want young people from Trout Run to get saddled with an arrest record that will follow them forever. But you tell Laurel I can't turn a blind eye to her behavior forever. She needs to straighten out now."

"Okay. Yes, I will. I promise."

When Frank hung up, he found Earl grinning at him. "Very forceful. You do that scared straight stuff pretty good."

"My good deed for the day. Let's hope it works." Frank leaned back in his swivel chair. "Speaking of good deeds, what about Billy Flynn? How's he doing?"

"Trudy convinced him to sign up at the VA outpatient clinic in Saranac. But driving forty-five minutes each way for a half-hour appointment with a counselor..." Earl shook his head. "I doubt that's going to last long."

"He's got plenty of time on his hands. Why complain about the drive?"

"No gas money," Earl explained.

"The clinic in Saranac is the best Trudy can do?"

"She offered to try to get him admitted for in-patient evaluation at the big VA hospital in Albany, but he really wasn't having that."

"What he really needs is a job."

"I know. He's staying with his sister and looking for a job every day. At least she won't hassle him like his dad does."

Frank left Earl to hold down the office while he went out on the morning patrol. The mountains, cloaked in their early summer bright green, surrounded Trout Run protectively. On a beautiful morning like this, Frank understood why spiritual seekers from the city might want to follow Adam Fortway to the High Peaks.

He swung the patrol car around the bend and caught a glimpse of a car that had just pulled out of a side road. Then the road turned again, and the car disappeared from view.

Frank passed the Stop 'N' Buy, and the road stretched out straight before him. The small car appeared as a blur on the horizon.

Something made Frank speed up.

He drew closer to the car and now could discern that it was red. A little closer and he could see it was a Mini-Cooper. He still wasn't close enough to read the plates.

Frank flipped on the siren and the lights and sped up.

Immediately, the Mini-Cooper signaled and pulled onto the shoulder.

Frank pulled up behind the car and checked the plates: New Jersey RVB-973, the number Mrs. Dunleavey had given him.

He walked up to the driver's window. The young man behind the wheel rolled down the window and looked up at Frank. "Hi, officer. What's the problem?"

"License and registration, please."

The kid leaned over and took his registration from the glove box, then pulled out his wallet and removed his license. He handed the documents to Frank and smiled again. He had perfect teeth, probably the result of thousands of dollar's worth of upscale suburban orthodontia. Today the kid was clean, his cheeks rosy and shaven, his eyes bright under his straight, dark brows. A far cry from what he'd looked like at the DixTrailhead.

"The speed limit is fifty here, right? I was trying to keep under that."

Frank studied the papers feeling no need to answer the kid's questions. The car was registered to Patrick R. Dunleavey, Glen Rock, New Jersey. The license said Charles Dunleavey, same address.

"So, Chip, can I call you Chip? Last time I saw you, you were half unconscious on a stretcher being hauled off to the Adirondack Medical Center. Your mom and dad have been a little worried about you."

For a moment, the toothpaste-commercial smile flickered. Then it came back full force. "Wow, you were there when I got rescued? I don't even remember being taken off the mountain. Crazy, huh?"

"Look, Chip— "

"Charlie." He corrected Frank firmly.

"Sorry. Charlie, you haven't committed any traffic violations. I pulled you over because your parents have reported you and this car as missing. They're worried because they haven't heard from you in over a week, and when you disappeared from the hospital—"

"How did they even know I was in the hospital?" Charlie still had the smile plastered on his face, but there was an ever-so-slight edge of irritation in his voice. His hands gripped the steering wheel.

"Your mother called the Trout Run police department looking for you. I took the call, and it just so happened that I was there when the DEC rangers brought you down the mountain, so I told her where you were. Except you were no longer there when she called."

Charlie raised his hands palm-up in a casual whattaya-gonna-do. "Hospitals are a drag, man. They pump ya full of drugs. That's not my scene."

"Yeah, I'm no fan of hospitals either, but you can understand that your mother was worried when you left without being discharged. Why haven't you answered her calls?"

Charlie spread his fingers wide. "I threw away my phone. I'm no longer subject to its tyranny. Since I got rid of it, I feel liberated, free!" Charlie leaned his head out the little car's window and peered up at Frank. "You can call my mother and tell her I'm fine."

Frank could anticipate how that call would go. "She'll want to know where you're staying, how to get in touch with you. What should I tell her?"

"Tell her to stop projecting her worry onto me."

"What about the car? It's registered to your father."

Charlie Dunleavey removed the keys from the ignition and dropped them at Frank's feet. "Tell him I don't need his car."

Then he scrambled over the passenger seat and jumped out of the car. As Frank moved around to the passenger side, Charlie sprinted down the road like a track star, heading back in the direction from which he'd come. Before Frank could move toward the patrol car, Charlie plunged into the forest.

Frank contemplated the abandoned car and the keys in his hand. So far as he knew, no laws had been broken. It wasn't illegal for an adult to avoid his mother.

He sighed. Try explaining that to Maeve Dunleavey.

Chapter 13

After a cool, rainy week, the day of the first concert on the green dawned bright and balmy. Although predicting Adirondack weather was a fool's game, the clear skies promised to hold all the way through the evening.

People started arriving to set up their chairs by three in the afternoon. Old-timers knew it was important to stake a claim with a good view of the stage, but not too close to the loudspeakers. The Spouse's Auxiliary (formerly Women's Auxiliary until Megan Brandt joined the Rescue Squad, and her husband made the Auxiliary co-ed) of the Fire Department and Rescue Squad began setting up for the pie sale shortly thereafter. Of course the pies and cakes themselves would not make their appearance until much later, but the table and signs had to be arranged.

By four, Frank and Earl headed out to set up the traffic control cones and directional signs. Consulting their diagram, they shifted and fine-tuned, determined to avoid the mass confusion of every previous concert.

Ardyth Munger arrived on the green, staggering under the weight of a small box. Earl rushed to help her, and promptly dropped the thing on his toe.

"Ouch! What's in here? A block of lead?"

"It's the programs for the entire season of concerts. The print shop in Lake Placid stuffed them all into one box."

"Let me see what's coming up," Frank said. He and Ardyth held open a program between them, while Earl leaned over Ardyth's shoulder.

"The North Country Stompers will be playing the Fourth of July show, of course. But we've got some interesting newcomers this year." Ardyth tapped the program. "The Lakeside Jazz Quartet is supposed to be outstanding, and The Queen Bees are four young women who sing acapella."

"No repeats of the Marley Maddow fiasco?"

Ardyth shuddered at the memory of a performance so ear-jangling it had cleared the green before intermission, thus dooming the pie sale. Marley was some distant relation of Reid Burlingame, and the town council chairman had pulled strings to get her in the lineup without an audition, assuring everyone that the young woman sang like an angel. Her off-key renditions of Kelly Clarkson hits made the crowd restless, but her glass-shattering imitation of Celine Dionne's "I Will Always Love You" caused Rollie Fister's hound to point his nose to the sky and howl. There had been no recovering from that.

"The selection committee has been quite stringent about auditions this year," Ardyth assured them.

"Who's this?" Earl pointed to tonight's performers, who were listed as The Bright Lights. "I thought the Sturgis Family Band was supposed to be the season opener."

"A last-minute substitution." Ardyth pushed her hair back with the heel of her hand. "Will Sturgis had emergency gall bladder surgery just as the program was going to print. The Bright Lights auditioned late, and the committee thought they wouldn't be able to squeeze them in. Instead they get to be opening night headliners."

Will Sturgis was a fantastic fiddle player, and his family band were perennial favorites. The schedule change disappointed Frank, and he could see that Earl agreed. "But who are The Bright Lights?" Earl squinted at the fine print in the program. "I don't recognize the performers' names."

Ardyth threw back her shoulders. "The Concerts on the Green aren't just a local talent show, Earl. We've been drawing auditions from as far away as Speculator. I'm confident everyone will enjoy the show." Ardyth marched off with a bundle of programs to place on the pie table.

"Guess she told you."

Earl grinned and picked up a stack of orange traffic cones. He had known Ardyth all his life and didn't take notice of her occasional tart tongue. But Frank did think it odd that Earl didn't recognize any of the performers in The Bright Lights. Earl knew, or knew of, half the population of Essex County. And unlike Frank, his youthful brain could pull up a name faster than a Google search.

Frank followed his assistant with the directional signs. With or without Earl's endorsement of the band, the show must go on.

After finishing with the traffic signs, Frank and Earl agreed to meet back at the Green at six. Earl would take the first shift directing traffic while Frank watched over the crowd of listeners. At intermission, they would switch positions.

Frank returned to the office to find Penny hunched over Doris's desk. In her hand she clutched a sheaf of bright yellow papers.

Doris held one out in front of her and squinted. "He doesn't look familiar to me. The Vollmans have a black cat, but it's a scrawny little thing. Oh, and it's a girl, 'cause it had kittens once."

"I made a flyer to see if I can find Yogi's owner." Penny handed one to Frank. "I'm positive someone is heartbroken over losing him."

Found on Stony Brook Road

Black male cat with White-tipped tail

16 pounds

Very friendly

If you lost this handsome boy, call Penny Bennett at the Trout Run library

The center of the flyer contained a photo of Yogi lounging on Frank's favorite easy chair.

"Where is that porkchop right now?"

"I brought him with me to the library. It's hot today, and there's so much traffic with the concert this evening. It's not safe for him to stay outside."

"Your library reading chairs will be covered with cat hair, and he'll pee on the rug," Frank warned.

Penny waved away his complaints. "He did his business in his new litterbox. I left him snoozing by the window when I came over here. I'll bring him back to our house at the end of the day in his new cat carrier."

Penny posted the flyer of Yogi on the bulletin board right next to the wanted posters for a serial bank robber and an MS-13 gang member. "I'm going to hang the rest of them around town. Spread the word for me, Doris!"

Frank stood beside Doris's desk and watched his wife stride across the green toward Malone's and The Store. He figured Yogi's true owner was about as likely to be found in Trout Run as that gang member. "I bet some tourist dumped off the cat because they were tired of taking care of him."

"People are rotten." Doris elbowed Frank. "Looks like you got yourself a new pet."

When Frank returned to the green hours later, a long line of cars and trucks moved steadily past the gazebo and down to the parking area. Earl waved on anyone who hesitated or considered bolting toward a forbidden, traffic-blocking parking spot.

A sea of colorful lawn chairs and blankets radiated out from the gazebo stage. Kids chased one another through the maze, while the teenagers huddled in knots along the verge of the park. Frank found Penny and settled into his lawn chair, smiling at the periodic bleat of Earl's whistle. The kid loved that thing!

Some bongo drums, an electric keyboard, and two microphones stood on the stage. One guy with a guitar tested the sound system by playing a few random chords. The concert seemed close to starting. Penny waved to Edwin and Lucy picking their way through the labyrinth of lawn chairs and blankets. "Set your chairs up right here. We saved you a space."

"Thank goodness!" Lucy plopped into her brightly striped chair. "We served the Inn guests a cold picnic dinner, but Edwin still had trouble getting out of the kitchen." She leaned closer to Penny. "He makes everything too complicated. We didn't need to offer three different salads."

"You're here now. That's all that matters." Frank moved his chair to make room for Edwin. "What've you got in that cooler?"

Edwin opened up the insulated tote and pulled out a plastic container. "Marinated mozzarella anyone?"

A long arm reached over Edwin's shoulder and grabbed a snack. "Thanks, I'm starving."

"Bob! Squeeze in here with us."

Pastor Bob produced a small blanket and sat cross-legged at their feet. "I've been with the contractor all afternoon. I had no time to eat dinner." He looked up at the church steeple. "He patched the hole as best he could. It looks like crap."

Frank's eye was immediately drawn to the raw brown plywood nailed over the hole in the white steeple. It did look like crap, but he wouldn't say so. "It'll keep the critters out," was the best compliment he could come up with.

Luckily, he didn't have to say more. Reid Burlingame stepped up to the mic and launched into a long rah-rah speech about this being the eighteenth season of the Concerts on the Green, praising the organizing committee, thanking the sponsors, on and on.

"Let's get to the music, Reid," someone shouted from the crowd to loud laughter and cheers.

Reid tugged at the lapels of his seersucker sports coat and cleared his throat to regain the crowd's attention. "Without further ado, let's give a big welcome to tonight's performers, The Bright Lights!"

Two men and three women, all in their twenties and thirties, trotted onto the stage, joining the guitarist. As they picked up their instruments, a tall young man with auburn hair darted through the beam of the stage lights and disappeared into the crowd.

Frank craned his neck. "Was that Charlie Dunleavey? Who's he with?"

He twisted in his chair and tried to spot the young man in the sea of concertgoers. He wished he knew Charlie's connections in Trout Run. Were they local people or was he just crashing in some rented vacation home? Penny took his hand in hers and gave it a squeeze. "What does it matter? Sit back and enjoy the concert."

The guy on the lead guitar counted down three beats and the band began to play. The lead singer tossed her long blond hair and crooned into the mic with a lovely, rich alto—a far cry from Marley Maddow's caterwauling, thank God. The drummer threw back his head and half shut his eyes as he kept rhythm on the bongos. Transported by the music, he drummed, oblivious to the crowd. All the band members seemed like they were playing for one another, not the audience.

Frank relaxed in his seat. The band wasn't quite what he'd been anticipating—Will Sturgis's fiddle had no peers—but they weren't half bad.

After each song, the crowd clapped generously. But in one section, whistles and hoots augmented the applause and cheering.

"The band seems to have brought their own fan club," Frank said.

Penny stood from her chair and peered over at the cheering group. Then she sat back down. "Odd. Every single person in the band or in the fan club over there is wearing the same three colors: yellow, red, and electric blue."

Edwin squinted. "The kid on bongos is wearing a white shirt."

But he's got a yellow bandanna around his neck," Penny pointed out.

Frank assessed the band. The lead guitarist wore an electric blue plaid shirt, while the keyboardist sported a jaunty hat in the same shade. The bassist wore a yellow t-shirt and the singer wore a flowing red blouse. He turned to look at the cheering section. Penny was right: the same three colors cropped up throughout the group. Yet it wasn't a uniform. Every article of clothing was a different style.

The band started up again. This song thrummed with a strong bass line and all the band members sang, even the drummer.

Penny swayed in her seat. "Their music is catchy. It must all be original—I don't recognize the tunes."

Bob scowled. "It's praise band music."

"What does that mean?"

"Christian rock. The kind they play in megachurches with big projection screens."

"You think this band is from a megachurch?" Edwin asked. "I can hardly understand the lyrics. Did I miss something? Are they singing about God?"

"The refrain is 'Shine the light, be the light'—that seems pretty generic," Penny said.

Bob shifted on his blanket. "Maybe they changed the lyrics. I've definitely heard that tune before at a symposium I went to—Music to Attract Younger Worshippers".

"The way you just rolled your eyes, you must be taking lessons from Olivia." Lucy teased.

Bob seemed unamused at being compared to Edwin and Lucy's thirteen-year-old daughter. But Frank thought Lucy's crack was spot-on. And given the advanced age of the Trout Run Presbyterian congregation, it couldn't hurt to liven up the musical selections on Sunday. "So did you learn anything at this symposium?"

"Oh, just that everything I love and value about the church is all wrong and dooming our congregation to a rapid death."

Penny and Frank traded a glance above Bob's head. Lucy reached out and patted her friend's shoulder. "What's wrong, Bob? I've never seen you so dispirited."

"The church's finances were weak when I took this job, and they've only gotten worse over the last five years. The elders of the church seem to think

I should be adding all sorts of bells and whistles to the service to attract new members. Guitars instead of an organ. A projection screen instead of hymnals. A frozen yogurt machine at fellowship hour. And raffles!" He shuddered. "I didn't enter the ministry to run a carnival. If that's what it takes to keep a church going these days, maybe I should look for a different job."

Frank gazed at the familiar white clapboard church presiding serenely over the green. How had he been so unaware of these problems? In his experience. ministers always complained about money and carped about change—encouraging it or resisting it brought equal amounts of grousing. Were Trout Run Presbyterian's current problems more serious? Could the little church that had been at the heart of the town for over 150 years really be dying?

Before Lucy or anyone else could offer words of comfort to Bob, the band picked up their instruments again. This time, the audience recognized the song in the first few chords.

"Ooo, "Blinded by the Light"—they're covering the Springsteen song." Lucy danced in her seat.

"Springsteen covered Manford Man," Edwin reminded them.

"Whatever. It's a great song!"

At the refrain, the crowd all joined in, so the green was filled with the sound of hundreds of voices all singing "blinded" or "light" at slightly different times and wildly different pitches.

Frank smiled. A lively band. A happy crowd. No signs of trouble. Just the kind of evening he had hoped for.

"Blinded by the Light" was the big showstopper before intermission. Time for him to nail a piece of pie and trade places with Earl. He kissed Penny's cheek and slipped away as the band revved up to the climax of the song.

At the pie table, Frank tried to negotiate with the Spouses Auxiliary for early access. "I'm heading over to relieve Earl. I won't be back this way until the concert is all over."

Maureen McNulty crossed her arms across her ample bosom. "Pie sale doesn't begin until the band stops playing."

"There'll be nothing left but the raisin pie if I have to come back at the end of intermission." Frank clutched his throat and stuck out his tongue. "Have mercy on me."

Paula, the young clerk from the Store, slid her hand under the plastic wrap covering the table. "Chief Bennett likes strawberry-rhubarb." Using Maureen's body to shield the transaction from the hungry crowd, Paula passed him the slice of pie. "Three dollars. I can't make change."

Frank dropped a five in the collection tin and left, satisfied with the deal.

As he walked past the group of fans who'd come with the band, he saw Billy Flynn among them, laughing and talking with two young women and a young man about his age or a little younger. Maybe Billy was reconnecting with some old friends. That would take the pressure off Earl.

Frank wove through the sparser cluster of concert-goers at the edge of the green. No families here—only teenagers and young adults more interested in one another than in the music. This is where trouble tended to crop up later in the evening. Young men who'd come to the concert already buzzed got more full of bravado as the night wore on. He scanned the groups to see what they were drinking. They knew better than to bring open bottles of beer, so they sipped from red Solo cups. Frank knew they contained cheap vodka and fruit punch, and the kids knew he knew. They were at a truce this early in the evening. As long as there was no trouble, Frank wouldn't demand to smell the drinks. But at the first sign of rowdiness, all tolerance was off.

Frank smiled with a combination of charm and menace at a big knucklehead that Earl had written up on a DUI last month. He continued walking the perimeter of the park, approaching the foursome he'd rousted for smoking weed on the rocks under the covered bridge. Tonight no cloud of smoke hung over them. The boys kept their eyes focused on the band as Frank drew nearer, but Laurel looked right at him, unintimidated. The temporary lights strung through the trees illuminated a brightly inked tattoo climbing from inside her strapless top to her pale shoulder.

Frank met her gaze and nodded. His unspoken message to all of them: don't push your luck.

He left the green and walked toward the orange cones guiding the traffic toward the parking area. The sun had set, and in the dim glow of the lights strung in the green, Frank couldn't quite make out who Earl was talking to. Whoever it was, their conversation seemed quite animated.

Ten steps closer and Frank could see that Earl's conversation partner was an athletic young woman. She looked familiar....

"Okay, Earl—I'll take over here," Frank said as he approached them. "The crowd likes the band, so I think most people will stay to the end."

Earl startled. "Oh, er...hi, Frank. Didn't see you coming."

The temptation to say, "You wouldn't have noticed a meteor crashing in-to the gazebo," crossed his mind, but he swallowed the wisecrack. Frank rec-ognized the young woman now—it was Tess Keener the new DEC ranger. No longer wearing the utilitarian DEC uniform, she looked even more at-tractive in her civilian jeans and t-shirt with her wavy hair cascading onto her shoulders.

"I see you've met Rusty's new associate," Frank said to Earl. "She helped carry Charlie Dunleavy off Dix last week. And guess what? Charlie is here tonight."

"I'm glad that extraction had a happy ending." Tess smiled at Earl. "I'd better let you get back to work. Nice meeting you."

"I'll stop by the ranger office with a map to that trail I was telling you about," Earl called after her as she walked toward the green.

Tess glanced back over her shoulder and smiled again. "I'd like that."

Together, Frank and Earl watched her long legs moving beneath her tight jeans.

"A very nice addition to the ranger station," Frank commented.

"*Very* nice."

"Sorry to break up your little interlude, but we need to make a plan for the end of the night."

"No problem." Earl grinned. "Tess's working the desk at the ranger sta-tion on Monday. I'll be dropping by with a little information to help her get acclimated to her new posting. She just transferred here from the Lake George region."

"Your helpfulness is admirable. Now, I predict a mad rush after the last song. That's when kids end up getting separated from their parents, so keep an eye peeled. And this crew here," Frank nodded toward the drinkers, "is halfway to shit-faced already. I'll be watching them, but if you're close to the band, make sure you can still hear your radio. We may be providing rides home for some of them."

"Will do." Earl loped off into the crowd.

As he left, the full moon began its ascent in the eastern sky.

Chapter 14

With no traffic action during intermission, Frank leaned against the Welcome to Trout Run sign savoring his strawberry-rhubarb pie: flaky crust, perfect balance of sweet berries and tart rhubarb, filling neither too firm nor too runny. He debated who had baked it. Ruth Ann Givens? Marlys Vane? Definitely not Barbara Lubroski, who was known to use Pillsbury pre-made pie crusts. The Rescue Auxiliary considered it poor form for customers to ask who had baked what—they had a vested interest in getting as many people as possible donating homemade pies and cakes—but Frank suspected Paula had intentionally snagged him a slice donated by a highly regarded baker. He made a note to thank her next time he saw her at the Store.

A few yards away, Reid Burlingame's blue and white seersucker jacket glowed in the moonlight. Soon the town council chairman appeared beside him.

"Outstanding opening night, wouldn't you agree, Frank?"

"Not over yet, but yeah, we're off to a good start."

"Ah, Frank—always so cautious. I'm feeling quite optimistic, myself. We haven't had this big a turnout in years."

As the band continued to play, some of the young families drifted toward their cars pushing strollers loaded with tired and cranky toddlers. The old folks filtered out next, clinging to one another's arms and cautioning about where to step in the dark. The moon moved in and out of clouds, sometimes shining bright as a beacon, sometimes obscured by drifts of cirrus that might bring rain by morning. Frank shone his flashlight to illuminate the hazards of tree roots and loose stones on the shoulder of the road as the music lovers picked their way back to their cars. In the beam of light, he noticed Tess Keener talking to Billy Flynn.

Good thing Earl was on the other side of the park.

But the green was still three-quarters full when the band announced its last song, a true testament to the quality of the music. Frank grinned as he recognized the opening chords—a rousing cover of one of his favorites, the

Johnny Cash tune, "Ring of Fire." The Bright Lights' delivery was a little more cheerful than Johnny's gravelly ode to the fires of despair.

The audience surged to its feet. At each refrain, the crowd shouted back, "*the ring of fire!*" After five verses, the song ended, but the citizens of Trout Run wanted more.

"Encore! Play another song!"

From where he stood, Frank couldn't see the action on stage, but he soon heard a male voice. "Thank you all so much for your enthusiasm tonight. I'm Pastor Adam Fortway of the Tabernacle of Living Light. Remember, you can hear the Bright Lights every week on Monday evenings right after our free community dinner. Come on over and join us. And now, the band would be delighted to play one more number to sing you home."

So that's where the band was from. Had Ardyth known all along, or had Fortway's appearance come as a surprise to her and Reid both? Free food and free music. Frank suspected the Tabernacle would pack in a big crowd this coming Monday after that promotional spot.

The drums and guitars fell silent and the singer's voice cut through the night in a clear acapella. The song seemed vaguely familiar, but off somehow. Then Frank recognized it—Van Morrison's "Moondance" sung in a dreamy, lullaby-like tempo, which soothed the crowd and signaled that the concert had truly ended. People began folding their chairs and gathering up their blankets, then shuffled out of the park, murmuring farewells. Traffic increased, and Frank had his hands full directing the flow from the side street onto Route 86, while periodically stopping cars to let pedestrians surge across the road. A mother showed up at his side with a howling child who was not her own, and in the furor of getting the little girl reconnected with her parents, Frank lost sight of the drinkers and the pack of boys surrounding Laurel Caine.

By ten, all the cars had driven off. The stage stood empty. The folded pie sale tables leaned against a tree waiting to go into storage until the next concert. Although the lawn would require the attention of the Garden Club in the morning, the concert had gone off without a hitch. Earl loped toward him and Frank raised his hand for a high-five.

"Good work, partner. I think we can both sleep late tomorrow."

"Yeah, the new parking plan real—"

A piercing scream silenced Earl. "No-o-o-o! Stop! Stop her!"

"That sounded like it came from the covered bridge." Frank took off running the block to the bridge. Earl soon overtook him. Breathless, they arrived at the short, steep descent to the river to find a knot of people staring up at the roof of the covered bridge. A shadowy figure crouched in the middle. As a cloud scudded away, the moon came out and bathed the bridge in silver light. The crouching figure rose—a slender young woman with long hair wearing shorts and an off-the-shoulder blouse.

Laurel Caine.

She extended one bare foot and took a step closer to the edge. A hush fell on the small crowd. In the silent night, the water of Stony Brook surged over the jagged boulders and slabs of rock in the riverbed below.

She stretched her arms up over her head, as if to pluck the round moon from the sky.

"Laurel!" a shout rang through the night.

Laurel bent her knees and sprang forward.

She fell through the air without a cry.

The next sound was the sharp crack of bone against stone.

Chapter 15

Half a beat and bedlam erupted.

Women screamed. Men cursed.

Frank and Earl charged into Stony Brook. Laurel Caine lay sprawled across the rocks, twisted as a little girl's doll flung out the car window by a spiteful brother.

Frank reached her first. Laurel's lifeless eyes stared right at him, as bold in death as they had been in life. The tattoo of a colorful bird in flight mocked him. In the beam of his flashlight, he saw the surging current carry her rich, red blood downstream. He checked for a pulse even though he knew he wouldn't feel one.

Earl crowded in beside him, and Frank felt the young man recoil. "There's nothing we can do for her. We need to move the body quickly, so it doesn't get swept away." Frank debated which assignment was worse for Earl: asking him to stand guard over the body or asking him to disperse the expanding crowd of gawkers. He quickly decided his authority was required to deal with the crowd.

"Check her pockets for a phone," he told Earl.

As he scrambled up the bank, he could hear people buzzing.

"I can't believe it. I saw her at the concert. She looked like she was having fun."

"She musta been high as a kite."

"You don't know that. The poor kid hasn't had an easy life."

Frank stood in front of the twenty bystanders. When they saw his grim face, they fell silent. "Please, everyone—go straight home. Keep what you saw to yourselves. I have to notify Laurel's father. Give me a chance to do that before you start beating the jungle drums."

Ruth Ann Givens started to cry. Chuck who worked at the hardware shook his head and backed away. Ellie Haskell opened her mouth to ask a question, but her husband yanked her toward their car. Frank knew that by morning twenty different versions of what had happened at the bridge would be circulating around town. All he asked was a fifteen-minute head start to get the truth to Laurel Caine's father.

Someone in the crowd had had the presence of mind to call the rescue squad. The ambulance parked at the head of the path to the brook. Frank gave the crew careful instructions. The body would need to be transported to Saranac for an autopsy. Most likely it would take a full week before the toxicology report came back to let them know just what Laurel had ingested to make herself believe she could fly.

———◆———

FRANK PULLED UP IN front of the Caine house. A light glowed in one of the front windows, but no one had left the porch light on for Laurel. Did her father even know where she was? Frank hadn't seen Matthew Caine at the concert, but he might have been somewhere in the crowd. Or maybe music and pie wasn't his idea of a fun Saturday night.

Frank knocked on the door, and the dog began barking inside. He thought he saw a flash of motion behind the curtained window, but no one answered the door.

Frank pounded louder. "Trout Run police, Mr. Caine. I need to talk to you. It's important."

The door opened a crack, and an eye peered out from under bleached blond bangs. "Matt's asleep." A smoker's rasp delivered the message. "What's Laurel gone and done now?"

"Ma'am, can you open the door please?"

With a disgusted huff, she yanked it open and stood on the threshold with her arms crossed over a long, ratty t-shirt. If she was wearing shorts, they were quite well concealed.

"Ma'am, I need you to wake up Mr. Caine. There's been an accident. I need to talk to him."

The woman looped a hank of stringy hair behind one ear. "What kinda accident? Laurel don't drive."

The kind of accident that makes no sense. The kind of accident that wipes out all a kid's fresh chances.

"She fell. Please go and get Mr. Caine."

Something in the finality of Frank's tone motivated the woman to do as she was told. She shuffled into the house, hurling a complaint over her shoulder. "Awright. But it won't be easy."

Frank stepped into the tiny living room to wait. The place looked like it had been pleasant once, with cheerful checked curtains and a display of framed family photos. But now the coffee table sported a pattern of beer bottle rings, and the sofa cushion oozed stuffing where the bored dog had gone to work on it. A cluster of ants crawled over a plate smeared with congealed egg and jam. The scent of cigarette smoke coated the back of Frank's throat.

Every moment he waited made Frank's task more distasteful. Was it worse to deliver terrible news to a happy family? Or did the evidence of Laurel's sad life make her death even more tragic?

Low voices and grunts reached his ears from the back of the house, followed by staggering footsteps and the sound of water running. Finally, a man appeared in the doorway to the living room. Like Laurel, Matthew Caine was tall and thin. His glazed eyes peered at Frank from a grizzled face.

Frank introduced himself and extended a hand to shake. Caine hesitated, as if this were some strange custom of an alien culture, but he finally responded. The physical contact seemed to wake him up fully. "Wha—" His voice cracked and shuddered into a painful, wracking cough. "Why are you here? What happened to Laurel?"

"Laurel was at the concert on the green tonight with some friends. After the show, she apparently went down to the covered bridge." Frank took a deep breath to steel himself for the worst part. "She climbed up to the roof."

Matthew's head tilted. "What? Don't tell me she was spraying graffiti. Jeez."

If only.

Frank pressed his lips together, then let the rest of the message pour out. "She jumped, Mr. Caine. Laurel jumped off the bridge."

Caine's mouth hung open. The girlfriend scratched her head. "Into the water?"

"The water's only a couple feet deep there. She landed on the rocks." Frank looked at the beaten down brown carpet and shook his head.

"Wait. Wait." Matthew Caine stepped closer. Frank could smell the alcohol sweating through his pores. "You're saying...."

"Laurel died, sir. I'm very sorry for your loss."

Chapter 16

Matthew Caine was too drunk and too shell-shocked to be interviewed. Frank left the father to the dubious comforts of the woman who'd answered the door and asked if he could go back to Laurel's bedroom.

Neither one objected, but neither offered to show him the way. In a house so small, Frank really didn't need a guide. He averted his eyes from the gray and tangled sheets on a queen-sized bed in one bedroom and opened the door to the only other bedroom.

What he saw made his eyes prick with tears for the first time in this awful night.

Laurel had kept her small room meticulously. The twin bed was made, covered by a worn pink and white daisy comforter appropriate for a much younger girl. Laurel's limited wardrobe hung neatly on hangers all facing the same way. A framed photo of a younger Laurel with a pretty woman in her thirties stood on the desk. A poster of the Eiffel Tower hung on the wall. Laurel had tried to create an oasis of order and beauty in this miserable house.

The mutt Frank had seen on his first visit lay on the far side of the bed with his head between his outstretched paws. He regarded Frank through one brown eye, then sighed and turned away.

Frank searched for a note or any other sign that Laurel had been planning to take her own life. But the room held no clues—no computer, no diary, no letters, no drugs. Just a stack of paperback books with dragons and swords on the covers.

He stood at Laurel's window and gazed into the black night. Tomorrow would be a day devoted to picking at a scab. What was there to investigate? Laurel had committed suicide. He and Earl and twenty other people had witnessed it. The autopsy would eventually reveal to what extent she was addled by drugs and booze. A chat with her friends might uncover a boyfriend who'd dumped her or some mean girls who'd hassled her. But in the end, her suicide would be inexplicable. How could someone so young feel such despair? But even as that thought passed through his mind, he knew he was asking the wrong question. When you were old, it was easy to forget the passions of youth. Looking back forty years to his teen years, he could see now that being cut from the high school baseball team hadn't ruined his life. But at the time, he thought he'd never recover from the humiliation.

Had something so inconsequential driven Laurel to end her life?

Frank had once seen a video of a young man talking about surviving his leap off the Golden Gate Bridge. The kid said that the moment his fingers let go of the railing, he'd been flooded with regret. He'd realized that he *did* want to live. Had Laurel felt that? Of course, a leap off the Trout Run covered bridge didn't give a jumper much time for contemplation. Laurel had hit the rocks within two seconds. Was that enough time to feel regret?

Frank pictured her silent, graceful fall. He had to admit, she hadn't seemed sorry.

WHEN FRANK RETURNED to the huddle of misery in the living room, Matthew Caine rose from the sofa. The father lurched toward Frank like a zombie. "You're wrong. Laurel was fooling around with those kids she hangs out with. She must've slipped. An accident."

"I saw her with her friends earlier in the evening. But she was alone on top of the bridge. I got there just before she jumped." Frank put his hand on the man's shoulder. "I'm sorry, sir. Her action was intentional. Had she been depressed?"

Caine scanned his living room like a raccoon who'd wandered into a house and couldn't figure out how to exit. "I know my daughter. She wouldn't...Laurel would never..."

Frank figured if he had a dollar for every parent who'd ever uttered the words, "I know my child would never..." he could buy a fancy house on Mirror Lake. "Did you notice any mood swings?"

"All teenage girls are moody," the girlfriend offered.

Caine spun around. "Shut up!"

The woman shrugged and left the room.

So there was no need to enquire how Laurel had gotten along with her father's companion. "How was Laurel spending her summer? Did she have a job?"

Caine shook his head. "We only have the one car. That makes it hard."

The house was more than two hilly miles from the center of town—walkable for the right motivation. But the tourist attractions that hired seasonal workers were much further away.

"So how did she spend her days?" Frank pressed.

Caine raked his fingers through his already wild hair. "She'd be asleep when I left for work. Out with her friends when I got home." He held out his hands for understanding. "If they offer me overtime, I gotta take it. Laurel told me she could manage her own dinner. I, I— " Caine didn't mention the long nights he spent at the Mountainside. "How long ago did Laurel's mother die?" Frank asked gently.

"Almost three years now. It was hard, so hard. But I thought Laurel was doing okay. Her grades were good. She didn't cry anymore."

There was a limit to how many tears a person could shed. Frank knew that well enough. But dry eyes didn't mean the grieving had ended.

"I told you last week that Laurel was smoking weed. Did you talk to her about it?"

"She told me you were mistaken. She and her friends were just hanging out. One of the boys had a cigarette."

Frank gave the father a long stare. "The kids tossed away the joint by the time I got down to them. But I assure you, I know what marijuana smells like. I didn't have evidence to arrest her. But Laurel was pretty stoned. Maybe her habit was more serious than either one of us realized."

Caine gripped the ratty blanket draped across the back of the sofa. "You think the drugs made her do it?"

In Frank's experience, PCP or meth could make a sane person do something deranged. Weed didn't have that effect although he'd heard of people who smoked themselves into a psychotic break. "There's no point in speculating before we get the autopsy results."

Caine's eyes widened. "Laurel...where is she? Don't I have to...?"

"Her body was taken to the Adirondack Medical Center. They won't release it until they've done an autopsy. Probably on Monday."

"But my baby...I want to see her."

"I'll drive you over there tomorrow to make the identification."

"ID? So maybe it's not Laurel."

"It's a formality, Mr. Caine." Frank turned away from the desperate hope in the father's eyes. "Laurel had a tattoo on her shoulder, correct?"

Caine collapsed on the sofa and buried his head in his hands. "A bird. A beautiful bird and the numbers 5/6/15. She got it in memory of her mother's death."

Chapter 17

Frank had planned to go to church on Sunday to support Pastor Bob, but Laurel's suicide made this Sunday a work day. When he entered the office, he found a large bowl of uncooked rice on his desk.

"What the hell's this?"

"I'm drying out Laurel's phone," Earl explained. "I found it in her front pocket. The way she landed, it didn't get broken, but it did get wet. I took it home last night and put it in rice. I was waiting for you to come in before I try turning it on."

Frank watched as Earl put on a pair of gloves and fished the phone out of the rice. "That works?"

"Worked for my cousin Donald when he fell out of his canoe. The phone might need to sit longer. We'll see."

But when Earl pressed the power button, Laurel's phone remained stubbornly dark. Frank scowled and turned away. "Old wives' tale."

"The rice will work eventually. We just need to have patience."

"You know I've got none of that. I need to talk to those three boys who were with Laurel at the concert last night. Did you see them?"

"One of them was Tyler Voorhees. Not sure about the others—didn't see them that clearly," Earl said.

"I only need one to get started. Track him down and get him in here, please."

Tyler arrived within the hour, red-eyed and shaken, accompanied by his mother. The boy was a minor, so she had every right to be there, but Frank knew her presence would complicate his work.

"This is terrible, terrible." Lydia Voorhees started talking before Frank even said hello. "But Tyler doesn't know anything about why she did it, do you honey?"

"Have a seat, please." Frank plastered his most reassuring smile on his face. "All I want to do is establish the timeline of events last night."

"Tyler just ran into that girl for a little while at the concert and then he came home with us, right honey?"

"I just want to ask Tyler a few questions, ma'am. As I said, no one's in any trouble." Frank turned to the boy. "Now, Tyler, I saw you and Laurel and two other boys together at the concert before intermission. What are the names of those other guys?"

Tyler gulped, and his eyes darted back and forth. He opened his mouth and shut it again without a sound.

"You're not ratting out your friends," Earl reassured him. "Lots of people saw you guys together. We can figure it out. It'd just be easier if you'd tell us."

Tyler sighed and spit the names out in a rush. "Jimmy Metz and Gordon Brophy. You won't be able to get ahold of Jimmy. He left before dawn on a backwater camping trip with his dad. St. Regis Wilderness. I bet he doesn't even know what happened to Laurel."

Frank exchanged a glance with Earl. They'd follow up as soon as this interview ended.

"Laurel didn't have a car. Did one of you pick her up?" Frank continued.

Tyler nodded. "Jimmy got her."

"Is—was—Jimmy Laurel's boyfriend?"

Tyler made a face. "They were talking, that's all."

Frank had learned that teenagers no longer dated. Talking apparently preceded a full-fledged romance. He would definitely need to meet with this Jimmy.

"What kind of mood was Laurel in last night?"

The shoulders moved up. The head hunched down. "I dunno."

Of course Tyler didn't know. If Frank had asked him how the engine of Jimmy's car had been running, the kid probably could have rambled on for five minutes describing it. Ask him about a girl's emotions, and he was clueless. "Did she and Jimmy argue? Did she seem sad? Any tears?"

"No, there was no fight. They didn't say a lot. But Laurel never talked much."

"Tyler hardly knows this girl, right honey?" The mother was up on the edge of her seat, ready to spring.

"You both go to High Peaks High School—rising seniors, correct?"

"Yeah, but...."

"But what?"

Again the elaborate shoulder contortion, as if he were trying to physically roll out from under Frank's questions. "Laurel was...different."

Frank steepled his fingers and leaned back in his chair. "How so?"

"She did what she wanted. She didn't care about the same stuff as other kids. She didn't care about the football team, or the junior prom, or the class trip."

"What did she care about?"

"I, I—I dunno."

"Did she care about grades?"

Tyler shook his head. "She never raised her hand, but if a teacher called on her, she always knew the answer. She didn't try, but she always did okay."

Tyler shuffled his big, sneakered feet. "I can't explain it. Laurel was weird, but like, not in a bad way."

Who knew what that meant? Frank could tell that asking for clarification would be pointless. He could only hope that one of the other kids on the list was more eloquent. They were all boys, so his hopes weren't high.

"What girls was Laurel friends with?"

Tyler squinted his eyes in deep thought. "Not sure. She didn't hang out with girls much."

"Uh-huh. So, why were you hanging out with her?"

"She was with Jimmy and Jimmy is friends with us."

"Last week, were the four of you together under the covered bridge?"

A brilliant flush rose from Tyler's chest, raced up his neck, inflamed his cheeks, and threatened to set his hair on fire. "No."

The lie was laughably inept, but Frank let it go. Tyler would never tell him about the weed-smoking in front of his mother. Frank would see what the other boys told him and then come back for round two.

"After the music ended last night, what did you four do?"

"I went home with my parents," Tyler nodded toward his mother. "Laurel and Jimmy and Gordon were near the gazebo when I left."

"What were their plans?"

Tyler raised his hands palms up. "Just hang out, I guess."

"Thank God you weren't with them," Lydia Voorhees said. "Tyler wanted to stay, and I said no. What is this hanging out? There could be nothing worthwhile to do in town after the concert was over."

Tyler examined the ceiling with a pained look on his face.

"If more parents kept a closer watch on their kids, these terrible things wouldn't happen."

"M-o-m-m!"

Frank stood up. "Okay. Thank you for your time. You've been very helpful."

Tyler staggered to his feet looking stunned that his ordeal was over so soon.

Mrs. Voorhees headed for the door nattering nonstop about tragedy and never knowing and personal responsibility. When the mother's back was turned, Frank slipped his card into Tyler's shirt pocket and gave the kid's shoulder a little squeeze. "If you think of anything else, let me know."

With mother and son gone, silence descended on the office.

After a wait, Frank asked, "You know this Jimmy kid who was the boyfriend?"

"Seen him around. He's into hunting and fishing." Earl scanned his notes. "I think we might have better luck with Gordon Brophy. He was in my little brother's Boy Scout troop. My brother hated him."

"And why will that bring us luck?"

"Because he's the kind of kid who's always trying to suck up."

Chapter 18

Frank left Earl to track down Gordon Brophy and verify that Jimmy Metz had truly gone camping while he took Matthew Caine to identify Laurel's body.

The forty-minute drive to Saranac passed in painful silence. Frank asked if the Caines had a computer, but Matthew said their old one had died, and he had cancelled their internet service to save money. Then Frank asked about the possibility that Jimmy Metz had been Laurel's boyfriend, but Matthew didn't even recognize the name.

"I, I—I didn't know there was a boy. She never said. Her mother would have—" He turned his head and stared out the window. His hands clenched and unclenched in his lap. "You think that's why she...."

"Not necessarily. I haven't talked to the kid yet, but his friend said Laurel and Jimmy didn't argue. At least, not that he knew."

"I'll kill him." Mathew punched one hand into the other. "I'll kill him if he hurt her."

Frank knew it was the father's own guilt talking, but he offered silent thanks that Jimmy was camping on a tiny island somewhere in the maze of lakes and streams that made up the St. Regis Wilderness. Frank took his eyes off the road for a moment. "I'm going to try my best to figure out what happened. But we may never know why Laurel jumped. There's rarely one straightforward reason. At least, not a reason that makes sense to those left behind."

"I've got Gordon Brophy scheduled to come into the office at two," Earl reported. "Jimmy and his dad definitely went camping. His mom said he didn't even take his phone 'cause it's new and he didn't want it to get wet. Hey, speaking of which—I got Laurel's phone to turn on. Ask her dad if he knows her password."

"Don't get your hopes up. He doesn't even know her friends' names."

"It's usually something obvious, like a birthday."

"Okay, I'll try to get him to brainstorm."

But when Matthew Caine emerged from the morgue, he looked too much like a zombie for conversation. On the way back to Trout Run, he didn't speak a word. Frank's mind drifted as he drove. It wasn't until he pulled up in front of the Caine home that Frank remembered what Earl had asked him to do.

"Say, Matthew—my assistant has gotten Laurel's phone dried out. It might be helpful to see who she'd been in contact with on Saturday. Do you know her password?"

Caine paused with his hand on the car door. Frank could tell that he wanted to help. Then he shook his head.

"Maybe we can guess it. What's her birthday?"

Frank jotted down the date. "Your birthday?"

Caine's head swung back and forth. He looked even more miserable, if that were possible. "She wouldn't use that. Maybe her mother's birthday." He rattled off the numbers.

"Okay, thanks. We'll try these. I'll be in touch as soon as I know anything."

Frank drove back to the office and turned over to Earl the dates supplied by Laurel's father. Earl tried each one.

"Nope." Earl gripped the tantalizing prize of the phone, its secrets so firmly locked away.

"I just thought of something," Frank said. "The date of her mother's death was part of Laurel's tattoo. Five, six, twenty-fifteen. Try that."

"We're in!" Earl's fingers flashed across the screen. "Let's see who she was texting with that night."

From behind his desk, Frank watched Earl's expression change from excitement to shock to horror.

"What?" He moved to Earl's side and picked up the phone.

The screen showed a string of messages with no replies, the last words Laurel would ever see. They all came from the same number, a number without out a contact name.

You know your challenge.

Are you ready?

This is your moment.

Go!

Chapter 19

The phone dropped through Frank's fingers and clattered onto the desk. "Goddam. Someone coaxed her to jump."

Earl picked up the scratched Galaxy in its purple and silver case. He read the words aloud to make sure they weren't imagining this evil. Then he looked at Frank. "Promoting suicide is illegal in New York. A Class E felony."

"Yes, but to get a conviction, you have to prove intent. The DA will say those words aren't enough." Unlike prosecutors who made the national news by filing charges in controversial cases, the Essex County DA was a conservative man, uninterested in the spotlight and unwilling to engage in fruitless work. "We need to find out who sent the texts and then look for more corroborating evidence of motive. It's possible we're jumping to the wrong conclusion."

Earl returned his attention to the phone. "The first three messages came in at 9:30 through 9:47. Right as the concert was ending."

"And the last one?"

"10:02."

"And then she jumped. What kind of sick bastard—" Despite his warning to Earl that they had to proceed cautiously, Frank felt a knot of outrage building in his gut. He envisioned Laurel's uncanny calmness as she stepped off the bridge. The person encouraging the girl had produced that, he suspected.

"It can't be one of the boys. They were with her. They wouldn't need to text her." Earl fiddled with the phone. "It's not a number in her contacts. And the area code isn't local. So it's unlikely the texter is a kid from school."

"But how could a stranger have such influence?" Frank paced around the office. "The Caines only have one car. The kid barely had a way into the center of town, let alone access to other areas."

"Maybe she connected with some creep on the internet."

"Possibly. But there's no computer or wi-fi in the house. That phone would be her only link."

"She doesn't have any social media apps on here. Not even Facebook."

Frank returned to look over Earl's shoulder again. As was typical of a kid, all the contacts in the phone were listed simply as first names. And as Tyler had told them, there were more boys than girls. Tyler, Gordon, Jimmy and Dad were on the list. There were some other boys' names, but only three girls: Abigail, Franny, and Shannon.

Frank jotted the numbers of the girls, then handed the phone to Earl. "Get a trace on the texter's phone number."

"Sure. What are you going to do?"

"I'm calling the girls on the list. They're more likely to know what was going on with Laurel."

As Earl began the lengthy process of getting the number traced, Frank moved onto the girls on the list. Dialing from the office phone, he knew that "Trout Run PD" would show up on the recipient's caller ID. Would the girls answer, or would he have to track them down? Neither Abigail nor Franny picked up, but before he could make the next call, the principal of High Peaks High School called him.

"I'm devastated by this news. Teachers and parents have been calling me all morning. Is there anything you can tell me?"

Frank had no intention of sharing the information about the text messages. But he figured the principal might have some useful information. "Was Laurel bullied?" he asked.

"No." The principal's answer came quick and certain. "I mean, we adults can never know all the social dynamics going on among our students. But Laurel wasn't a girl that other students picked on. In fact, they seemed a little intimidated by her."

"You seem to know her well."

"It's a small school, and I taught English here for twenty years before taking over as principal. I still teach a class, just to keep my classroom skills sharp. Laurel was one of my students." The principal continued, "Laurel didn't have a lot of friends, but I suspect that was by her choice. She didn't have much patience for silliness and gossip. Instead of being part of one group—the nerds or the jocks or the AT Vers—she seemed to pick and choose. One day I'd see her eating with the girl who will definitely be valedictorian of her class. The next day I'd see her with a guy who's going to flunk out if he doesn't stop play-ing video games."

Frank inquired about the three girls in Laurel's contact list. The principal quickly supplied the last names of Abigail and Franny, but even after he checked his records, he couldn't find a Shannon registered at High Peaks High School.

"So Laurel didn't strike you as vulnerable?" Frank probed.

"I didn't say that. Laurel was deeply affected by her mother's death. Maybe her pain is why she kept her distance from the other kids. But she wasn't the kind of kid that other kids target."

"Not the kid with 'kick me' written on her back," Frank clarified.

"Exactly. I always hoped," the principal's voice broke and he coughed to cover his distress, "hoped that once Laurel got through this rough patch after her mother's death, she'd go on to bigger and better things. She was bright and, and—"

Frank waited while the principal searched for the right word.

"Imaginative. Conceptual." He sighed. "Trout Run was too small for her. She probably couldn't see a way out. Maybe that's why she did it."

As Frank hung up with the principal, Gordon Brophy, one of the other boys who'd been with Laurel at the concert, arrived for his interview.

Before the kid entered the inner office, Frank lowered his voice and spoke to Earl, who had finished initiating the trace. "Don't mention anything about Laurel's phone and those text messages. I don't want that circulating around town."

As soon as Gordon came in, Frank could tell that Earl's assessment was accurate. Goofy-looking and anxious, Gordon was the kind of kid who caved to authority. He not only answered Frank's questions, but also offered up more information. "We saw some other kids from school, but Laurel didn't want to hang with them. They were fooling around and making noise, and Laurel wanted to listen to the band. She was really into the music."

"This other group of kids—were Abigail and Franny in that group?"

Gordon nodded energetically, with none of Tyler's reluctance to give up names, and no curiosity about why Frank was asking.

"What about Shannon?"

Gordon scrunched his face in thought. "Shannon who?" Frank let it go and moved on to ask about the end of the evening.

"Laurel kept checking her phone," Gordon said. "Jimmy wanted to know who was texting her, but she wouldn't say. He tried to grab her phone to see, but she pulled it away."

"He thought she was texting with another boy?"

"I guess. So Jimmy got mad and said he was going home and wasn't going to drive her. She said she didn't care and told him to go ahead and go. That's when Jimmy and me left. Jimmy kept looking back over his shoulder at Laurel. She was walking toward the covered bridge."

"Alone?"

"There were other people on the road, but no one was walking with her."

"When she was reading these other texts—how did she react?"

Gordon stared at him as if he needed a clue, but Frank didn't want to plant ideas in his witness's mind.

Gordon breathed through his mouth.

"Not upset," he murmured as if he'd successfully eliminated one answer on a multiple-choice quiz. "Kinda like...eager. Like when you've been waiting a long time for your turn and then it's finally time to go."

Chapter 20

After Gordon left, Frank picked up the phone again. "Let's see if we can find out who this Shannon is." He dialed, and immediately a female voice answered. In just the word "hello"—suspicious, edgy—Frank knew he'd reached a woman, not a teenage girl.

"Is this Shannon?" Frank asked.

"Maybe. Who are you? Why are you calling from the police? Who's in trouble?"

"There's no trouble, ma'am. This is Police Chief Frank Bennett. I'm calling about Laurel Caine."

"Who?"

"Laurel Caine. I'm investigating her suicide. I found your name and number in her phone contacts."

"Wha—? Wait, you mean that kid who jumped off the bridge?"

"Yes, ma'am. Just your first name was in her contacts. Could I have your last name please?"

"What? No. I don't know that girl. I've never talked to her. Why would she have my number?"

Why was she so belligerent? He hadn't accused her of anything. "It's just a routine follow-up, ma'am. I'm calling everyone in Laurel's contact list."

"And I'm telling you, I don't know her. I never gave that girl my number…. unless—"

"Unless what?"

"Nothing. Nothing."

"Can I have your last name, ma'am?"

"Mo-m-m-e-e-e." A child's shrill scream came through the phone.

"Derek, stoppit! You're gonna get hurt." These words were spoken away from the phone. Then Shannon's voice got louder. "Look, I've gotta go. My kids are gonna kill each other." And the line went dead.

Frank looked at Earl. "Any chance you know a young mother named Shannon with at least two little kids, one of whom's named Derek?"

Earl's eyes widened. "Shannon Wilton. That's Billy Flynn's sister. What's the connection?"

"Shannon told me she didn't know Laurel," Frank said. "She sounded genuinely confused. Then she seemed to think of something but didn't want to elaborate."

Earl sat still and toyed with a paperclip on the desk.

"What?"

Earl shook himself. "Nothing."

"Something," Frank insisted.

"Billy can't afford his own phone. Now that he moved out of his parents' house and in with his sister, Shannon said he could give out her cell number as a contact when he applies for jobs."

"So you think Billy used his sister's phone to call Laurel?"

Earl's eyebrows drew together as he searched Frank's face for reassurance. "Why would Billy be calling Laurel? She's just a kid, a high schooler. Maybe Shannon called her as a babysitter once, and she just forgot."

Frank handed Earl Laurel's phone. "See if there's a call from Shannon in her recent calls."

Earl took the phone like it was a hand grenade. His face told Frank everything he needed to know. "There's a call from Shannon on Friday afternoon." He tossed the phone back onto the desk and rocked back in his chair. "What could the connection be?"

"She was a pretty girl. He's a lonely guy."

Earl slammed upright. "C'mon—she's seventeen! Billy doesn't have to stalk young girls. He could have any woman he wants."

"Back in the day. Not now. He's unemployed, practically homeless, and prone to violent outbursts. I don't see a line of eligible women forming. But a young girl might be flattered by the attention of a good-looking older guy. Especially a troubled young girl."

Earl jumped up. "Don't go pinning Laurel's suicide on Billy! He's got enough trouble without you fitting him up for this. And Shannon's number isn't the number that sent the texts."

"I'm not pinning anything on him. But it's not that hard to imagine those two having a connection. In my experience, troubled people gravitate to each other."

Earl poked the phone as if he were pushing away a gross bug. "The texts didn't come from Billy."

"They didn't come from Billy using Shannon's phone. He could've borrowed someone else's phone to send them." Frank held up his hands to ward off the anticipated objection. "I'm just brainstorming."

"Let's stop *brainstorming* and actually get some facts." Earl pulled out his own cell phone and called Shannon's number. "Hi, this is Earl Davis. I'm a friend of Billy's—"

Earl held the phone away from his ear. Frank could hear an agitated stream of words as he watched Earl's tense face. He didn't need to decipher them all to understand the irritation.

"Okay. Sorry to bother—" Earl massaged his temples. "She hung up on me. Said she's tired of Billy's friends using her number to contact him. Said she was blocking my number."

Frank clapped Earl on the shoulder. "We'll go talk to her face-to-face tomorrow and get to the bottom of this."

Chapter 21

First thing Monday morning, there was still no news on Laurel's toxicology report and still no news on who owned the number that sent the goading messages to her right before her death. Frank had, however, succeeded in getting through to the parents of Laurel's friends, Abigail and Franny. But his conversations with each girl hadn't yielded much of interest. Apparently, they'd been assigned to work together on a group project in history class during the spring semester. After the project was completed, neither girl had been in touch with Laurel. "We weren't really friends," Abigail explained. "She was nice. But she was different."

Franny said she'd invited Laurel to a sleepover, but she hadn't come. "She told me she was busy, but I don't think she was."

Lonely. Different. Out of the high school mainstream.

Open to a friendship with an unhappy veteran?

Time to talk to Billy Flynn. And Frank made up his mind to go without Earl. If he had to pressure Shannon to get information about her brother, he didn't want Earl intervening to protect Billy. When his assistant set off on the morning patrol, Frank drove to Shannon Wilton's house.

When he pulled up to the modest ranch house, Frank saw a man in his early thirties—steel-toe boots, Stevenson's lumberyard shirt—in the open garage fixing the flat tire on a child's bike. When he saw Frank, he smiled and rubbed his right hand against his pants before offering it to shake.

"Frank Bennett, Trout Run and Verona Police Chief."

"Jeff Wilton." The man's smile stayed in place, but Frank saw a shadow of concern enter his eyes.

"I'm actually here to talk to your brother-in-law, Billy Flynn. Is he around?"

Now the concern flared to full-scale alarm. "No. Why? What's he done? Oh, God."

"He hasn't done anything wrong, so far as I know." But Frank found it interesting that Jeff immediately assumed that Billy had. "I just need to have a word with him. Do you know when he'll be back?"

Jeff shook his head. "I don't know where he's staying now. He left two days ago."

"Billy's not living with you anymore? Why did he leave?"

"Having him live with us didn't work out." Jeff clasped his hands and looked down at the floor. "Billy means well. He's trying to help out with the kids. But sometimes he plays too rough with them and gets them all wound up. And the other day, he loaded them both in his canoe and took them out on Heart Pond without life jackets. Our daughter came home and told her mother and Shannon went ballistic. She told Billy he was totally irresponsible and had put the kids' lives at risk and that he wasn't welcome to stay with us anymore."

Jeff looked up. "All this happened while I was at work. Shannon and I work different shifts, so we don't need a babysitter for the kids. When I got home, they were fighting. Obviously, putting two little kids who can barely doggy paddle in a canoe without life jackets wasn't too smart. But no one got hurt, so I said lesson learned and let's move on. But Shannon wasn't having it. She kept yelling at Billy until he packed his duffel bag and took off in his truck."

Frank listened with rising anxiety. It sounded like Billy had lost the small corner of stability he'd only recently found. Could this expulsion from his sister's house have tipped Billy over the edge? A horrible thought popped into his head. What if this had been a suicide pact? What if Billy had urged Laurel to jump because he too planned to kill himself? Did he persuade Laurel they could meet up on the other side?

Wasn't that the kind of romantic bullshit a teenage girl would be drawn to?

"And you haven't talked to him since?"

Jeff shook his head. "He doesn't have his own phone."

"Had Billy been giving Shannon's number as a way to get in touch with him?"

"Yeah, she told him it was fine to do that when he was applying for jobs. But then she started getting calls from random drinking buddies and girls, and she got mad. That was another part of their fight."

"Do you know the friends' names?"

"Nah. You'd have to ask Shannon. She's at work now." Jeff picked up a wrench and went back to work on the bike.

"She works at Stevenson's too?"

"Yeah—in the office." Jeff's head bobbed up from his project. "But don't bother her there. She won't like that."

It wasn't lost on Frank that Jeff seemed as unwilling to antagonize Shannon as his mother-in-law Martha was to antagonize Shannon's father, Gene.

"The office staff leaves at four, right?"

Jeff's forehead furrowed. "Yeah, but.... What's this about? Shannon told me you called yesterday about that girl who jumped off the bridge."

"Just a routine inquiry." Frank turned to leave.

"You don't really think Billy had anything to do with that girl?" Jeff called after him as Frank walked toward his truck.

Frank stayed silent.

"Oh, shit."

THE DRIVE BACK TO THE office would take him past the Rock Slide, the outdoor equipment store where Martha worked. While he drove, he called Trudy Massinay.

"When's the last time you spoke to Billy Flynn?"

"Last week. But I heard from his counselor at the VA this morning. Billy didn't show up for his last appointment."

Frank cursed and updated the social worker on what was happening in Billy's life. But he didn't mention the texts to Laurel. "Any chance he could be suicidal?"

"The suicide rate among vets with PTSD is high. I asked him about suicidal ideation, but he said no."

"Did you believe him?"

"I believed he wasn't thinking of it immediately before I talked to him. That doesn't mean he couldn't have changed his mind. Suicide is often an impulsive act."

Not when you've been working on persuading someone to join you.

"I'm worried about him, Trudy. How unstable do you think he is?"

"Imagine spending five years in the hot, dusty, ugly desert. There are long periods of boredom interspersed with short stretches of intense fear. There's someone yelling at you, telling you what to do every minute of the day. To get through the days, you fantasize about home. You remember your parents as the two sweetest people on the planet. You picture the beautiful green mountains and valleys and cool streams of Trout Run. You fantasize about being free to do whatever you want, whenever you want. You imagine your friends there are all just hanging around where you left them, waiting for you to rejoin the fun.

"Then you come back. Trout Run is still beautiful, but there are precious few jobs. Most of your friends have left, and the ones who stayed have moved on with their lives. They're too busy to hang around much with you. You have freedom—too much freedom. You don't know what to do with yourself, how to manage your own time. Your family are the same imperfect people who caused you to want to leave home in the first place." Trudy sighed. "When he was in the military, he missed the peace and comfort of home. When he's home, he misses the camaraderie and structure of the military. Is it any wonder Billy can't adjust?"

"Thanks for your insights," Frank muttered and signed off with Trudy as the Rock Slide came into sight. A rustic log-cabin style building housed the outdoor equipment store. Red, yellow and blue kayaks rested against the porch, and an old-fashioned birch-bark backpack adorned the front door. A bell tinkled to announce his arrival.

Three customers browsed through the racks of clothes, hiking gear, and rappelling equipment. Two were engaged with the store's owner in a lengthy discussion on the merits of a particular type of climbing harness. Meanwhile, Martha spoke patiently and at length to a woman trying to decide between two rain jackets.

Frank thanked the Lord that he was stuck in a hiking store, not a dress shop. At least there were things to look at here that interested him. As he browsed, he eavesdropped on Martha's sales pitch.

"This Marmot is Gore-Tex. It's more expensive, but it's the only rain jacket you'll ever need. Good for hiking and walking around town."

"Hmm." The woman examined the beige jacket Martha recommended, but her gaze kept darting to a teal jacket on another rack. "What about this North Face jacket?"

"That's also a great jacket. Lightweight and that color looks good with your hair."

The customer smiled and tried it on. "But it's probably not as rainproof as the other one?" She sounded wistful.

"Do you do a lot of all-weather hiking in the backcountry?" Martha asked.

Frank smiled. The customer was in her forties with perfect hair and makeup. He was sure Martha understood the woman might occasionally take a little walk up Baxter Mountain or Hurricane and then adjourn to go shopping in Lake Placid. But she was the kind of person who wanted the best of everything.

"No-o-o. Is the beige one made for that?"

Martha adjusted the hood of the teal raincoat. "Yes, that one is for back-woods types. Look, this one has a special feature—a visor to keep drips off your face. I think this one will be great for you."

The woman beamed. "You're right! Thanks for giving me such great advice."

Frank watched the happy customer hand over her credit card. After she was gone, Frank approached Martha. "The Gore-Tex jacket is better."

Martha smiled. "Oh, definitely. But that's not what she wanted to hear. She had her heart set on the teal jacket."

"The customer is always right, eh?"

The store's owner appeared at Martha's side. "A few people genuinely want advice. Most simply want validation for what they're determined to do anyway." He patted Martha on the back. "Martha's good at knowing the difference. That customer probably would've left empty-handed if I'd been waiting on her, trying to persuade her that nothing beats Gore-Tex."

Martha looked pleased at the praise, but she still eyed Frank uneasily. She waited until her boss wandered off to a new customer before asking, "Is something wrong?"

"I wondered if you'd heard from Billy. Your son-in-law said Billy's not living with them anymore."

"He's not." She didn't offer more. The expression on her face: *what's it to you?*

"Jeff told me Billy and his sister argued. Did Billy call you after that?"

"No, Shannon told me he left."

"I need to talk to him, and I wondered if you knew where he's staying."

Martha stepped away from Frank and began re-folding an untidy stack of t-shirts. "Talk to him about what?"

"His counseling. He made a deal with me to go to the VA clinic after the incident at The Store. He skipped an appointment."

Martha's lips compressed into a thin line. "Forcing him to go won't do any good. People have been bossing him around his whole life. His father. The army. His sister. You leave him be. Let him find his own path."

Frank hadn't come here to argue. "Has Billy come back to your house?"

"No. And he won't come there."

"What truck was he driving?"

Martha shrugged. "Gene let him use a blue GMC, but then someone wanted to buy it, so Billy took a different one."

"Which one?"

"Couldn't say."

For a woman who was so deferential to her husband, Martha certainly didn't object to challenging police authority. "You still haven't answered my question. Do you know where Billy is?"

"I don't." Her hands stopped their restless motion with the shirts. "It's not for me to know."

WHEN FRANK GOT BACK to the office, he found Earl dealing with a middle-aged couple who looked to be tourists. The man—intense, irritated—wore khaki slacks, tassel loafers and a navy blazer, so if he wasn't a tourist, he must be headed to a funeral. The woman was nearly as tall as her husband, but fluttery and distracted.

"Here are the keys," Earl said to the man. "The car is parked out back. You can take it as soon as you sign this release form."

Ah, it must be Patrick and Maeve Dunleavey. With all the commotion around the concert and Laurel's suicide, Frank had never had a moment to wonder why they hadn't yet claimed the Mini-Cooper abandoned by their son.

The wife leaned in close to Earl. "What are you doing to find our son?" Mrs. Dunleavey, a pale skinny woman with a cloud of wavy blond hair, twisted her purse strap around and around her hands. "Are there search teams out there?"

Earl glanced at Frank, and he jumped in to answer. "I'm Police Chief Bennett. I think I explained on the phone that Charlie isn't missing, ma'am. He doesn't want to come home. And he's perfectly healthy. Running in top form."

"But he doesn't know how to surv-i-ive on his own. He's just a ch-i-ld." This came out in a long crescendo that began at F and ended around middle C. "How will he eat? He doesn't even have a job."

"And now, with no car, he'll never get one." Patrick Dunleavey pursed his lips. "Chip...*Charlie*... loves a dramatic gesture. But he never thinks through the consequences of his performance."

Maeve shot her husband a filthy look. "Our son is *missing*. He could be abducted by drug dealers, or skinheads or, or *sex* traders. They don't just go after girls, you know."

Patrick rolled his eyes. "For God's sake, Maeve—look around you. We're in freakin' Mayberry. They sell coffee on the honor system at that store. We saw a bluebird out there." He jabbed his finger in the direction of the office window. "A bluebird! I haven't seen one since I was twelve years old. Chip must've met someone at college who lives up here and followed him home. When his friend gets tired of Chip's freeloading, Chip will wash back up on our doorstep."

Frank smiled sympathetically at the father. The guy came across as a jerk, but at least he was a jerk who wasn't making unreasonable demands on Frank's time.

Maeve jumped up. "I want to see the spot where my son disappeared!"

She spoke as if she hadn't heard one word of her husband's diatribe. As if her son had dropped through a wormhole into another dimension, not run away from a cop on a pretty country road. "I'll sketch you a map," Frank said. He grabbed a piece of paper and drew the three turns they'd need to make to take them to the spot. Not that there was anything to see there. A stretch of pavement. A stand of forest. The majestic spike of Whiteface piercing the blue sky.

Patrick Dunleavey took his leave with a curt nod of his head. Frank watched at the window as Patrick drove off in his big, black Mercedes, with Maeve trailing behind in the Mini-Cooper.

The Dunleaveys were an unhappy family. If that were a crime, his work would never be done.

He turned to Earl. "Have you heard from Billy? His sister kicked him out of her house. His mother says he hasn't come back to the family home. Trudy says he missed a counseling appointment. No one seems to know where he is."

Earl's eyes narrowed. "I thought we were going to go talk to Shannon together?"

Frank had anticipated this and had an excuse handy. "I had to drive over in that direction to check on that vacation home with the broken window. On my way back, I passed right by the Wilton's house. Jeff was out in the garage, so I stopped to talk to him. He told me Billy and Shannon had an argument, and she tossed him out. Did you know that?"

Earl spun his desk chair away from Frank. He answered the question with his head buried in a file cabinet drawer. "I'm not surprised. Billy says his sister is a lot like their dad. Always sure she's right. I wondered how long those two living together could last."

"Any idea where he'll go now?"

"No." Earl kept digging in the drawer.

"I'm worried about him, Earl. Suicide is very common among vets. What if he planned to kill himself after this fight and persuaded Laurel to join him. The timing is right."

Earl slammed the file drawer. "No way. When we were out at the Mountainside, Billy talked a lot about the Marine Corps code of honor. How when you're a Marine, you abide by that code forever. He'd never kill himself. And he'd certainly never talk a girl into doing it with him."

Frank could see that despite all Billy's issues, Earl still admired his friend. It was pointless to argue with him about Billy's propensity for suicide. They needed to find the guy. If he was alive, to question him about the possible crime surrounding Laurel's jump.

And if he was dead by his own hand, well, that would end the investigation too.

"Look, Earl—we need to find Billy. Even if he didn't send those texts, he clearly knew Laurel. And if he's still around Trout Run, he knows by now that she's dead. That and the fight with his sister could push him over the edge and make him do something crazy again. Where would he go?"

Frank could see this logic got through to Earl. He was worried about his friend. "I don't know who else Billy would turn to. I already talked to my folks in case things went south with Shannon. They said Billy could stay with us for a while. But I've got no way to invite him unless he calls me."

He faced Frank. "And I haven't heard from him."

Chapter 22

What was left of the morning passed in tense silence. Frank knew he'd pulled an end-run around Earl by going solo to see the Wiltons, and he was pretty sure Earl hadn't fallen for his excuse. Would Earl go so far as to hide it from him if Billy checked in? Would he go so far as to shield Billy from questioning?

Surely not.

Frank pretended to read reports as his mind churned. Then he swiveled at the sound of a familiar voice.

"C'mon honey—let's go!" Penny popped into the office. "There's already a line forming, and you know how you hate to wait."

He'd forgotten that the long-awaited Grand Opening of the Hungry Loon had finally arrived. His wife intended to be among the first customers.

The events of the morning had left Frank with a gnawing in his stomach. He wasn't positive the feeling could be assuaged with a gourmet sandwich, but he was willing to give it a shot. He escorted his wife past Doris's desk. "We're going over to check out the Hungry Loon."

"Would you like Frank to bring you something back?" Penny, ever magnanimous, offered.

"Thanks, but I'll be going over myself just to look." Doris swiveled back to her keyboard. "Besides, if Frank had to buy lunch there for you, him and me, he'd have to put in for some serious overtime."

"Doris has already decided she's not going to like the Hungry Loon?" Penny asked as they crossed the street.

"Are you kidding? Even if she doesn't buy anything, that place will open up a whole new vista of commentary for Doris. I guarantee she'll be on the phone all afternoon reviewing every detail with her flock of hens."

The house where the Hungry Loon had opened was too close to the main road into town to be a desirable residence, but the wraparound front porch made a great place for tourists to eat their take-out lunches, and the large flat lot provided some off-street parking.

As Penny and Frank approached, a horde of little kids clutching free cookies tumbled down the front steps. They all sported stickers of a goofy cross-eyed waterfowl with a cartoon bubble saying, "I'm a Loon-a-tic."

Inside, the front room of the house had been turned into a mini gourmet market. "Ooo, balsamic vinegar... artichoke hearts...*capers*! Just like the market in Keene." Penny squealed. "Wait'll Edwin sees this."

Frank grabbed his wife's elbow before she waded any deeper into this retail nirvana. "Let's get our lunch order placed, then you can explore."

They pushed through the crowd into the room that contained the café and refrigerated cases of perishable foods. The staff wore red t-shirts emblazoned with the same bird that said, "I'm a Loon-a-tic about freshness" or "I'm a Loon-a-tic about flavor."

Frank and Penny finally got within a few customers of the head of the order line. And there, with his back turned to the crowd as he focused on preparing a sandwich, was a familiar auburn head.

Charlie Dunleavey, working at the Hungry Loon.

His parents had missed encountering him by a couple of hours and a couple hundred yards. "That's the kid I was telling you about," Frank whispered to Penny.

Charlie worked steadily, occasionally joking with the other staff. He kept his back to the line of customers and stayed focused on his work.

"He seems perfectly normal," Penny said. "Working at a café may not be the job his parents want for him, but he seems happy with it."

"I can't believe Charlie was right on the other side of the green when I had his parents in my office. I could've sent his mother over, so she could see for herself that he's all right." Frank leaned forward to try to catch Charlie's attention.

Penny hauled him back. "From what you've told me, she wouldn't have been content to leave him here. He needs some space. You did your job. Let Charlie manage his relationship with his parents."

Frank supposed she was right. Caroline had given him and Estelle a fair share of trouble as she fought for her independence. Of course, it had all passed by the time she was Charlie's age. But kids these days, especially boys, seemed to take longer to grow up. A few months of living on his own and working at the Hungry Loon was probably exactly what Charlie needed.

The customers in front of them stepped away, and Frank let Penny do their ordering.

Penny looked at the chalkboard menu hanging on the back wall. "We'll both have the marinated tarragon chicken sandwich."

"I hope this sandwich doesn't have some weird, gloppy sauce," Frank complained as he stuffed the paltry change he'd received from a twenty into the tip jar and they both shuffled down to the order pick-up area.

"Just some sundried tomatoes. You like them." Penny patted his arm. "Edwin has served them to you many times at the Inn." She peered into the food prep area with interest. "Look, Reid Burlingame's granddaughter is working here. And isn't that Kristen Mooney?"

Reid materialized out of the crowd. "The Hungry Loon has made a commitment to hire all local people. They've brought in the manager from somewhere else, but the rest of the staff is from Trout Run and Verona."

Frank raised a finger to point out that Charlie Dunleavey was a rich kid passing through from New Jersey, but Penny elbowed him into silence, and a beaming Reid continued to work the crowd, fanning enthusiasm for the new business in town.

"Let him enjoy the big opening day," Penny said.

"What's this?" A loud voice boomed from the direction of the refrigerated cases. Gabe Thune held up a plastic container with a white blob floating in cloudy water.

"Fresh mozzarella. It's delicious with homegrown tomatoes, a little olive oil and balsamic vinegar," the manager advised.

Gabe grimaced. "Looks like brains in a jar, like at a carnival freak show."

Just then, Pastor Bob joined the line waiting to place orders. Gabe turned his attention to the minister. "Hey, Pastor Bob—you coming over here to buy some food for Fellowship Hour?"

Bob's brow furrowed over the menu. "I'll be lucky to afford my lunch."

"You know, over at the Tabernacle, they don't just pass out stale cookies. They give everyone a whole dinner, free. And they're not always hittin' ya up for money."

Bob met Gabe's gaze. He kept his tone light, but the smile on his lips didn't reach his eyes. "Our volunteers strive to make Fellowship Hour as welcoming as possible. And you're welcome to join the Finance Committee if you think your donations to our congregation aren't well managed."

"Oh, Gabe don't wanna work," some wiseguy shouted from the crowd. "He came in here lookin' for free samples, right Gabe?"

Gabe held a cookie aloft and waltzed out the door.

Bob watched him go with a stricken look on his face.

"Don't let that freeloader get under your skin," Frank said.

"It's not just Gabe." Bob tapped his menu against his palm. "Scores of people have told me about this community dinner that the Tabernacle puts on. We have a hard enough time organizing the annual Harvest Potluck. How can I possibly compete with a weekly free dinner?"

Frank understood the competition between The Store and the Hungry Loon. He hadn't ever considered churches competing for members by offering better service and improved products.

"Surely they can't keep it up indefinitely," Penny said. "They're just trying to attract some attention because they're new."

"It's certainly working." Bob's lips pressed into a thin line. "Playing the lead-off concert in the summer series. And then using that to plug the dinners." The Presbyterian minister seemed in physical pain as he relived the memory.

"People are just curious," Penny reassured him. "But in the long run, they don't choose a church with their stomachs."

"Don't be so sure of that." Bob would have continued complaining, but he was interrupted by someone thanking him for the good job he'd done on her friend's memorial service.

"See that—people appreciate Bob." Penny smiled as she watched her friend comforting the old lady.

"True. But he does more funerals than baptisms."

Chapter 23

When Frank returned to the office, he found Earl had already left on the afternoon patrol. He wondered if Earl had departed in response to a call, but Doris said no. They usually touched base after lunch, but Frank supposed Earl needed to assert his independence after their skirmish over Billy.

Of course, that meant Earl was now not available to accompany him to Stevenson's Lumberyard to talk to Shannon. Despite Jeff's warning not to approach her during work hours, Frank headed out.

Trout Run's largest business was a bee hive of activity at this time of day. Forklifts trundled two-by-fours between open-sided storage sheds. A 16-wheeler loaded with logs backed up to the sawmill. Frank parked near the main building and entered through the door used by contractors ordering supplies. Behind the sales desk, a room filled with cubicles held the book-keepers and inventory managers who kept the business rolling. Frank asked for Shannon, and the man at the sales desk shouted her name without looking up from the order he was reviewing with a customer.

A young woman came to the door of the outer office. The broad shoulders and strong jawline that made Billy and Gene handsome made Shannon imposing rather than pretty. She wore her hair short and had a red pen stuck behind one ear.

Shannon looked Frank up and down. "Can't this wait? I have a lot of work to do."

Frank waved her toward the door to the parking lot. "Let's just step outside for a moment. I won't keep you long."

With a scowl and a huff, she followed him. Outside, Shannon folded her arms across her chest and angled her chin upward. "What?"

Chip off her father's block, that was for sure. "I need to talk to Billy. Any idea where he went after he left your place."

"Nope."

"What kind of truck was he driving?"

"I can't remember. He had one of my dad's trucks. Blue? Gray?"

"You're not worried about him? What if he's sleeping in his truck because he has no place to live?"

"Ha! My brother can always find a girl willing to take him into her bed. No worries there."

"Do you know the current girls' names?"

"No." Shannon moved to get past Frank. "I don't want to hear about his sex life."

He blocked her path. "Have they been calling your phone? Can I see the incoming numbers?"

She put her hands on her hips. "I blocked the numbers and deleted them. Why are you after my brother? He's a pain in the ass, but he hasn't done anything illegal. Leave our family alone."

Ah, there it was. I'm disgusted with my brother, but I'll defend him to the death to anyone outside our family. "I'm not after anyone." Frank tried to keep his voice low and reassuring, but the roar of the sawmill made it difficult. "Billy and I had an agreement that if he went to counseling, I wouldn't charge him for the damage he caused at The Store. He's not holding up his end of the bargain. Your brother is unstable, Shannon. He needs...*deserves*...help."

Billy's sister dialed back her belligerence, but she still couldn't quite bring herself to look Frank in the eye. "Some days, Billy knows he needs help, wants it even. But other times he just wants to forget everything that happened to him over the past six years and pretend it's the summer after his high school graduation."

And wouldn't a pretty seventeen-year-old girl fit that fantasy?

"Has Billy ever mentioned killing himself?"

Shannon's eyes widened. "Don't even say that. Don't—"

"Yo, Shannon—it's that trucker from Albany you've been trying to get ahold of," a voice bellowed from the office.

"I have to take this." She trotted toward the office while shouting back at Frank. "I'm sure Billy's crashing with friends. He'll turn up soon."

———————◦———————

BUT WHEN FRANK AND Earl put their heads together at the end of the day, they came up blank. Earl had reached out to every high school friend still living in the High Peaks, and no one had heard from Billy. Frank had contacted every gathering place, bar, and store in Trout Run and Verona to ask that they contact him if they saw Billy. Everyone agreed, but no one had called with a sighting. Frank called Gene's business number to find out what truck Billy was driving but had to leave a voice message. At the end of the day, Frank had no choice but to go home empty and hope the next day would bring more leads in Laurel's death and Billy's coincidental disappearance.

He arrived at home calling for Penny.

Instead of a greeting from his wife, he got a disinterested yawn from the cat.

Frank sorted through the mail. In among the catalogs and brochures for cruise vacations they would never take was a padded envelope from Amazon. He slit it open and a bright red collar slid out. Frank read the words engraved on the heart shaped tag.

Yogi Bennett.

"Great. Now you've got my last name."

The cat paused in the methodical licking of his nether regions. Then his ears pricked up and he raced to the door.

The knob turned, and Penny entered. Yogi stood on his back paws, stretched his full length, and began to knead her thigh.

She scooped him up and buried her nose in his neck, whispering endearments.

"Hey, what about me?' Frank groused.

"I missed you, too." Penny gave him a perfunctory kiss on the cheek and took the cat collar from his hand. Then she scrounged in her large purse and pulled out a bright yellow sheet of paper.

"Look what someone wrote on one of my found cat flyers."

Thank you for this news. He was right.

"Who was right?"

Penny stroked the cat, but he leaped out of her arms. "It sounds like Yogi's first owner is still around Trout Run. He or she seems to be glad to hear that Yogi is okay. I found this flyer pushed under the door of the library this morning."

"Maybe Yogi lived with an old person who couldn't afford to take care of him anymore," Frank suggested.

"So they just tossed him out to fend for himself?" Penny sat on the sofa and patted her lap. Yogi jumped into it, and she fastened his new collar around his sizable neck. "An elderly person who'd had a pet for years wouldn't do that."

"Maybe the old person had to go live with relatives and couldn't take him along."

Penny latched onto this suggestion and elaborated. "And maybe the 'he' is the person she had to move in with who told her the cat would be all right. Do we know anyone in that situation?"

"Not off the top of my head. But I'll ask Doris. She doesn't know where she filed my accident reports, but she'll know that."

Penny continued to stroke the cat's back, eliciting a rumbling purr. "But if the owner was worried about Yogi, why didn't they call me? Or stop in and talk? Why write this weird note?"

"Maybe they're ashamed that they tossed him out."

Yogi stood in Penny's lap and wrapped his paws around her neck. "Oh, my sweet boy. If only you could talk."

Chapter 24

Frank entered the office Tuesday morning to find Earl whistling "This Land is Your Land" while cleaning the screens of their computer terminals.

"You're in high spirits. I didn't know you were a Woody Guthrie fan."

"I stopped by the DEC office yesterday after work. The song was playing there, and I can't get it out of my head." Earl dusted the crumbs out of Frank's keyboard. "They've got this really cool footage from their wildlife cam—it shows a bobcat hunting a squirrel in broad daylight. Very unusual—they normally hunt at night. She sneaks along and then, bam—she pounces. People I know have seen bobcats, but I've never been so lucky."

Frank shot his partner a sidelong glance. "You drove clear to Ray Brook to see a bobcat movie?"

Earl grinned. "Tess happened to be on duty. We've been so busy since the concert that I never got a chance to go over there to tell her about those unmarked trails like I said I would."

"A man's gotta be true to his word."

"So this bobcat was about twenty pounds—about as big as your cat."

"Penny's cat," Frank corrected.

"She was probably out hunting during the day because she's got kittens to feed. They give birth in the spring. There's an abandoned beaver dam near the wildlife cam, and the bobcat might have made her den in there."

"You're full of information today."

"Tess told me all this. She's very knowledgeable."

"Sounds like you were at the DEC office for some time."

"She got off work an hour after I arrived, so we went out for a burger and a beer at the Trail's End. She'd never eaten there."

"So that's why you're so cheerful. You lined up a second date?"

"This wasn't a date. I tried to pay the check, but she insisted on splitting. She's kinda, you know..."

"A feminist?"

"Yeah, but not like..."

"A ball-buster?"

"She's smart and focused. And she has a plan for her life. I like that in a person."

Frank smiled but stayed silent. He wondered if Tess's life plan included marrying a local boy and living in the High Peaks forever. Because Earl sure didn't want to leave.

"She's had a very interesting life. Her dad is in the Army, so they moved a lot when she was a kid. When he was stationed in Alaska, they went to Denali all the time. That's when she got into hiking and camping and knew she wanted to be a ranger."

Earl completed his cleaning frenzy and sat down at his desk. "Hey, Tess asked me a question that I couldn't answer. She was in the school plays in high school and college, so she wondered if there's a community theater group around here she could get involved in. Ever hear of one?"

"Not my area of expertise—ask Penny."

Earl immediately followed up and took notes on whatever Penny told him. Then he jammed the paper in his pocket when he noticed Frank observing him. Earl changed the subject before Frank could tease him. "Hey, my cousin Sandy and her family went to check out that new church last night."

"On a Monday?"

"Yeah, that's their thing—the Tabernacle of Living Light has services on Monday night. That way all the people like Sandy who work weekends at tourist-type jobs can go to church."

Frank had a hard time keeping track of Earl's huge extended family although he recalled that Sandy worked at the café on Whiteface. She and her husband were real salt-of-the-earth types. He couldn't imagine them subscribing to Adam Fortway's mumbo-jumbo. And since when did churches get to unilaterally change the day of the Sabbath?

"So what's the church like? Are the Chinese lanterns left over from the Asian Bistro hanging from the pews? Is Sandy going to sign up for a spiritual retreat?"

Earl didn't react to Frank's sarcasm. "Sandy says everyone is super friendly, but a lot of the people are not from around here. They had a big buffet dinner you didn't have to pay anything for or even bring a dish. And then they had ladies who played with the little kids to keep them busy. And the church service was mostly singing songs and they had a good band. So she said it was more like going on a date than going to church."

"Did Sandy see anyone who usually goes to Trout Run Presbyterian?"

"Yep. A gang of high-schoolers. A couple families with young children. One mom told Sandy her kids cry when she tries to get them to go to church, but they liked this one."

"Better not tell Pastor Bob that."

"I dunno. Maybe people should tell Pastor Bob. He needs to up his game before all his pews are empty."

Before Frank could defend Pastor Bob, Doris announced a call from the medical examiner. He snatched up the phone. "What do you have for me?"

"Nothing. There was nothing in Laurel Caine's system."

"No booze? No weed?"

"Nothing. She jumped off that bridge stone cold sober. All she had in her stomach was a piece of apple pie."

"Was she pregnant?"

"Nope. Sorry I can't offer you any reason for why she killed herself." The medical examiner paused. "Wasn't there a full moon that night?"

EARL WENT OUT ON THE morning patrol while Frank tried again to reach Gene Flynn to find out what truck Billy was driving. When the phone rolled to voicemail every time, he knew for sure the man was avoiding him. Frank doubted Martha would tell him where Gene was working that day, so he'd have to track him down tonight.

He sat at his desk gazing into space, trying to think like Billy. Where could he have gone? His old high school friends had cut him loose, so it seemed unlikely that one of them would hide Billy and lie to the police about it. Was Billy back with his parents, the dramatic fight with Gene forgotten? He could drive over there now, look around while he knew Martha and Gene were both at work.

Frank slipped out while Doris was on the phone, not bothering to tell her where he was going. As he drove along the river, Frank saw a bicycle propped against a tree near the scenic overlook. A familiar figure sat on a park bench. He parked his truck on the other side of the road and walked toward Charlie Dunleavy, who was gazing into branches of a maple tree with a pair of small binoculars.

"Any birds up there?" Frank dropped onto the bench beside the kid.

"Not that I see. But I'm not good at noticing them." Charlie continued squinting upward. "I'm trying to get better."

"Bird-watching is all about training your eye."

"Yes, exactly!" Charlie turned toward him in excitement. Then he recoiled slightly when he realized who he was talking to. His voice changed from dreamy to aggrieved. "It's not illegal to watch birds, is it? Do you always pull over to talk to people who are observing nature?"

Frank took a deep breath. Already this conversation was running off the rails when he really had intended it to be a friendly chat. "Your parents drove up here on Monday to pick up your car. Your mother seems to think I should be conducting a house-to-house search for you. I told her you weren't missing, as far as I'm concerned."

Charlie's shoulders relaxed. "Good. Thank you."

"How do you like working at the Hungry Loon?"

Charlie's head swiveled toward Frank. "How do you know I'm working there?"

"Cops have to eat too, you know. I saw you working behind the counter."

"I suppose you told my parents." Charlie scowled.

"No, they'd already left when I saw you. And it's not my job to report on your whereabouts. But if you're in hiding from them, the Loon isn't the best place to work."

"I'm not hiding. I'm simply living my life, or trying to, without their constant interference."

"Your father seems willing to let you explore. It's your mom who's so worried. Maybe you could send her a postcard to let her know you're alive."

"Her idea of alive and my idea of alive are entirely different. She exists in a constant state of fear. And my *father* is just waiting for me to fail. He thinks I should be doing what he does—helping the rich get richer."

Frank had to admit, the kid had a pretty keen understanding of his parents. But at the same time, there was something dreamy and otherworldly about Charlie, which made Frank feel the Dunleaveys' concerns were not wholly unjustified. "You getting around Trout Run okay on that bike? We've got some steep roads."

Charlie extended his long, skinny legs. "I'm building strength, both physical and mental."

"I suppose. But the hill between here and the green will make your heart explode. You want to put your bike in the back of my truck, and I'll give you a ride into town? I don't mind backtracking."

Charlie shook his head. "No thanks. Shortcuts aren't part of my plan."

<hr />

WITH HIS OFFER REJECTED, Frank continued on his way to the Flynns' house. When he got to Robinson Road, he chose to park on the shoulder rather than pull into the driveway. If Billy happened to be hiding out there, Frank didn't want to alert him to his arrival. He hadn't even set foot on the driveway when he heard the loud barking of the Flynn's dog. The mutt must have an impressive nose if he could detect Frank at this distance.

When he got to the top of the driveway, Frank surveyed the line-up of vehicles: one rusted-out Chevy truck without plates, two newer but hard-driven Ford pick-ups (one with plates), and a late-model silver/gray GMC with plates. Within the line-up there was space for another truck, and muddy tracks to show one had been parked there recently. Was the gray truck the one Billy had been driving? Was he here, or had he come back to swap out the truck for another vehicle? Or swap the plates from one truck and put them on another?

The dog hadn't stopped barking. It's high-pitched, frantic baying echoed through the yard. Frank thought back to his first visit here. The dog hadn't barked until Frank had entered the house. Why was it so hysterical now?

If Billy was home, he certainly must be aware he had a visitor. Frank flattened himself against the side of the garage and crept around to the rear of the house. Now he could hear the dog flinging itself against a door, probably the sliding glass door that led to the deck.

Frank crouched and peered around the corner.

A thick coil of black rope lay on the deck in front of the slider. Frank took a step closer and saw the rope wasn't solid black; it had shadings of pale yellow between bands of black.

It had scales.

Frank jumped back. A huge timber rattle snake, four feet long—the biggest he'd ever seen. Its five-inch segmented rattle came to a point at the end closest to him and its triangular head faced the house as it sunned itself on the deck.

No wonder the dog was going crazy. Once his heart stopped pounding, Frank contemplated the scene. The snake wouldn't be basking there while a dog barked furiously a couple feet away. Rattlesnakes were shy creatures who avoided larger animals.

Was it dead?

He approached the big snake cautiously in case it was just stunned. It didn't move.

Odd that it had died fully extended.

When he got within two feet, he noticed blood on the snake's head.

When he stood over it, he saw the entrance wound of the bullet that had killed the creature.

Frank dropped to his knees to study the snake. Flies, but no smell, and in this heat the decay would begin quickly. So the snake hadn't been here long. It didn't make sense that Flynn would shoot a snake before work and leave it lying on his deck. Frank nudged the snake's head with his boot.

The bullet hadn't gone through the deck floor. The snake had been shot elsewhere and moved here. He nudged it further down its body but encountered resistance.

The snake had been nailed to the deck.

Artfully arranged as a message to the Flynns.

Chapter 25

There could be no rational reason for this crime, so that left the crazy. Billy must have used this as some angry warning or taunt to his father. The young man was unravelling fast.

Frank took pictures of the scene with his phone, called the Department of Environmental Conservation because rattlesnakes were a protected species, and tried once again to get in touch with Gene Flynn.

No success, of course. He called Martha at the Rock Slide, but it was her day off. The owner gave Frank Martha's cell phone number, but she didn't answer.

What was with this family?

Finally, Frank succeeded in tracking down Shannon's husband Jeff at Stevenson's Lumberyard. Frank told the young man what had happened at his in-laws' house. "Can you get Shannon to call her father? He won't answer my calls, and I really need to get him over here."

"Ooo, that's not happening," Jeff said. "She refuses to speak to him after the toilet paper incident."

Frank had started yesterday with the intention of asking Billy one simple question about Laurel, and now he felt like he was tumbling down Alice's rabbit hole. "Toilet paper incident?"

"You wanna start World War Three—just tell my father-in-law you buy Charmin toilet paper." Jeff coughed. "No lie—Shannon was at Hannaford's last week and there's a sale on Charmin, plus she's got a coupon. She runs into her dad there, and Gene tells her to put the toilet paper back because the perfume in Charmin will give you ass cancer. That's the world according to Gene. My way or the highway. And he's screaming at her there in the supermarket because she won't put back the Charmin and buy the Gene-approved toilet paper. Shannon was so embarrassed, she had to run out of the store and left her cart half full of groceries behind."

"So Shannon will refuse to call her father even when there's been a crime committed at his home? Even when her brother might be dangerously unstable?"

"That's what I'm tellin' ya—it's nuts. I love Shannon, but honestly, her whole family is way too high strung. I come from people who are very go-with-the flow, know what I'm sayin'? When Shannon is away from her family, she's fine. But between Billy and all the crap with Gene, Shannon's gone a little off the deep end herself. I'm not even going to tell her about this." He hung up.

Another stonewall.

Frank considered calling in the State Police. But how could they help when he didn't have a vehicle description or license plate number to give them? And the only crime that had definitely been committed—the shooting of the snake—was a misdemeanor more likely to be punished with a fine than jail time. The state troopers wouldn't be dropping everything to help with this. What he really needed was to lean on the phone company to speed up finding out who had sent those texts to Laurel. If the texts could be traced to a phone Billy had access to, he could launch an all-out manhunt.

Frank went back to the office and called the phone company again. His request had made it through two more levels of bureaucracy. Only one more to go, the man assured him. As he hung up with the phone company, Earl returned from lunch, and Frank updated him on what he'd found at the Flynn's house.

"I'm worried about Billy, Earl. I think he's unraveling. He could be a danger to himself and others. We need to find him."

Earl nodded, but he seemed distracted. He walked away from Frank and stood staring out the office window with his hands jammed in the pockets of his uniform.

Frank waited, but the silence soon became oppressive. "What's wrong?"

"That snake. I don't think Billy would do that no matter how pissed he is with his father."

Was Earl reflexively defending his friend, or did he have some evidence beyond a gut feeling? Frank reminded Earl of the facts. "Billy is a hunter and was a trained marksman in the Marines. It would take a good aim to kill a snake with one bullet through the head."

Earl spun around. "I didn't say he *couldn't* do it, I said he *wouldn't*. Remember, Billy is afraid of loud noises. When I was at the Mountainside with him, some guys invited Billy to come out to their property to do some target shooting to prepare for deer season. Billy turned them down cold. I thought it was strange at the time, since Billy used to love hunting and he was looking for friends to hang with since he's been back. But after the incident at the Store, I realized he must've turned them down because he can't stand to be around gunfire."

Frank pursed his lips. "Possibly. But there's a difference between being around a bunch of guys all firing guns at once, and Billy's taking one clean shot with his own gun."

Earl simply shook his head.

"Well, there's no use speculating. I need to talk to Gene and Martha, but I haven't had much luck this morning. All the Flynns seem to have gone to ground."

Frank's speech was punctuated by a loud rumble from his stomach. "Geez, it's one o'clock and I haven't had lunch yet. Hold down the fort until I get back." He left Earl lost in thought about his friend and headed across the green to Malone's Diner for a late lunch. Passing the Hungry Loon, Frank saw the sun beating down on a line that spilled out the door and onto the front porch. Not surprising that tourists liked the place so much, but he wondered if the locals would keep eating there after the novelty had worn off. Honestly, he was already tired of all those unfamiliar ingredients and strange presentations. Wraps. Paninis. What was wrong with two slices of rye bread as a platform for roast beef and cheese?

Even the short walk in today's heat made the back of his shirt damp with sweat. A welcome blast of chilled air greeted Frank as he opened the diner door. Sure sign of a heatwave: cheapskate Marge had grudgingly turned on the AC.

"Don't stand there with the door open." Marge bustled by balancing four plates on her ample arm. "I can't afford to cool off the whole valley."

Ah, the comforts of the familiar! Frank sat at the counter out of habit, but he could have had a table to himself. There were quite a few vacancies.

He glanced at the plate of the Stevenson's worker beside him. "Is that chicken pot pie?"

"Yep—really good. She hasn't had this as a special in quite a while." He glanced over his shoulder to check Marge's whereabouts and lowered his voice. "I think she brought it back 'cause she's feelin' the heat from that new place." He jerked his head in the general direction of the Loon.

Marge reappeared. She moved surprisingly fast for a woman her size. "What'll it be, Frank?"

"I'll have a big slice of that pot pie."

"They're all the same size," she snapped. Frank relaxed back in his seat. It was good to be home.

While he waited for his food, he listened with a half-tuned ear to the conversations around him. ".... can't believe he got so much for that little house...". "....says he could sell anything these days..." "Hot enough for ya?" ".... must be the economy improving..." "no new jobs around here—my son's still outta work...." ".... all outside money..." ".... but no one would want that place as a vacation home..." "Man, there's a big crowd swimming under the bridge today. Too hot to hike."

"Hope all the blood's washed off the rocks by now."

The last remark came from a smart aleck a few seats down from Frank. Marge slammed her iced tea pitcher on the counter before him. Conversation stopped. "That's an awful thing to say. If you're going to talk like that, go eat somewhere else."

"Sorry." He hung his head until Marge went into the kitchen.

The Stevenson's worker stood and counted out money for his check. "Laurel's mother waitressed here years ago, before she got sick," he explained to the other guy. "Marge is a little touchy about the girl."

Frank filed away that information.

Marge burst through the kitchen's swing doors and deposited Frank's pot pie without pausing. Even though the diner wasn't full to capacity, the lunch rush was not the time to question her. He might return for information during the afternoon lull. He tucked into his meal: flaky crust, big chunks of chicken, nice normal vegetables, simple gravy. Marge might be prickly, but she was a damn good cook. While Frank focused on eating, someone slid into the seat vacated by the Stevenson's worker.

"Nice to see you again. What do you recommend?"

Frank glanced over at the guy: baseball cap, sunglasses, tee shirt, shorts. He looked like a tourist, but still vaguely familiar.

Frank smiled. "Pot pie can't be beat."

The guy took off his hat and switched his shades for regular glasses. Adam Fortway. No wonder Frank hadn't recognized him. The Tabernacle's leader was so nondescript, he could blend in anywhere. "I keep hearing about how good your community dinners are. You must have some good cooks in your group. Maybe Marge's food won't compare."

"All food prepared with love is delicious."

"You never ate my Aunt Viola's roast beef. All the love in the world couldn't tenderize that."

Fortway gazed at Frank earnestly, unamused by his quip. "Food nurtures both the body and the soul."

Geez, this guy had a platitude for every occasion. Did people really pay money to hear totally unoriginal lines like that? "How's the retreat business? You all filled up this week?" he asked as he stabbed a piece of chicken.

"Yes, we welcomed a new group of acolytes this weekend." Before Fortway could elaborate, Marge's helper arrived to take his order.

Frank waited until she went back to the kitchen to find out more. "So, these, er, acolytes—where do they come from? Do you advertise?"

"As long as there is disharmony in the universe, there will be truth-seekers striving for the light."

Oh, brother. Frank swallowed the last bite of his lunch and tossed a ten on the counter. He'd rather over-tip Marge than wait for change listening to more of this drivel. "See you around, Adam. Don't get burned by all the light outside today."

Outside the diner, Frank squinted into the afternoon sun as he walked back across the green. A skinny woman slumped on a park bench smoking a cigarette. He was three steps beyond her when she spoke. "Hey, can I talk to you?"

Frank back-tracked. The woman shaded her eyes to look up at him.

Matthew Caine's girlfriend.

Frank dropped on the bench beside her. He needed to share the results of the autopsy directly with Laurel's father, not this woman. So he planned only to listen, not talk. "How are you and Matthew doing?"

"Life sucks. Matt hasn't stopped drinking since Laurel jumped. They gave him time off work, but if he doesn't sober up soon, he's gonna get fired."

Is that all she cared about? That her meal ticket was about to expire? Frank waited, making an effort to keep his expression neutral.

"He keeps asking, 'why, why, why?' and when I tell him what I think, he gets mad." She turned her head and Frank noticed a fading, yellow-ish green bruise on her cheek. "Maybe if he hears it from you, he'll listen."

"Hears what?"

She leaned toward him. "Laurel was sneaking out to meet someone. Matt thinks his daughter was Little Miss Perfect, but I know different."

"Oh?" Matthew Caine clearly was no prince, but Frank really disliked this woman who'd been jealous of her boyfriend's child when she was alive and was jealous still now that Laurel was dead. But he didn't have to like her to get useful information from her. "Who was Laurel meeting?"

"About a week ago, she started walking down to the end of our road. She wouldn't tell me anything, so I didn't even bother to ask where she was going. But she would wait and eventually a truck would pick her up."

That was probably Jimmy, the kid she'd gotten a ride to the concert with. But Frank knew Jimmy hadn't coaxed Laurel to her death. "What kind of truck?"

She ground her cigarette butt under her dirty sneaker. "That's what's so weird. It was always a truck, but always a different truck."

Frank felt the tick of excitement sparked by progress in an investigation. Billy Flynn had access to all those different trucks his father bought, repaired, and sold. "Did you see who was driving?"

"Nah. I couldn't make out the driver from that distance. But that little skank was up to no good, trust me. And she probably killed herself 'cause she knew she was in over her head."

Frank stood up. "Thank you. I'll keep that in mind."

As he walked away, he heard her voice again, too low to make out the words. He turned toward her. "Excuse me?"

She raised her voice but wouldn't meet his eye. "I said, 'yer all the same.'"

Chapter 26

Back in the office, Frank's phone chirped the arrival of a text. He glanced at it and froze.

Leaving now. Will arrive after dinner, so we'll go straight to the hotel. Meet us there for a drink. Can't wait to see you!

My God, how could he have forgotten that Caroline, Eric and the kids were coming today? The visit had seemed like it was a long way off, but Laurel's suicide and Billy's disappearance had made the days fly by. He'd already made plans to take two days off, but he needed to review the outstanding work with Earl.

When his assistant returned from the afternoon patrol, they sat down to make a plan.

"I'll go over and talk to Mr. and Mrs. Flynn tonight after they're home from work," Earl said.

Frank opened his mouth to object but shut it again. He would have preferred to go himself, but that was out of the question. And maybe Earl could get more out of the parents talking to them as Billy's friend.

"Okay, but be careful. And call me if there are any problems. And don't let them—"

"Frank. Relax. I got this."

"I know. I know you do." Frank spoke more to reassure himself than to reassure Earl. "Hey, one more thing." He told Earl what Matthew Caine's girlfriend had said about Laurel going off in different trucks. "That could be her meeting up with Billy. Ask his parents if Billy knew Laurel."

"She could have been meeting different friends each time," Earl protested. "Most people in Trout Run drive trucks."

"Yeah, but we know Laurel didn't have a wide circle of friends."

Earl sighed. "Okay. I'll ask."

They reviewed a few other matters, and Earl finally succeeded in shoving his boss out the door. "See you on Thursday. Have fun with the kids."

Frank drove home to shower and change. He found Penny clad in her underwear with a tangle of clothes strewn over the bed.

"We're only meeting them for drinks on the patio of the hotel. You don't have to get dressed up."

"I know. I'm just…" Penny ran her fingers through her hair. "You know."

He did know. Penny was a nervous wreck around Caroline. Only six years separated the two most important women in his life. They both rejected a mother-daughter relationship, but they hadn't quite figured out how to be friends.

Frank glanced at a plain beige skirt on the bed that he'd never noticed Penny wear before. "Are you looking for something step-motherly?"

"I thought it would be best not to be too, too—"

Sexy? Beautiful? Frank supposed Penny was right. He knew Caroline didn't like thinking about the implications of her father's late-life romance. He pulled her into his arms. "Just be yourself. You'll be fine."

Penny swayed for a long moment in his embrace. Then she snapped into action. "I brought home some books from the library for the boys. And I bought a lot of food for a picnic tomorrow. The weather is supposed to be perfect. I thought we'd take them swimming at Heart Lake."

"Sounds like a plan. Let me change, and we'll take off for Lake Placid."

———●———

"GRANDPA, GRANDPA, GRANDPA!"

Excited squeals and the pounding of little sneakers preceded Frank's entrance into the bar of the Mirror Lake Inn. His grandsons launched themselves into his arms, nearly knocking him into an elderly couple in golf attire. Not for the first time, Frank wondered why Caroline and Eric had chosen the fanciest hotel in Lake Placid when they were traveling with two seven-year-olds. But Eric wasn't one to rough it; he required luxury to be happy.

After hugs and kisses and exclamations over the boys' growth, they moved outside to the deck overlooking Mirror Lake. Both Penny and Caroline seemed exaggeratedly polite, like the first ladies of two rival countries forced to have tea together. The boys raced to the railing and peered through the slats at the water below. Although they weren't identical twins, they were the same height and their tousled brown hair made them indistinguishable from behind.

"Can we go swimming?" That was Jeremy, always up for an adventure.

"Are there fish in there?" Joshua, the more contemplative twin.

"Let's go on a boat ride!"

Frank tore his attention away from the boys and studied his daughter and son-in-law. Did they seem happy? Their marriage had gone through a rough patch a couple years back, and Frank never stopped worrying that Eric's tense, competitive nature would undermine his daughter's happiness.

But Eric laughed and chatted and hadn't once pulled out his cellphone to take a call from work. Suddenly Frank's own phone felt like a hot coal in his pocket. He wondered if Earl had talked to the Flynns. Would he call if he needed help?

Frank dragged himself back to the here and now. He asked Eric about his new job and heard about Caroline's latest consulting project. His daughter asked his wife about the Trout Run library and seemed genuinely interested in Penny's answers.

Frank smiled. The evening was going well.

Finally, Penny outlined the plans for tomorrow. "Sleep as late as you like, then come over to our house. We'll go to Heart Lake and the boys can swim, and fish, and go out in the canoe. And we'll have a picnic."

"Yay! I wanna catch a barracuda!" Jeremy threw his arms out to their full spread.

Joshua tugged on Frank's sleeve. "Won't the barracudas bite us when we're swimming?"

The evening ended with laughter and reassurances.

Frank and Penny drove home with full hearts.

Chapter 27

It was nearly eleven by the time Eric, Caroline, and the kids showed up the next morning. Frank used the delay to check in with Earl, who reported he'd had no luck connecting with the Flynns. Their house had remained dark and locked up well into the evening.

Rather than unload the kids and their extensive gear from the minivan, Frank and Penny climbed into Caroline's vehicle to set off on the day's adventure. As Eric drove toward the lake, Caroline spotted a sign and pointed. "Ooo—Farmer's Market and Craft Fair. Is that today?"

"Yes, it's every Wednesday and Saturday from June through October."

"I love farmer's markets. Can we go?"

"No-o-o." The boys chorused.

"We want to swim," Jeremy insisted.

"Don't make us go to some dumb market," his brother chimed in.

"We'll go on the way home," Eric reassured them.

"The market will be over by the time we're done swimming and fishing," Penny said. "Here's an idea. We'll drop you and Frank off at the market. Eric and I will get us settled at our picnic spot, then I can drive back and pick you up. It's not far."

Frank smiled at his wife's efforts at peacemaking. She knew he wanted some time alone with Caroline. And this had been engineered perfectly, as if he weren't even part of the plan.

"Fantastic!" Caroline gushed. "Everyone's happy."

Five minutes later they were at the big field beside the volunteer fire department where tables and portable awnings dotted the landscape. Penny shouted out the window as Eric turned the minivan around. "Get some peaches and blueberries. And buy them from the organic girls, not that old grouch with the cigar."

Frank ushered Caroline into the market. "They used to put the food on one side and the crafts on the other, but they discovered everyone did better business with them mixed up."

Caroline grinned. "That means we'll have to walk up and down both sides, not just dart in and buy fruit."

"Browse to your heart's content. Just don't let me forget the two things I'm supposed to buy."

They strolled along, with Frank waiting patiently as his daughter examined pottery cream pitchers and quizzed an old hippie on how the beeswax candles were made. He bided his time, waiting for the perfect moment to ask how things were going between her and Eric.

"Smell this honeysuckle goat's milk soap." Caroline waved a bar under his nose. "Isn't that heavenly? I'm going to get three bars. And will this goat cheese keep if we put it in the cooler?"

Jackie the goat lady assured her it would, and as Caroline opened her wallet to pay, Jackie's goat came over and buried its nose in Caroline's purse.

"Eeek—what's he doing?"

"You must have some food in there." Jackie smiled beatifically. "Gilbert can always tell."

"It's the boys' pretzels," Caroline laughed as Gilbert emerged chewing. "Oh my God, he's eating the baggie and all."

"That won't hurt him. Goats eat everything."

Frank grabbed Caroline's package and nudged the goat with his knee to give his daughter an escape route to the next booth.

"Too bad Eric's not here," she said still laughing. "That goat could have tested his exposure therapy for germ phobia."

Here was his opening. "He's still struggling with that?"

"Oh, he's much better. His therapist is helping him overcome his perfectionism. And he's much more relaxed since he's gotten settled in his new job."

"So, everything's okay between you two?"

Caroline looked up at him and smiled. "Yes, Daddy. We're fine. You can stop worrying."

Frank steered Caroline toward a booth surrounded by a crowd of customers. "Here are the organic girls, where we're supposed to get the fruit." Frank looked longingly at the booth directly opposite where a grizzled old man clenching a stub of unlit cigar stood scowling at his lack of business. Frank thought his peaches looked fine, but he was under strict orders. Frank queued up. "This may take a while," he grumbled.

He introduced Caroline to Ardyth Munger, who happened to be ahead of them in the line. They chit-chatted for a while, but when Ardyth started quizzing Frank about running a speed trap near the Stop'N'Buy, Caroline drifted off to another booth.

Ten minutes later, Frank finally had his wholly organic fruit. He searched for Caroline and spotted her bright pink shirt far down the row of booths. When he arrived at her side, he found her examining the grain of some polished salad bowls at a woodworker's booth. The edges were uneven, following the ripples in the grain, making each bowl in the set slightly different.

"Aren't these gorgeous, Daddy? So unusual."

Frank dabbled in woodworking himself, so he found the bowls much more interesting than pottery or soap. "I wonder how he gets that effect?" Frank ran his finger over the bowl. The craftsman had his back turned, thanking a departing couple and offering a business card in case they wanted to order more.

"I use a jig saw." The craftsman, who'd obviously been keeping an eye and ear on them, finished with his other customers and came over to talk.

"Really! How does that—" Frank looked away from the bowl and into the man's eyes and realized with a start that he was talking to Gene Flynn. He stumbled over his words, then made an effort to keep talking as if he'd never wrestled this man to the ground. As if Gene hadn't been dodging his calls for days. "How do you get that beveled edge? It's a nice effect."

"Gorgeous," Caroline chimed in. "They're so original. Beautiful, yet useful."

Gene seemed pleased by the praise. "Yep. I don't believe in making stuff that doesn't serve a purpose. But I enjoy the challenge of doing something different. Anyone can crank out ten matching bowls on a lathe."

Caroline began asking him about the type of wood and the finish and how the bowls should be cared for. Gene spoke expansively, his large hands tracing the bowls like a lover caressing a woman's cheek. "There's not a lot of hickory in the High Peaks, but it's the best wood for this purpose. It grows west of here."

Frank watched as the man engaged with his daughter. Caroline would never dream that this artist was the same person who'd shoved his own wife and threatened his own son. He had a hard time believing it himself.

After lengthy consideration, Caroline made her selection. As Gene wrapped the purchases, happy with making another significant sale, Frank risked a question. "How's Billy these days? Heard from him?"

Gene didn't lift his gaze from the box he was packing. "I got your messages. Billy's taking some time off. Staying away from the bars and other...distractions."

Like seventeen-year-old girls?

Gene handed Caroline the well-packed box with a big smile. "Enjoy your bowls. Think of the High Peaks when you use them."

Frank turned his daughter around. "There's a guy over there who makes little toy canoes the boys could float in the lake. I'll meet you in that booth."

Her eyes questioned his, but she left without comment.

Frank turned back to Gene. "I need to talk to Billy."

"I don't actually know where he is." Gene straightened some cutting boards and jewelry boxes. "All he told his mother was that he needed some time alone."

"Was that before or after he nailed a rattlesnake to your deck?"

Gene bristled. "That had nothing to do with Billy. It was some bad blood between me and another tree man over a job."

"Then I'm sure you'll want me to arrest him. Give me his name."

Gene thrust out his chest. "I can handle my own problems. I don't need your help."

"Shooting a rattlesnake is a crime. If you don't want to press charges about the damage to your deck, that's your business. Give me his name."

The two men glared at each other.

"Give me his name." Frank lowered his voice. "Or I'll arrest you for obstructing an investigation."

"Obstructing an investigation of snake murder." Gene barked a harsh laugh. "Go ahead. Ruin your visit with your daughter. She's not from around here, is she?"

A shrewd play. Frank had a better move.

"Let's go," Frank grabbed Gene's elbow. "I'll let Earl process the arrest. I'm sure some other vendor can look after your booth." Frank glanced at a woman fingering some wooden bangle bracelets. "Keep people from walking away with the merchandise. You might be back by closing time."

Gene jerked his arm out of Frank's grasp. "Fine." He scrawled a name and number on a scrap of paper and thrust it at Frank. "He'll deny it."

Frank slid the paper back toward Gene. "While you're at it, write down the license plate, make, and model of the truck Billy is driving."

"I don't know off the top of my head. I'd have to check my records."

"Fine with me. I'll give you a ride."

Gene scowled, pulled out his phone, and scrolled through some emails. Eventually he found what he was looking for and wrote a license plate number on the paper. "It's a blue Ford pick-up, 2010. But he won't be driving it around. I told you, he's holed up somewhere."

"Does Billy have friends from the Marines around here?"

Gene shrugged. "Possibly. I don't know anything about his social life."

Frank pocketed the paper. "Thanks. Hope you sell a lot of bowls."

Caroline walked toward him juggling all her packages. Frank took the bowls from her and Caroline waved to Gene as they walked away from the booth.

"What a nice man," Caroline said.

"Mmm—he's certainly talented."

"What's the matter, Daddy? Suddenly you seem a million miles away."

"Nah, I'm fine. Let's get out of here. Penny will be waiting for us."

———————◦◉◦———————

THE REST OF THE DAY passed blissfully. Frank found a moment to pass along to Earl the information he'd gotten from Gene, so Earl could initiate the search for the truck. After that, Frank succeeded in focusing his attention on his family.

The boys splashed and dug on the little beach at Heart Lake. They got filthy, but Eric seemed to tolerate the dirt pretty well. Frank took his grandsons to a large flat rock that jutted into the deeper water of the lake.

The boys crowded close to him as he opened his tackle box.

"What are these for?" Joshua pointed to the different size sinkers arranged in a tray.

"That's what makes our line go down deep to where the fish are," Frank explained.

"And look at the toy fish—why do you have toys in here, Grandpa?"

"Those are lures. We use them to trick the fish. They think it's a tasty little fish that they can eat."

"But they're wrong!" Jeremy laughed. "They're so dumb!"

"I like this green one. It's pretty."

Frank took the lure from Joshua's hand before he impaled himself on the sharp hook. "That's called a tailspinner. This shiny part on the back creates a flash as it moves through the water that attracts the bigger fish. And then the fisherman reels them in. But we're going to use worms today."

The boys tossed fishing lines into the water, getting them tangled repeatedly, but they managed to catch two little sunfish. Joshua wanted to take the fish home, but Jeremy cried at the thought of them being separated from their fishy families. Frank showed the boys how to release the fish back into the lake, and they waved good-bye to their catch.

After their picnic, they all went back to Frank and Penny's house. The boys squealed with delight when they met Yogi. Wisely, the cat took his first opportunity to escape into the backyard. They ended the day sitting in Adirondack chairs gathered around the fire pit, using sticks to roast hot dogs as a main course and then marshmallows as dessert.

"We don't wanna go back to the hotel," Jeremy complained as his mother began gathering up all their stuff. "Why can't we stay here with Grandpa and Penny?"

"Because there's not enough room for us all, silly."

Frank had a flash of inspiration. "How about if the boys stay here and you and Eric stay in the hotel? You can have a little alone time. And I could take them to see the goats at Jackie's farm in the morning."

"Yes! Yes!" Jeremy and Joshua high-fived. Caroline's face lit up and she traded a glance with Eric. He looked pleased, too. Only then did Frank notice the tight press of Penny's lips.

"Is that okay with you, Penny?" Caroline asked.

Penny smiled. "Sure. No problem."

But Frank knew the difference between Penny's polite smile and Penny's gushing enthusiasm smile and this smile fell far short of the gush mark. He supposed he should have discussed it with her first before he blurted out his invitation.

Penny picked up a stack of dirty glasses and headed into the kitchen. Frank encouraged Caroline and Eric to take the boys down to Stony Creek to see if the blue heron who fished there at dusk had arrived. Then he headed into the lion's den.

"What's wrong?"

Penny banged glasses into the dishwasher. "I told you before their visit that I had an important meeting with some library donors at eight a.m. on Thursday."

"I'm sorry. I totally forgot."

"You forgot because my job is unimportant to you. You think it's just a hobby to keep me occupied."

"I do not think that. The meeting simply slipped my mind. I got carried away because I was having fun with my grandkids. Is that so terrible?"

Penny gripped a serving bowl with two hands. When she spoke, her lips barely moved. "I have to prepare for the meeting tonight. I have to be out of the house early tomorrow. I can't help you with the boys. I can't go with you to the goat farm. You're on your own."

"Okay, no problem." Frank kept his tone upbeat. "You sit down here and do your meeting prep. I'll give them a bath and read them a story upstairs. You won't even know they're here. We'll go to Malone's for breakfast and then visit the goats. I'll handle everything. Earl can hold down the fort until I get to work."

Penny arched her eyebrows. "You better hope there's no crime wave between now and noon tomorrow."

Chapter 28

Some commotion erupted when Eric and Caroline left, and some screaming when Frank made the bath water too hot, but Penny kept her head bent over her laptop in the living room. Frank wrestled Joshua and Jeremy into clean tee shirts since their pajamas were at the hotel and smeared some toothpaste across their teeth. The bathroom looked like the main deck of the Titanic after it hit the iceberg, but he could deal with that after they fell asleep. Soon the boys were snuggled beside Frank in the guest bedroom as he read aloud from their favorite Captain Underpants book.

Joshua's eyes drooped, but Jeremy remained resolutely alert, demanding another chapter. Frank read on. The potty jokes that had been cute when he started were getting tiresome with repetition. Towards the end of the chapter, he noticed Jeremy was no longer giggling.

He stopped reading and waited.

No complaints.

Frank slid out of bed. Joshua stirred, but rolled over and stayed sleeping. Jeremy opened one eye. "Where are you going?"

"Across the hall to my bedroom. You stay under the covers with your brother."

"I wanna nuther...." Jeremy's eyelids fluttered and closed.

Frank slipped out of the guest bedroom. Whew!

He paused at the head of the stairs, drawn by the sound of Penny clacking away on her laptop. Going down to deliver the news that he'd successfully put the boys to bed without her help tempted him, but he figured he'd better not bother her. Frank entered their bedroom and stretched out, but watching TV up here was out of the question for fear of waking the boys. He reached for the book on his bedside table but found it difficult to transition from the antics of Smartsy-Fartsy and Super Diaper Baby to the life and times of Andrew Jackson. So he settled for scrolling through the news on his phone.

As he squinted through the latest political coverage, his phone rang. Quickly he answered before the sound woke the twins.

"Frank? It's Bob. I'm sorry to bother you at home, but there's someone up on the roof of the church. I'm not sure what to do."

Frank sat up. "What? You mean someone's trying to break into the church?"

"No. It's a person—I think it's a girl, but maybe a small man—crouching up near the steeple. After what happened to Laurel— "

Frank sprang out of bed. The memory of Laurel poised on the bridge, reaching for the moon burned into his memory. "Is she trying to jump?"

"No, she seems to be hanging onto the side of the steeple, like she's afraid of falling. I called up to her, but I'm afraid I'll make the situation worse. I don't know how she could've gotten up there."

"I'll be there in five minutes."

Frank had his foot on the stairs when a tousled head popped out of the guest bedroom.

"Where are you going? I want another chapter. You promised."

"We'll read it in the morning. Grandpa's gotta go out for a minute now. I need you to stay in bed."

"No-o-o-o. You can't leave us alone!"

"You're not alone. Penny is downstairs." Frank herded Jeremy back into bed. Thank God, Joshua was snoring softly. "But I don't want you to bother her, okay? Just go to sleep now, and in the morning, we'll visit the goats. But you have to get your sleep now, so we can go to the farm early. Right?"

The goats were a powerful inducement. "Ok-a-ay," Jeremy peered at his grandfather suspiciously from under the covers. "Will you come and tuck me in again when you get back?"

"Definitely."

Frank crept downstairs and stuck his head into the living room. "The boys are asleep. I just have to run into town on a quick call."

Penny's head snapped up from the sprawl of papers on the table. "Frank! I told you I can't babysit them tonight."

"You don't have to do a thing. They're sound asleep." He had no time to argue and ducked out of the house without looking back at his wife's furious face.

Frank jumped in his truck and raced up to the green. What the hell was going on? Was this a copycat suicide? No one knew about the texts Laurel had received urging her to jump.

No one but the person who'd sent them.

When he arrived at the green he found Bob Rush standing in front of the church peering up at the steeple. The moon had been waning since Laurel jumped, and tonight a distant half-moon barely illuminated a cloudy sky. The point of the steeple disappeared into darkness, but at the base Frank could dimly discern a small figure crouched in the gutter where the steeple joined the roof. He'd grabbed his binoculars from the truck and now focused them on the person.

He was afraid to shine his flashlight on the person yet, and dim light made it hard to bring the figure into sharp focus. Sneakers...jeans...a sweatshirt...shaggy bangs. Maybe a boy, but Frank sensed it was a girl.

He moved the binoculars to see the person's hands. They seemed to clutch tightly to the edge of the plywood sheeting that had been used to patch the hole in the steeple. A good sign, he thought. She didn't seem to want to jump the way Laurel had. If she regretted her decision to climb up there, she'd be easier to rescue. Still, it was a delicate situation.

One wrong move could spook her into jumping. The vision of Laurel sailing through the air and the horrible thump of her landing flooded his memory. This couldn't happen again.

Frank handed Bob the binoculars. "See if you recognize her."

"Definitely young, but I can't see her face clearly."

"Did you shout up to her?"

"Once. I noticed someone was up there as I was driving down the hill from Verona. It was lighter then, and I saw someone standing next to the steeple. I stopped the car and ran over. Suicide hadn't crossed my mind. I've been so preoccupied with our building problems; my first thought was that something had come undone with the repair, and Herv or one of the other handymen in the congregation had crawled up to fix it. So I shouted, "What's wrong? Why are you up there?""

Bob shuddered. "She swayed when she heard my voice and saw me down here. I realized it was a kid. A kid in trouble." Bob folded his hands and shut his eyes. "I could've scared her into jumping or falling. That's when I called you."

"You watch through the binoculars while I talk to her. Let me know her reactions."

"Hi there!" Frank shouted through cupped hands. "We'd like to help you come down from there, okay?"

"She's just hanging on for dear life, watching us."

"You're not in any trouble. No one is angry at you. We just want to help you down, so you don't get hurt. If that's okay with you, nod your head."

"Her head twitched a little. I don't know if that counts as a nod," Bob reported.

Frank evaluated options as he continued talking to Bob. "Any idea how she got up there? Could she possibly have jumped onto the roof from one of those big trees behind the church?"

"No, we had them trimmed after a falling branch damaged the roof in the spring." Bob looked through the binoculars again. "The way she's holding on to that plywood—I think it's not nailed down flat anymore. Maybe she went up into the steeple and pushed herself out through the hole."

"You mean she came up through the inside of the church? How would she get into the building?"

"The ladies' restroom window doesn't have a lock. You can slide it up from outside." Bob looked down at his shoes, embarrassed to confess this security lapse.

"But how would she know how to access the steeple?" Frank had been attending Trout Run Presbyterian since he'd moved to town six years ago and he didn't know how to get up there.

Bob let the binoculars dangle from his hand. "She must be someone who grew up in the church."

Chapter 29

Bob handed over the key to the church and explained where to find the tiny staircase that led to the steeple. The pastor agreed to stand watch over the girl while Frank went inside. Frank heard his friend praying as he walked away.

Prayers were as valuable as anything else he could do.

Frank went to his truck for some supplies, then shouted to the girl one more time. "I'm coming up to get you now. Everything will be okay soon."

He hoped he was right.

Inside the dark church, Frank stumbled past the empty pews and around the baptismal font to the front of the sanctuary. He soon found the three-quarter height door built to look like part of the wainscoting in the choir loft. In all his years of staring at the choir from the congregation, he'd never noticed it before.

The door opened onto a narrow, steep staircase that turned several times as it led up to the steeple. Frank flicked on his flashlight, and the powerful beam showed footprints on the dusty stairs: the large treads of work boots, but also, along the side closest to the railing, the imprints of much smaller sneakers. Frank started up, pausing briefly to listen for the sound of scratching rodent feet. The last thing he wanted to encounter on his climb was an enraged squirrel or raccoon.

He turned onto the last flight. Ahead he could see the big cast-iron bell hanging from beams laced with cobwebs and birds' nests.

Heart pounding, Frank arrived at the base of the steeple. He shined his flashlight on the plywood patch. A hammer lay on the floor. The claw end had been used to pry out some of the nails and pull away more of the rotten wood of the steeple. By pushing outward, the girl had created a gap just big enough for a small person to squeeze through.

But coming back in the way she had gone out was trickier.

Inside, she had been standing on the firm level floor as she pushed herself out.

134

Outside, she was on a slippery, steeply sloping surface, making it nearly impossible to pull the plywood open while edging back inside. As he studied the problem, he noticed the tips of eight fingers clutching the rough edge of the wood, the fingernails white with pressure.

Frank spoke softly, peeking through the small opening where he could see the arm of a blue sweatshirt. "Hi, honey. How are you doing out there?"

The only response, a gasping sob.

"I'm going to slide this rope through the opening. I want you to let go with just one hand and wrap the rope around your waist, then slide the end back in to me."

The girl heaved a shuddering sob but did as he instructed. Once the rope was around her, Frank tied a strong hitch knot as close to her body as he could reach through the crack. Then he tied the other end to a beam inside the steeple.

"You're tied to a beam in here," Frank explained. "Even if you slip, you won't fall off the roof. Now you have to trust me. I need you to let go of the plywood. I'm going to push it open, so I can get you back through."

"Okay, let go."

The fingers held tight.

"Honey, I know it's scary, but this is the only way." Frank tugged the rope. "Feel that? I've got you. But you have to trust me and let go."

He heard her take a deep breath. The little fingertips disappeared.

Frank pushed on the plywood.

Outside, he heard the sound of feet scrabbling on the slick cedar shingles.

The girl screamed.

Frank used his shoulder to keep the plywood wedged open. Then he pulled on the rope and the girl came through, falling into his arms and knocking them both onto the floor.

When he got up and recovered his flashlight, he saw a smear of blood across the girl's face. But a closer examination showed it was just from a scrape where she'd caught her wrist on the rough edge of the plywood.

The girl pulled her wounded hand out of his grasp and curled up with her head between her knees and her arms wrapped around her legs.

That's how Bob found them when he popped through the door seconds later.

"Is she okay?"

"She's fine." Frank untied the rope. "You're back to square one with your steeple repairs, though."

The girl's shoulders shook with sobs. Some garbled words that might have been "I'm sorry" emerged from the little bundle of misery. Bob crouched down beside her and murmured consoling words.

Relief at having saved the child's life manifested itself as irritation. "See if you can figure out who she is and where she lives." Frank turned his back on the girl and focused on winding up the rope. His hands shook as he made the coils.

Behind him, Bob spoke so softly that Frank couldn't make out his words. Then his voice rose in surprise. "Jenna!"

Frank spun around. The girl had lifted her head from the fetal position. Her tear-streaked face looked very familiar.

"It's Jenna Burlingame. Reid's grand-daughter." Bob sat back on his heels, stunned.

Frank lowered himself to the dusty floor. "Jenna, what made you go out there?"

Her eyes were as wide as a cat's at night. She rocked back and forth.

"Jenna, telling me the truth is very important. Did someone encourage you to do this?"

A high, keening sound echoed through the hollow steeple. If Frank hadn't already checked for animals, he would have sworn it was inhuman.

Jenna's entire body trembled. A sheen of sweat coated her forehead.

"She's going into shock," Bob said. "You can't question her now. We'd better get her home, and you can talk to her in the morning."

Frank could see Bob was right. He thought it might help to have Trudy Massinay present when he questioned the girl.

So Bob and Frank half carried, half dragged Jenna out of the church.

When they got her outside, Frank's phone began buzzing crazily.

He glanced at it. Five texts in a row:

Where are you?

The boys are crying.

I can't handle them.

Get home. Now!

Jenna slumped against Bob.

"Come on, Jenna. I'll drive you home," Frank commanded.

She shook her head and clung to Bob.

"I'll take her, Frank. She doesn't live far from here."

Again the phone chirped in his pocket, and Frank agreed. "Tell her parents to keep watch over her all night. I'll be there in the morning to question her."

Bob turned Jenna around and pointed her toward his car. As they walked away, Frank spied Jenna's phone jutting out of her back pocket.

He trotted after her and plucked it out.

The girl didn't seem to notice. She kept trudging along beside Bob.

Frank looked at the phone in his hand. What he'd done was illegal. But he wasn't going to risk having Jenna delete her messages.

And once he told Reid why he'd done it, he knew the man wouldn't object even though he was a lawyer.

Chapter 30

Every light in Frank's house blazed.

He walked into bedlam: one voice howling, one voice whimpering, one voice shouting. That stupid cat tore past him, taking advantage of the open door to dart outside.

Frank followed the sounds to the bathroom where Penny yelled at the medicine cabinet as she hurled tubes and boxes to the floor. "Oh my God! Where is it? I know we have it."

Jeremy sat on the edge of the bathtub screaming through hands pressed to his face. Joshua lurked in the hallway, hiccupping with sobs.

"What's going on?"

At the sound of a new voice, Jeremy dropped his hands. A deep red scratch bisected his cheek. Blood and snot and tears smeared across his face.

Frank ran to his grandson. "My God, what happened?"

Jeremy flung his arms around Frank's neck. "Yogi h-u-r-rt me!"

Frank pried the boy's arms away, so he could get a look. An angry welt rose on either side of the scratch. He looked up at Penny, who had finally found a tube of antibiotic cream. "That damn cat did this? How could you let this happen?"

Penny's eyes widened as she kicked aside the wet tee shirts on the bathroom floor. "How could *I*? How could *you* run off and leave me? The boys were both out of bed not five minutes after you left. Racing around...chasing Yogi...."

"Enough! If that cat knows what's good for him, he'll stay away. If he comes back here, he's going straight to the pound."

Penny pushed past him. "I'm going to Edwin and Lucy's. There's a nice quiet room for me at the Inn." She tossed the antibiotic cream at his chest. "You know so much, you handle this."

The front door slammed, then opened again. "And leave my cat alone!"

138

Frank finally got the boys settled down. Jeremy fell asleep quickly, exhausted by all his crying. Joshua clung to Frank, begging for more stories. Finally, he drifted off.

Frank sat in the living room, nursing a scotch. Of course, he should have told Penny why he had to answer that call, but there had been no time for explanations. Couldn't she trust him that he wouldn't have broken his word if it hadn't been vital to go? And of course he shouldn't have threatened the cat, but he'd been so on edge after saving Jenna that seeing Jeremy injured caused him to lash out. He massaged the bridge of his nose. Somehow, he'd have to make all this right in the morning.

And take the boys to see those damn goats.

His phone vibrated in his pocket. Thank God, Penny was calling him to make up.

But when he looked at the screen, another name flashed.

Reid Burlingame.

The distraught grandfather started talking before Frank even said hello. "My God, Frank, what happened? Thank you for saving her."

"Do you have any idea—"

"She hasn't said a word. It's like she's in a coma with her eyes open. We called Gloria Martin, and she came over and gave her a sedative. Gloria says she'll sleep for at least ten hours."

Gloria was a nurse-practitioner who lived right in town, closer than any doctor. Frank checked his watch. Already past midnight. "Fine. Call me as soon as she's awake. Don't let her out of your sight, and don't let her talk to any of her friends before I get there. By the way, I have her phone."

Above his head, Frank heard a slight noise. He ended the call with Reid and looked up to see Joshua crouched on the steps watching him through the spindles of the bannister. Frank closed his eyes. He couldn't read *My Sister is an Alien* again. He couldn't.

"Go back to bed, buddy."

Joshua shook his head and crept a few steps lower. "I have to tell you something," he whispered.

Frank extended his arm and Joshua scampered down and snuggled into his grandfather's embrace. "Don't send Yogi to the pound, Grandpa. It wasn't his fault. Penny told us not to tease the cat. But Jeremy didn't listen. When

Yogi's tail did this—" he swished with his left index finger— "Jeremy did this" –he grabbed his left finger with his right. "And after Jeremy did it a lotta times, Yogi did this." Joshua made his fingers into a claw and scratched the air.

"So Jeremy pulled Yogi's tail. How come you're telling me this now?"

"Jeremy asked me to," Joshua said. "He was afraid to tell you himself. But he doesn't want Yogi to go to the pound. They kill cats there, Grandpa. We saw it on TV."

"Okay, buddy. Thank you for telling me the truth. We won't send Yogi to the pound. He'll be back in the morning. Don't worry—he knows how to take care of himself."

Joshua twisted out of his grandfather's arms and looked around. "Where's Penny? Are you going to get a divorce?"

"What? No! What made you say that?"

"Our friend Madison says that when grownups fight a lot, that means they're going to get a divorce. That's what happened to her parents."

"Well, I'm sorry to hear that. But sometimes grownups just have a little disagreement. It doesn't mean anything. Penny and I don't fight a lot."

Joshua's big brown eyes blinked. "Yes, you do."

———◉———

AT THREE IN THE MORNING, Frank woke up. Had he been dreaming? Had one of the boys cried out? He lay still and listened.

All quiet.

The bed felt large and cold without Penny. He sighed and tried to get comfortable. Then he heard it. A faint, steady scraping.

And a long, plaintive meow.

Frank got out of bed and went downstairs. He opened the back door, and Yogi strolled in.

The cat sat down at Frank's feet and contemplated him through clear green eyes.

"All right—I apologize. But you know, if you weren't so fat, you could jump up on something high and get away from those kids."

Yogi licked his left paw.

Frank's stomach rumbled. Hot dogs and S'mores didn't stick with a man. "Oh, come on. Let's have a tuna sandwich."

Chapter 31

Breakfast without Penny had proved a little rocky. Frank poured too much milk in Joshua's cereal and put both butter and jam on Jeremy's toast instead of jam alone.

Tears ensued.

But the visit to Jackie's goats quickly restored Frank's status as best grandpa in the world. They found Gilbert the billy goat grazing in the meadow next to Jackie's house, surrounded by a harem of nanny goats and two adorable kids who jumped and pranced. Frank had cleared out every box of stale crackers and unpopular breakfast cereal in the kitchen, so the boys would have some snacks to attract the goats' attention.

The twins shrieked with a mixture of delight and outrage when Gilbert snatched a package of Wheat Thins from Jeremy's hands and calmly proceeded to munch the crackers, cardboard box and all.

"Hey, you dumb goat—don't eat the box!"

"Grandpa, make him stop!"

Frank took one look at Gilbert's beady eyes glowering under his very pointy horns and decided that the goat had won this round. "I'll hold the boxes. You offer the girl goats one cracker at a time."

This approach kept the entertainment going for a good half-hour until all the treats were gone, and the goats wandered away. With perfect timing, Caroline texted that she and Eric were checking out of the hotel and would pick up the boys within the hour.

Frank heaved a sigh of relief. He didn't think his nerves or his marriage could withstand much more family togetherness. Once his daughter and grandsons were on the road, he knew he had a lot of reconciliation work to do with Penny.

Frank chose a different back road to drive back home. Along the way, he passed a house with a huge flower garden growing along the fence next to the road.

"Lookit all the pretty flowers!" Joshua called out from the back seat.

Frank slowed and noticed a hand-painted sign: Flowers for Sale. He pulled over and turned around.

"Why are we stopping? I don't want to go to a dumb flower garden," Jeremy whined.

Frank parked in the house's driveway, next to a pick-up truck. "I'm buying some flowers for Penny." He turned around and fixed his grandsons with a stern glare. "You had plenty of fun this morning. Now, we're doing something nice for someone we love. You can be patient for five minutes. Just sit tight in your car seats and I'll be right back."

Jeremy's eyes widened in disbelief. "You can't leave us alone in the car. We could be kidnapped!"

"I'll never be out of sight of the car." Frank walked toward the flower-seller's house thinking of "The Ransom of Red Chief."

"We could bake to death in here," Jeremy called.

"It's 72 degrees and the windows are open," Frank shouted back without looking. Honestly, Caroline needed to stop filling their heads with horror stories.

"This is il-leee-gal!"

"I'm the police chief."

Frank knocked on the door, hoping that after all this debate he wouldn't have to leave empty-handed. But a cheerful woman in her mid-thirties soon answered. "I'll be right out and cut you a bouquet to order," she told him.

Frank strolled over to the flower garden as the boys watched his every move. He supposed they'd be quick to report this abuse to their mother. And he'd have to explain the scratch on Jeremy's cheek although it had faded a lot overnight. Maybe it would be best to get a bouquet for Caroline too. When he got to the narrow path winding through the lush flower beds, he envisioned what the picturesque scene would look like with the flowers trampled and the plants uprooted. He knew he'd done the right thing leaving the boys in the car.

The flower farmer walked toward him from the other direction. Her tanned face showed some early lines from hours working in the sun and her hands had some permanent grime around the cuticles, but she was pretty in a wholesome way. "Do you want the flowers for a special occasion?" she asked.

"I want a get-out-of-the-doghouse bouquet to give my wife."

"Oh, so a b-i-ig bunch!" She began cutting fluffy white flowers.

"What are those called?" Frank trailed after her as she worked. "I think my grandmother had them in her yard back in Kansas."

"Hydrangea. There are lots of varieties."

"Can I have some of those blue ones—my wife likes blue."

"Of course—delphiniums are beautiful, but they're delicate. We'll give you some long-lasting asters too." The basket she carried grew fuller.

"You'll arrange these for me, right?" Frank grew anxious at the thought of presenting Penny with a wild tangle of flowers.

She turned and smiled at him. "Of course! I'm going to make it really pretty for you. You'll see."

Frank relaxed at that news, but then tensed up again. "It won't take too long, will it? My grandsons are in the car."

She laughed and set her basket at her feet. "You're a real worry-wart, aren't you? I bet that's how you got in trouble with your wife."

Frank supposed she was right. He'd over-reacted to the scratch because he was so worried about keeping his daughter happy. And he hadn't paused to explain the call because he was so worried about another suicide.

Of course, he'd been right to worry there. But he didn't want to talk about his shortcomings with this woman. He changed the subject. "So, you don't just sell flowers to passers-by, do you?"

"Oh, no—that wouldn't be profitable. I sell at three different farmer's markets. And I deliver to several restaurants and inns for their lobbies and dining-rooms."

He was always curious how people managed to make a living at unusual occupations. The Adirondack growing season was short. Surely flowers didn't provide her with a year-long livelihood. "Flowers keep you busy all year?"

"Pumpkins and gourds in the fall, Christmas trees and wreaths in December, and forced bulbs in the spring. I have a greenhouse out back and ten acres where I grow Christmas trees."

"Were you at the Trout Run market on Saturday? My daughter and I were there."

"Yep. Every week." She sat at a small table outside a shed at the back of the garden and quickly stripped excess leaves off the flowers' stems and trimmed the flowers to different lengths. Her hands worked nimbly, and in just a few minutes she handed Frank a gorgeous bouquet tied with blue ribbon. "There you go—twenty-five dollars."

"Thank you....?" Frank paused for her to supply her name.

"Nadine. Nadine Witchel."

Frank happily handed her thirty. "Say, could my grandsons have a couple of flowers to give their mom? Something resilient –they'll crush them on the way home."

Nadine followed him to his car and cut some plumy spears with thick stems along the way. She passed them through the window to the boys in the backseat while Frank laid his precious bouquet on the front seat.

After they backed out of the driveway, Frank turned to wave to Nadine. By this time a tall man had emerged from the house. Frank watched in his rear-view mirror as the man walked toward the truck. Nadine approached him, and they embraced.

Frank slowed so he could continue watching.

The man bent Nadine backward and they kissed as she clutched his broad back.

They separated.

The man was Gene Flynn.

Chapter 32

Frank delivered the boys to Caroline and Eric full of tales about their goat adventure. Neither child mentioned the Yogi incident, so Frank stayed mum. With any luck, Eric wouldn't notice the scratch until they were home. He waved them off just as Reid texted him to say that his granddaughter had awakened. Frank jammed his bouquet of flowers in a bucket of water knowing that Penny must be at her library donors meeting by now and headed toward Jenna's house.

Reid's son and his wife and daughter lived a couple miles from the green. As Frank drove, he checked in with Earl, telling him what had happened last night and learning that the alert for Billy's truck had produced no results.

Frank pulled up in front of the lovely old stone house, rang the doorbell, and waited. For the first time it dawned on him that someone must've given Jenna a ride to the church last night—the kid was only sixteen. When he discovered who that person was, he was sure he'd have the answer to what had happened to both Jenna and Laurel.

Reid's son, taller and more athletic than his father but with the same nervous energy, pulled open the door. "Thanks for coming." James Burlingame pumped Frank's hand. "We don't know what to think. Jenna's not telling us anything. My wife and father are sitting with her. Maybe you can get something out of her."

Maybe. But Frank had his doubts. Reid, normally the soul of law and order as chairman of the Town Council, was a lawyer and a grandfather foremost. He'd never let his granddaughter say anything incriminating. Frank knew teenagers rarely came clean with their parents present unless he could hold a threat over their head. And he couldn't threaten his boss's granddaughter.

Frank stayed in the foyer. "I've asked Trudy Massinay, the county social services director, to join us. Before I talk to Jenna, tell me what you know about her movements last night."

James ran his hand over his close-cropped hair. "The three of us had dinner together. In retrospect, I guess Jenna was a little quiet, but she was acting perfectly normal. You know how teenagers can be. After dinner, my wife and I went into the family room to watch a documentary. Jenna wasn't interested in that, so she went up to her room. She's got a laptop and her own TV, so that wasn't unusual." James paced back and forth in the narrow foyer. "We thought she was up there all evening, but she must've sneaked downstairs and gone out. She's never done such a thing! The next we knew, Pastor Bob was here with Jenna, telling us this crazy story that she was up on the church roof, and that you rescued her."

"Any idea how she got into town? Did someone pick her up?"

James pounded his fist on the newel post. "She took her mother's car! We realized it was missing this morning. We called Bob and he says it's parked across the street from the church. Jenna only has a learner's permit. She's only practiced driving a few times. I'm stunned she'd take such a risk. She's never been rebellious or wild. If anything, she's too reserved. Her mother is always encouraging her to go out more, get involved."

"Does Jenna know Laurel Caine?"

"The girl who jumped off the bridge?" James's eyes grew wide with fear. "No...wait, you don't think Jenna was going to—" He couldn't bring himself to speak the words aloud. "No. No! This is just some kind of teenage prank that got out of hand. Jenna's a happy girl. A normal girl."

"Does she know Laurel?" Frank repeated.

"I don't know. She's never mentioned her. Jenna doesn't go to High Peaks High School, you know. She goes to the North Country Academy. Her mother felt it was a better fit for her."

Frank considered the implications. James Burlingame worked as a financial advisor, with wealthy clients in Lake Placid and Keene Valley and probably even further afield. Even in a small town, there were class divisions. Certainly, the Burlingames travelled in different social circles than the Caines. The North Country Academy had at one time been a school for troubled teens, but now it was a "progressive" school—a private school where students called their teachers by their first names and spent more time on the arts than sports. The kids who went to Trout Run Elementary and High Peaks High school had a not–so-friendly rivalry with these private school kids, many of whom weren't local. Still, it was possible that Laurel and Jenna knew each other through church youth group or 4-H or the summer softball league. Jenna would have to answer that question.

Frank pulled Jenna's phone out of his pocket. "I took this from her last night because I didn't want her to erase any messages. Has she been asking for it?"

"No." The father took the phone and quickly tapped in the password. "We insist on knowing her password. We check her phone periodically. There's never been anything ...er...inappropriate."

Different from Laurel, who had no such supervision.

Together the two men scanned the most recent messages on Jenna's phone. They were from four different girls and seemed to be the usual mash-up of emojis and abbreviations that were meaningless to adults. "All of these girls are her friends from school," James confirmed.

Frank checked her contacts. Laurel Caine was not on the list. Neither was Shannon Wilton. Jenna probably knew it wasn't safe for her to receive texts from anyone her parents didn't approve of. Still, he was sure two episodes of teenage girls climbing to high places had to be linked.

Frank heard the crunch of gravel outside. Trudy had arrived.

He stepped onto the porch, so he could speak to her privately before they sat down with Jenna and her family. "Thanks for coming, Trudy." Frank gave her a quick run-down of what had happened last night and this morning. "So you can see the parallels with Laurel. Jenna put in a lot of effort to get into town and get out on that roof. Thank God Bob spotted her."

Trudy sat quietly, thinking. "Did she ever seem like she was ready to jump?"

"Well, at the time, Bob and I sure were worried that she'd just let go and slide off that steep roof. But now when I play it back in my mind, she seemed pretty terrified the whole time. She clung onto that plywood. Whatever made her go out there, she changed her mind once she saw the drop to the ground."

Trudy nodded. "And that was different from Laurel?"

Frank swallowed the urge to object. Trudy wasn't challenging his theory, just trying to understand these two girls who had much in common yet were also very different. "Laurel stood on top of that bridge and raised her arms to the moon and then she just stepped off. Never uttered a cry. Never even looked at all the people gathered below, begging her to come down." Frank shivered. "Honestly, it still unnerves me. I've never seen anything like it."

"But Jenna was scared?"

"Yes, definitely."

Trudy studied her wide, sensible shoes. Then she looked up. "I'd like to talk to her alone, please."

"Fine with me. Just be sure you ask her about Laurel. Let's see if her parents will agree."

When they returned to the house, they found everyone in the living room gathered around the sofa where Jenna lay on her side with her head turned into the cushions. Mrs. Burlingame stroked her daughter's back, while Reid looked about ready to explode.

"Trudy. Frank. Thank you for all your concern." Reid glared at the figure on the sofa. "It's time for my granddaughter to sit up and take some responsibility for what happened last night. We need an explanation."

Trudy placed a careworn hand on Reid's shoulder, while making eye contact with the mother. "I'd like a chance to speak to Jenna alone."

Frank noticed the girl's shoulders tense. But Trudy projected such an air of calm competence that Reid and the parents nodded and edged out of the room, glad to have turned an impossible project over to someone better able to cope. Frank followed them, turning back to look at Trudy to mouth "Laurel" as a reminder before he left.

Once he was alone with the Burlingames, the blame game began.

"This has something to do with that stupid school," James said. "The weird kids there goaded her into this."

Mrs. Burlingame's eyes flared. "You don't know anything about North Country Academy. You didn't even attend her end-of-year assessment. She's thriving there."

The mother turned to Frank to explain. "Jenna is such a perfectionist. She was becoming obsessed with getting perfect scores on all her assignments in public school. At the Academy, they don't have a grading system. The kids are free to learn at their own pace, and the teachers provide detailed encouragement on the assignments."

James rolled his eyes. "That's not how it's going to be in college. Or in the workplace."

Mrs. Burlingame folded her arms across her chest and glared at her husband and father-in-law. "I think this has something to do with that job you forced her to take at the Hungry Loon. God only knows who she's come into contact with there. There's no need for her to be working. She's just a child."

Reid puffed out his chest. "A job teaches a kid responsibility. It's not about the money."

Frank had no interest in their squabbling, but his ears pricked at the mention of the Hungry Loon. He'd forgotten that he'd seen Jenna working there on opening day. "How did Jenna get the job there?"

James glanced at his father. "Dad lined it up for her, right?"

"No, I didn't," Reid answered. "She dropped by my office one day and told me she'd been hired. I congratulated her. Told her I was proud of her. I assumed you suggested she apply."

Mrs. Burlingame frowned. "Jenna's very shy. I always have to encourage her to try new things. I can't imagine she'd march in there and ask for an application all on her own."

An interesting development. The kid didn't need money, so what had motivated her to get that job at the Loon? He wished he could get Trudy to ask, but he couldn't risk interrupting her. Maybe it would come up naturally.

Mrs. Burlingame made a pot of coffee and laid out some cookies while they waited for Trudy to emerge. Frank tried not to fall on the offering like a marauding lion, but breakfast with the boys seemed like it had happened years ago.

Finally, Trudy appeared with her arm around Jenna's shoulder.

"I'm sorry for causing so much trouble," Jenna recited. "I'll never do anything like this again." Then she ran upstairs.

Reid dropped his teaspoon with a clatter. "What? That's it?"

Trudy sat down and broke a cookie in half. She looked at James and his wife steadily before she spoke. "Jenna is troubled. She feels like a failure. She feels she's let you all down."

"What?" her mother said. "Where would she get that idea? I tell her I love her every day. I always tell her how proud I am of her."

"Children often feel that they're the cause of everything that happens in their world. Perhaps there's been some tension between you two lately?" Trudy arched her eyebrows.

James and his wife exchanged a glance. "It's nothing. We're fine. All couples have disagreements sometimes."

Frank swallowed another cookie. *Tell me about it.*

Reid waved his hand dismissively. "What's this got to do with her climbing onto the church roof?"

Trudy ignored his question and kept talking in her soothing manner. "Jenna's perception is that you consider her incompetent and timid, and that's why you moved her from High Peaks High School to the North Country Academy. She believes you don't think she's capable of surviving in public school."

"What?" her mother squawked. "Jenna was unhappy there. I just wanted her to be in a more nurturing, supportive environment."

"I'm passing along Jenna's perceptions. I'm not saying they're grounded in reality." Trudy sipped her coffee. "If you ask a teenager, 'Why did you do this?' the answer you get 99% of the time is, 'I don't know.' And that answer is literally true. Young people's brains are not fully developed, and even the most intelligent teenager often lacks the judgment and self-awareness to understand her own motivations. So asking kids 'why, why, why' is counterproductive." Trudy paused and made eye-contact with Reid to make sure he was paying attention. "I simply talked to Jenna about what was making her unhappy. The theme that emerged was that 'everyone,'" Trudy made air quotes to emphasize that the word was Jenna's, "perceives her as weak. She wants to be seen as strong. This episode was an attempt to prove her courage. A failed attempt. That's why she's still so distraught."

"So was she trying to...to commit..." James still couldn't utter the word suicide.

"I don't think so. But teenage suicide is often an impulsive act. If the means present themselves at a moment of despair—a break-up, a failed class—it can happen."

"Oh my God!" Mrs. Burlingame began to weep. "We'll have to watch her constantly."

Trudy coughed. "Actually, that's the worst thing you can do. Jenna is seeking more autonomy, more indications that you believe she's competent. I think she's aware that what she did last night set her back significantly in that regard. Nevertheless, try to give her the benefit of the doubt. She seems to really enjoy her job at the Hungry Loon, so let her keep working there."

"But we don't know enough about who she's meeting there," Mrs. Burlingame objected. "Maybe that's where she got this idea to take our car and—"

Reid stood up and dusted a cookie crumb from his shirt. "She can't get in much trouble making sandwiches. I think Trudy has a point. You shelter that girl too much. She showed some initiative in getting that job. Let her keep it."

"But we still don't know if someone goaded her into this." James thunked his coffee mug on the table. "Didn't you ask her?"

"All of you asked her and she said no. I don't possess a magic truth serum," Trudy said.

"Did you ask her if she knew Laurel?" Frank pressed.

"She says she never met Laurel, but she admires her courage and confidence."

"Confidence?" Reid spluttered. "A confident person doesn't jump off a bridge."

Mrs. Burlingame jumped up and grabbed her phone. "Enough of this! Someone in this town is a bad influence on our daughter. We're sending Jenna to stay with my sister in Chicago for the summer."

Chapter 33

Frank drove away from the Burlingames' dissatisfied with the results of his strategy. Jenna's explanation for why she went out on the roof seemed bizarre to him, but, of course, he wasn't a teenager.

Jenna had committed a few crimes—driving without a license, breaking and entering, and property damage to start the list. But he hadn't caught her in the act of driving, so that charge would never stand. Not when Jenna had the town's foremost lawyer representing her. And Bob Rush certainly wouldn't press charges against a founding family of the church who happened to be his biggest contributors.

No doubt someone had seen Bob and him out there last night. And Bob would have to get the steeple repaired again, which would require an explanation. It wouldn't be long before the news of Jenna's escapade would be all over town.

And that's when his headaches would really intensify.

Because people would want to know why Jenna Burlingame didn't receive the same justice that would have been meted out to a poor, unknown atheist.

FRANK CHECKED HIS WATCH—JUST past noon. Penny's meeting with the library donors must be breaking up by now. He raced home and grabbed the bouquet, then headed to the library. As he pulled up, he saw Penny at the door shaking hands and smiling at her departing guests. Perfect timing.

He waited until they'd all driven off, well aware that Penny had seen his truck. Then he took a deep breath and strolled through the door, holding his flowers like a shield to protect him.

"How did the meeting go?"

Penny sat at her desk with her back to the door, pounding her keyboard as if it were her husband's head. She declined to turn around, but Frank suspected the strong scent of lilies would eventually get to be too much for her.

Sure enough, she swiveled. "Fine." Her face remained grim, but Frank saw her eyes gleam at the flowers.

He held them out to her. "I brought you a peace offering. I'm really sorry for last night."

She squinted without taking the bouquet. "Where did you get those?"

"Nadine Witchel. She runs a flower farm outside of town." He knew better than to say it was around the corner from the goats, and he had stumbled upon it in a stroke of luck.

"How did you know about her?"

In Frank's mind, this cross-examination was a good thing. At least Penny wasn't giving him the silent treatment. He smiled and boldly perched on the corner of her desk. "I'm the Police Chief. I know all kinds of things."

"You don't know how to keep a commitment." She scowled and took the flowers. "But there's no point letting these beauties wilt."

She stalked toward the restroom with an empty vase. Frank trailed after her.

Ah, he had one foot in the door! The trick now was to close the deal without setbacks. "Yogi has forgiven me. He came back in the middle of the night and we shared a tuna sandwich. And this morning he got to drink all the leftover milk from the boys' cereal bowls."

Penny spun around. "It's not a big joke, Frank. You ran off and left me with your grandsons. The boys are your responsibility. You could've sent Earl on the call, or the state police. You couldn't have run off to answer the call on your own last year, before we were married. What made you think you could do it now?"

Eeew. Steely rationality took him off guard. Agree. Keep agreeing.

"You're absolutely right." Frank raised his hands in surrender. "But can I just tell you what the call was about?"

Penny tucked the vase under her arm. "What? Some drunk stole the fake Olympic flag from the window of the Mountainside?"

"Reid's granddaughter climbed onto the roof of the church and was threatening to jump."

Penny raised her hands to her mouth and the vase thumped to the carpeted floor.

"Bob called me. He saw a girl up on the roof next to the steeple. He didn't know who it was at that moment, but after what happened to Laurel, I had to get up there."

Penny chewed at her thumbnail. "Of course. Of course you did."

"But I could've paused to tell you what was up. I just got panicky. And I really thought the boys would stay put."

Penny picked up the vase and went into the restroom to fill it. "They were out of bed before your car left the driveway," she shouted out to him.

Knowing the library was empty, Frank followed his wife into the restroom. "Joshua told me what really happened with the cat. I feel terrible. I shouldn't have flown off the handle. I know what a handful they are, believe me. I guess I was still rattled by what I had to do to pull Jenna to safety."

"Oh, Frank!" Penny set the full vase on the counter and rested her forehead against his shoulder. "I hate being angry. You could have saved me so much heartache by just telling me what was going on."

He pulled her closer and murmured into her sweetly scented hair. "I realize that now. I've been operating alone so long, I have to relearn how to be part of a team. Will you help me?"

She pulled away and cocked her head. "You certainly don't need any guidance in how to tug at my heartstrings."

"I'm being sincere. I know what my faults are. I'm impatient, and I always want to be in charge, and I'm sure I can fix everything. Unfortunately, I only see them in retrospect. You need to point out crimes-in-progress."

"Ten-four, chief." And then she kissed him.

Chapter 34

When Frank finally got to the office, the work day was half over. Earl had a lot to report.

"No sightings of Billy's truck. Not by the state police or the Lake Placid or Saranac PDs either. I called the Mountainside and a couple other bars to ask them to keep an eye peeled."

Frank sat down and sifted through the stack of paperwork awaiting him. "You think any of those bartenders would turn a customer into the police just because we want to talk to him?"

"Billy's not their most popular customer. He orders more than he can pay for and starts arguments. I kinda implied if they did us a favor, they'd be storing up some goodwill for the future. In case they ever needed it, ya know."

Frank smiled. The kid was learning. "Good work. What about the man Gene claims nailed the snake to his deck?"

"Whew! I got an earful from him! He says Gene's crazy and has it in for him ever since he got a job that Gene wanted. He says he's never been to Gene's house and he couldn't possibly have killed that snake because he's a lousy shot—blind in one eye. And then he popped out his glass eye to prove it." Earl shuddered. "Freaked me out."

"Huh. Pretty compelling evidence. You'd have to have a damn good aim to hit a snake's head with one clean shot. So Gene clearly sent us on a wild goose chase and didn't mind causing trouble for this other guy in the process." Then Frank told Earl what he'd seen at the flower farm. "Looks like Gene is gettin' some action on the side. And it was pretty early in the morning, so he must've spent the night there. Either his wife doesn't care where she sleeps, or she's too intimidated to complain." Frank took a deep breath and locked eyes with Earl. "Seems more and more likely that Billy's the one who left that snake on the deck. Gene knew that and came up with this other guy as a cover story. Billy's a great shot. And now I see he has an additional reason to be pissed at his father."

Earl swiveled away from Frank's intense gaze. "Yes, Billy's a good shot. And yes, finding out your dad is cheating on your mom would make any son angry. He'd beat his dad up—that I could see. But killing an innocent animal for spite, even a snake? That's not his style."

Frank took a breath to respond, then exhaled in silence. Leave it. What good could come from endless speculation about Billy's troubled mind? He and Earl agreed on one thing: Billy must be found.

If Earl was right, they'd exonerate Billy from any complicity in Laurel's death.

If Frank was right, they'd get some justice for the girl.

"Could Billy have taken off in the truck to meet up with some buddy from the Marines? Did he mention anyone?"

Earl shook his head. "From what he said to me, it seemed like his closest friends were still serving. And he's really broke. If he was going on a long road trip, he'd need money for gas and food. And if he was traveling on the interstates, the state police would've spotted him by now." Earl stood and gazed out the window. "No, I think he's still nearby. Holed up. I just don't know where."

AT FOUR, DORIS STUCK her head in the office to say good-bye as she always did. Her presence reminded Frank he had something to ask her. "Penny and I think it's possible that the cat we found belongs to an old person who had to go live with relatives. Do you know anyone like that?"

Doris thought for a moment and shook her head. "Are you two still worrying your heads about that cat? He's probably just a barn cat who wandered off."

"He's too fat and slow to be a barn cat," Frank said. "And he likes people. Not skittish at all. Someone left a message on one of Penny's posters." Frank had remembered to bring it with him and handed it to her. "It seems like the former owner doesn't want Yogi back but was happy to hear he was okay."

Doris squinted at the note. "That's not an old person's handwriting." She shifted her canvas tote bag from one arm to the other.

"How do you know?"

For once, it was Doris who was exasperated by Frank's failure to comprehend. "Everyone our age and older studied penmanship in grade school. You remember, the Palmer Method." She crossed to his desk and put an arrest report in Frank's handwriting and a phone message in her own writing side-by-side. "See, our cursive is all connected and slanted, and we make our S's the same. "But look at Earl's writing." She grabbed one of Earl's reports. It was written in a combination of printing and cursive. The letters were round and straight up-and-down.

Doris sighed. "They don't even teach cursive in school anymore." She tapped the poster with the note. "That note looks more like Earl's writing than ours. It was written by a young person. But it's neat. Probably a girl."

Frank studied the note as the secretary walked out the door. Damned if Doris wasn't right. No older person he knew wrote like this.

So much for that theory.

Chapter 35

On Friday morning, the phones started ringing early and never let up. Frank took a call from a disgruntled homeowner who claimed he'd been robbed when vacation renters hadn't locked up his house properly, while Earl patiently took down details of a missing mountain bike that might have been stolen but might have bounced off the back of a bike rack somewhere between Verona and Trout Run. Earl hung up, and immediately took another call. The entire time Frank took notes on the items stolen from the house, Earl watched him like a dog observing his owner eat a steak. When Frank hung up, Earl pounced.

"The phone company called. The owner of the number that sent those texts to Laurel was Dunleavey. The people who were in here the other day to pick up that Mini Cooper. That number is one of three numbers in their family plan."

Frank leaned back in his chair. "It must belong to Charlie. But he told me the reason he wasn't in touch with his parents was because he discarded his phone. So he wouldn't be oppressed by it or something. Maybe someone else found it."

Billy Flynn?

"Sure, Charlie told you that, but what college kid would really go around without a phone? And even if he did throw his phone away, it's not like someone who found it would be able to use it. Phones are all password protected now."

"Shit! Now I wish I'd figured out where Charlie is living in Trout Run." Frank kicked the leg of his battered metal desk. "I can see him befriending Laurel. They're both sort of lost souls. But persuading her to kill herself?" Frank met Earl's gaze. "I kinda like the kid. He sure didn't come across as mean."

"Maybe they made a suicide pact and he chickened out." Earl stretched in his seat, so he could see out the window. "Charlie still works at the Hungry Loon, right? You can track him down there."

Frank jumped up. "The Loon! That's the connection to Jenna. Charlie and Jenna both work at the Loon. He could be the one who persuaded her to go out on the church roof." He headed toward the door. "I don't know what's going on here, but I'm sure as hell going to find out."

Frank practically ran across the green to get to the new café. But when he walked in the door, he found himself mired in a mob scene. He'd arrived at lunchtime, and both locals and tourists packed the place. Frank edged through the crowd trying to get closer to the counter to see if Charlie was working. A tourist delivered a sharp jab with her elbow, determined not to let even a cop jump the line. But when he peered over the counter, he saw two women working the prep area and Kristen Mooney taking orders and payments.

"Is Charlie Dunleavey working today?"

"No. But we could sure use him. Jenna was supposed to be here, and she never showed up." Kristen turned away from Frank. "May I help the next person?"

"I'll have a tarragon chicken sandwich."

"We don't have that anymore." Kristen pointed to the menu board above her head. "Just what's up there."

"Why not? That chicken is killer."

"I don't know. Look, can I take the next customer while you make up your mind?"

An exasperated Kristen returned to processing her line of customers. Frank glanced around for the manager he'd seen on the grand opening day. He vaguely remembered the guy as tall with sandy hair, and he spotted someone in the market section who met that description. As he wormed through the crowd, he saw that his target was restocking shelves. Definitely the manager.

"Hi. I need to talk to Charlie Dunleavey. Is he working today?"

The manager scanned Frank's uniform but kept working. "Not today. He'll be on tomorrow."

"Where does he live? This can't wait."

The manager finished placing jars of Kalamata olives on the shelf and folded up the box they'd come in. "What's the problem? He's a good worker. I can't afford to lose him."

"He's not in trouble. I just need to talk to him. Where does he live?"

"I don't know. I'd have to check is personnel file."

"Overring! I need the register key," Kristen's voice boomed over the murmur of the crowd.

The manager pushed toward to register. "Look, we're swamped. Can it wait until after lunch?"

Frank might've been sympathetic if it weren't for his vision of Charlie spending his day off persuading some other young girl to do something crazy. "Take care of the register. Then I need you to get me Charlie's address and whatever phone number he put on his application."

The manager stalked toward the counter, indicating with a brusque jerk of his head that Frank should follow. He straightened out the overring, then led Frank to a small office beside the kitchen where he opened a laptop and jabbed furiously at the keys.

"You from around here?" Frank asked as he waited.

"Schroon Lake."

"That's a long drive."

"I only agreed to work here for the summer. By winter, I'll be back in the Keene store." The manager scowled. "If I ever get someone trained to take over here." He grabbed a pen and scribbled on a scrap of paper.

"I need ones!" Kristen bellowed from the register.

The manager tossed the paper at Frank and ran back to the front lines.

The address on the paper was on a road near where Charlie had abandoned his car and run off, but the phone number had the local 518 area code, so Charlie had not applied for the job using the phone that had sent the text to Laurel as his contact number.

Frank decided to drive to the house rather than call.

He turned onto Cooper's Vista Drive, squinting at the few marked mailboxes to get a sense of the numbering system. Fifty-three looked to be half a mile down the road on the left. The lots were large here, and the road followed a ridge that gave some of the houses a view of Cooper's Mountain, a small peak that nestled in the shadow of Whiteface. As was often the case in Trout Run, a few beautifully designed vacation homes stood among modest ranches and Cape Cods owned by locals. He expected fifty-three to be a vacation home if Charlie's father was right, and the kid was crashing with someone he'd met at college. But when he pulled up to the crooked, unmarked mailbox that followed number fifty-one, he found a ramshackle two-story house with a sagging wrap-around porch and peeling brown paint. It did, however, have a view. Maybe Charlie's friends hadn't had a chance to renovate.

Frank picked his way up the porch steps, worried his foot might plunge right through the rotten boards. Despite the crumbling condition of the rest of the house, the front door was brand new, made of steel with a sturdy lock. Frank knocked, the sound of his knuckles hitting steel disrupting the quiet summer afternoon.

The door opened. A waiflike woman in her early twenties stood on the threshold regarding him wordlessly.

"Hi. I'm looking for Charlie Dunleavey."

Aside from one blink of the eyes, the girl's expression didn't change.

"Does he live here?"

The girl nodded.

Frank had dealt with his fair share of sullen teenagers, but he hadn't done anything to make this one clam up. Was there something wrong with the girl? "I need to talk to him. Can you tell him I'm here?"

The girl gazed down at her sneakers. Then she quietly shut the door.

What the hell?

Frank stepped away from the door and looked up at the many windows that lined both stories of the house, each one covered with heavy curtains. What was the point of having a house with such nice views if you kept them all blocked out? Now he noticed one of the curtains in an upstairs room flick open. The sash in that room was raised. He didn't think the strange girl could've made it up there so quickly. Frank waved. "Hello? I'm looking for Charlie Dunleavey!"

A minute later, the front door opened again. This time, a slender woman in her forties stood framed in the opening.

"Charlie isn't here." She spoke to Frank without introduction.

"Police Chief Frank Bennett. I need to talk to Charlie. Do you know where he is?"

"Yes."

The woman said nothing more, gazing at him with the same level of curiosity shown by the average dairy cow. Was she the mother of the younger woman? If so, the lack of communication skills must be genetic.

Patience. He must learn patience. "Where can I find him?"

"You can't find him. He must find himself."

The patience pledge was already wearing thin. Frank chose and enunciated each word carefully. "Where was he headed the last time you saw him?"

"To Haystack Mountain."

Another wilderness hike. He hoped Charlie had learned his lesson from his hike on Dix and set off well prepared this time. That was a two-day hike at a minimum. He'd need a tent, sleeping bag, water purification equipment, and plenty of food. "When do you expect him back?"

"He'll stay as long as it takes."

"That's my point ma'am. Normally it takes two days. When did he leave?"

She thought for a moment. "The day before yesterday."

So, right after Laurel jumped. But if this woman was to be believed, Charlie was away when Jenna made her climb. If he had already been gone two days, he should be back by tonight or tomorrow at the latest.

"Was he with a group?"

"A group? Oh, no—this is a challenge that must be undertaken alone."

Must be? Frank wasn't up for lecturing her on how inadvisable it was to hike solo in the High Peaks Wilderness. "Ma'am, the last time Charlie went hiking alone, he had to be rescued by forest rangers. Does he have a phone with him this time in case he gets in trouble again?"

She shook her head. "No, Charlie has spent too much time in the thrall of 21st century perversity. That's why this journey will be so purifying for him."

What the hell did that mean?

Frank pulled out his notebook. "What's your name, ma'am?"

"Linnea."

"Last name?"

She shook her head as if this were a tedious detail she'd forgotten.

"And how are you connected with Charlie? Is he a friend of one of your kids?"

"We are all friends here." She smiled at Frank in the manner of one seeking to avoid the purchase of Girl Scout cookies without being rude.

Then she closed the door.

Chapter 36

Frank stared at the blank gray steel six inches from his nose. He could pound on the door, but the woman didn't have to answer more of his questions. He had no way to pressure her and not enough evidence yet to justify an arrest warrant for Charlie or a search warrant for the house. On a whim, he pulled out his phone and dialed the number Charlie had provided on his Hungry Loon job application. But he didn't hear a phone ringing inside the house.

What was going on in that house? For the first time since talking to Charlie's mother, he felt some uneasiness for the kid. Why was he so determined to hike alone? And who was this woman, Linnea?

When Frank walked into the Town Office, he tossed the scrap of paper with Charlie's address on Doris's desk. "Find out who owns that property."

She continued chatting on the phone, but nodded and picked up the paper, giving him some confidence she'd actually do the assigned task.

When he entered the inner office, he found Pastor Bob instead of Earl.

"Hey, what's up?"

"Earl went out to do the afternoon patrol. He said I could wait here for you."

Frank poured himself a cup of stale coffee and sat behind his desk, merely raising his eyebrows to indicate he was ready to hear whatever the minister had to tell him.

"I had to tell the Buildings and Grounds Committee why we need to get someone out on the roof to repair the steeple again. They were shocked that Jenna caused the damage. Rollie Fister says he thinks that new church, the Tabernacle, encouraged her to vandalize Trout Run Presbyterian."

"Whoa, Bob. Slow down. There's no evidence of that. Jenna didn't seem to be intentionally trying to damage the building. That was a side effect of her going out there."

"But why did she choose the church roof if she wanted to commit suicide? I've been to the Burlingames' home before. They have a big stone terrace out back. Jenna could've crawled out her own attic window and thrown herself onto those flagstones if she wanted to kill herself. I think her mission was to cause more damage at the church, and she panicked when she saw how high up she was."

Frank took a breath, ready to dismiss this notion, but paused. Because of Laurel's suicide, he'd been laser focused on the theory that Jenna too had been planning to jump but had changed her mind. What if he was totally off-base?

"Ok-a-a-y, let's explore that theory. You're telling me the new church in town is actively trying to destroy the old church?"

"This is not some friendly rivalry between two denominations...Methodists vs. Lutherans in an annual softball game." Bob leaned forward. "I'm worried, Frank. At first, I thought the Tabernacle was a Christian evangelical church. But now I think it's some kind of cult. A mind-control cult."

Frank studied his friend's anxious face. Bob was normally quite rational even if his life's work was about taking matters on faith alone. Today he seemed lit up with agitation. Frank decided to let Bob get everything worrying him out of his system. "What makes you say that?"

"When I drove Jenna home last night, she stared straight ahead like a zombie. She wouldn't talk to me at all. When I parked in front of her house, I turned to her and asked her to tell me what was troubling her. I assured her that she could speak to me, her pastor, in confidence. And she looked at me for a long moment and then said, 'No. You're not...' and she broke off and jumped out of the car and ran into the house. So obviously, what she meant was, 'no, you're not my pastor.' Because that cult has twisted her mind."

"You know for a fact she's been going there? Did you ask her parents when you spoke to them last night?"

"Well, no. I didn't realize the significance then. It's only after I thought about it that it dawned on me what she must've meant."

Only after Rollie Fister had planted this crazy theory in his mind. "She might have meant, 'No, you're not going to understand.' Or you might be misremembering her exact words."

Bob held his hands out in supplication. "You don't believe me?"

"I didn't say that. But we don't even know if Jenna's been going to the Tabernacle. Her parents didn't mention it when I was there today. But I admit, I didn't specifically ask."

"Everyone goes. Half the town is there on Monday nights for that free dinner. The kids all go because they get a chance to fool around on electric guitars and drum kits."

"That seems like harmless fun. Better than sitting under the bridge getting stoned."

Bob recoiled as if Frank had slapped him. "So you're another one who thinks that our Presbyterian church family is boring and out of touch. That we don't offer anything that young people want or need."

"I didn't say that. But teenagers in Trout Run have very little to do at night, especially in the summer." Frank didn't want to add that the woman who ran the Presbyterian youth group had been doing it since her kids were teens and now she was a grandmother. She wouldn't be likely to add electric guitars to her agenda.

Bob gazed up at the ceiling. "I know we need someone younger to take over our youth group. But I can't find a younger parent willing to do it." Bob snapped back to his conversation with Frank. "I wouldn't care if the kids were just going over there to play music. But that man, that Adam Fortway—who, by the way, does not have a degree from any divinity school because I checked—is filling their heads with poison and preying on the most vulnerable."

Bob's normally kind, open face twisted with disgust. Frank felt like he was watching his friend spin out of control. The man had been investigating the credentials of his rival? Was Bob really this threatened by the arrival of the Tabernacle?

"Again, I say: evidence. Whose head has been filled with poison?"

Bob tugged at his clerical collar. "Rollie's nephew leads our men's Bible study class, and he decided to go to one of those dinners to see what was going on over there. He told me no one mentioned Jesus once the whole evening. That they sing songs and light candles and then Fortway comes out and makes a speech and everyone cheers." Bob stopped, obviously embarrassed by how mundane his recitation sounded.

Frank walked around to Bob's chair and rested his hand on his friend's shoulder. "Look, I met the guy. I didn't particularly like him, but he's totally ordinary. He spouts some trendy New Age patter about finding your inner light. I'm sure he's happy to separate people from their hard-earned money for one of his retreats. But he's no more dangerous than whatever self-help author happens to be on the bestseller list this week."

Bob wasn't giving up so easily. He jumped to his feet and faced Frank. "If he set himself up in Trout Run to hold retreats, why aren't we seeing droves of spiritual seekers arriving here from other places? Why is he recruiting people from Trout Run to go to his Tabernacle? And he doesn't even ask them for money. So what's he up to?"

Frank didn't know. But with Billy Flynn and Charlie Dunleavey both connected to Laurel's suicide and both suddenly MIA, he wasn't sure he really cared.

Chapter 37

Doris entered Frank's office as Bob left.

"That house is owned by something called 'Affiliated Holdings, Inc.' whatever that means. They just bought it."

Frank reached for the title transfer document, so he could see for himself. "Who's this seller?"

"That's Leon Hurdiman's granddaughter. He left the house to her when he died a few years ago, but she lives downstate somewhere and didn't want it. It's been on the market ever since. Guess she finally managed to find someone who wanted that old rattletrap."

Frank continued to study the paper in his hand. "Looks like Reid represented the seller. Who's this lawyer representing the buyer?"

Doris shrugged. "I don't know everyone, Frank. You'll have to ask Reid."

Before he called the lawyer, Frank Googled Affiliated Holdings. All that came up was that it was a company incorporated in Delaware. It didn't seem to have a website or any description of what the company did. He picked up the phone.

"How come some random company in Delaware bought the old Hurdiman place on Cooper Vista Road?" Frank asked when Reid answered.

"How should I know?" Reid snapped. "Neither the buyer nor the seller attended the closing. It was just me and some young lawyer from Au Sable Forks sitting in a room signing documents for our clients."

"Who was the real estate agent who handled the sale?"

"No agent. A private sale."

"Hurdiman's granddaughter found this seller herself?"

"Apparently, the buyer found her. She told me she got a phone call with a great all-cash offer. Honestly, this Affiliated Holdings paid substantially over the market value."

"Who called her? This lawyer from Au Sable Forks?"

"No, he was simply a local lawyer representing Affiliated for this transaction, so their lawyer wouldn't have to make a trip up here. It's done all the time."

Frank asked Reid if he knew who was living in the house now, if he'd ever heard of Charlie Dunleavey or a woman named Linnea. Reid grew crankier with every "no" he uttered. "One last question," Frank said. "You told me the Tabernacle bought some houses that have been on the market for a while. This Cooper Vista house isn't one of them?"

"No—The Tabernacle of Living Light bought three houses on the other side of town, near the church itself."

"And is the Tabernacle the owner of record? Not some company in Delaware?"

"Of course. The Tabernacle's name is on the deeds."

"That little church got mortgages on three houses?'

"No mortgages. They were cash transactions."

Now Frank sat at attention. Real estate in the Adirondacks might be cheaper than downstate, but it wasn't *that* cheap. How did Fortway have cash on hand to buy three houses? "Don't you think it's a little suspicious that a guy who runs his own storefront church and new age retreat center has enough money to pay cash for all his real estate?"

"Suspicious? No, Frank—I'm *grateful*. Grateful that the town doesn't have an empty, decaying Chinese restaurant blighting a main street. Grateful that houses are selling. Grateful that some new people are moving to town. And you should be, too. Remember, property taxes pay your and Earl's salaries. Now, I've got another call to take." And he hung up.

Frank scowled at the phone. He supposed Reid would be fine with Charles Manson moving to town as long as the man contributed to the tax base. He shook himself. In the space of a few hours, he'd gone from defending Fortway against Bob's accusations to skewering him to Reid. The truth, Frank was sure, lay somewhere in the middle.

Fortway might not be some crazy-eyed false messiah. But that didn't mean he wasn't up to something sketchy with his tabernacle and his retreats.

Frank went back to Doris and had her look up the owner of the building that once housed the Asian Bistro and now was home to the Tabernacle.

"Hmm. That's funny. Another company in Delaware." Doris handed him the title.

Seasonal Property Holdings. And when Frank looked it up, he found more nothing: no website, no phone number, no description of the company.

Chapter 38

When Earl returned from the afternoon patrol, Frank pounced like a mountain lion on an unsuspecting hiker. "Did you know that Delaware is the country's leading anonymous shell company provider?"

Earl raised his eyebrows. "No. And I don't know who's the country's leading opera singer either. Why should I?"

"Sorry. I've been doing some research while you were out. You walked in on the middle of my brainstorming." Frank backed up and explained what he'd learned about the ownership of the houses and the Asian Bistro building. "So it turns out that for years, Delaware made money from registering these anonymous shell corporations that rich people and criminals and even terrorists use to hide their money. But apparently, now the state has decided to crack down on them."

"So how does that connect to the Tabernacle?" Earl sat and propped his feet up on his desk, getting comfortable for a long discussion.

"Not sure. I read some news stories about it, but the whole operation is very complicated and secretive. But the bottom line is, Delaware is throwing on the bright lights and now all the roaches are scattering."

"Guess they need new places to stash their cash. But how would a shell corporation hide money in Trout Run?"

"Another thing I'm not clear on. Did you study money laundering at the police academy?"

"The basics," Earl said. "Drug dealers and other criminals take in a lot of cash. But they can't deposit tons of cash in the bank without bank regulators asking where it came from. So if they want to be able to use their illegal money to buy stuff in the legit world, they have to clean it through a legit business that takes in a lot of cash, like a laundromat, or a bar."

"Exactly." Frank pointed a pen at his partner. "But the process you described is too simple nowadays—the Feds are on to all the obvious schemes. I just finished talking to my son-in-law about this."

"Mr. Wall Street knows about money laundering?" Earl laughed. "I guess those investment banker types don't even bother to hide that they're cheating the rest of us these days."

"He doesn't know about drug dealers' money, but he says the key to sheltering wealth from the prying eyes of the Federal government is to move it around in so many different transactions that no one can follow it."

"So maybe Trout Run is one stop on the journey, eh?"

"We're off the grid, far from places like Miami or Vegas where this stuff goes on all the time." Frank spun around in his chair. "Think about this. A church is a tax-exempt organization, so that makes it a great place to stash money. And it's expected that people make donations to a church, so that could launder some cash."

"Except people say the Tabernacle never asks anyone to make a donation," Earl reminded Frank.

"That's my point." Frank leaped up and paced around the office. "Fortway doesn't need to take *in* any cash. He just needs to say that all the cash he deposits comes from church members and retreat followers. Any assets he receives are automatically tax-exempt."

"So you think he started the Tabernacle as a tax dodge? That he doesn't even care if people believe what he's preaching?"

"I don't know. Bob says Fortway never went to divinity school, so I guess he's a self-declared man of the cloth. Hard for me to tell what he really believes without going to one of his services. But he'd probably be suspicious if I showed up."

"I can go," Earl said. "My cousin Sandy invited me to the Tabernacle after she went last week, but I blew her off. I'll just tell her I changed my mind."

Earl made a quick call to his cousin. "Is that right? Tonight? Sure—sounds like fun."

"We're in luck," Earl told Frank after he'd hung up. "We don't have to wait for the regular service on Monday night. The Tabernacle is having a special fried chicken dinner and praise service to celebrate the end of the work week."

"Hallelujah!" Frank waved his hands to heaven. "You go to the Tabernacle. I'll do the Friday night on-call."

———————◆———————

FRANK AND PENNY COOKED dinner together at home, finishing by seven. Friday nights were the apex of criminal activity in Trout Run, so either Frank or Earl was always on-call, monitoring the phone from the comfort of their own homes.

Guys drank up their paychecks at the Mountainside and got into ridiculous squabbles about whether the Red Sox had better hitters than the Yankees and the Patriots had crooked coaches or not. And if Frank or Earl weren't needed to break up bar fights, then one of them would most likely have to answer a late-night domestic disturbance call when the outraged wife or girlfriend discovered how little of the week's pay had made it home.

No sooner had the last dish gone into the dishwasher than a call was forwarded to Frank's home phone from the office. Penny arched her eyebrows. "Starting early tonight."

"Matthew Caine passed out in the men's room at the Mountainside," Frank reported after he took the call. "His girlfriend can't get him home herself. I shouldn't be gone long."

When Frank arrived at the bar, he found the parking lot crowded, but not packed. Inside, the crowd was pleasantly buzzed, not yet belligerently smashed.

Except for Matthew Caine.

The bartender caught Frank's eye and pointed to the hallway leading to the restrooms and office.

Caine lay stretched out at the end of the dim tunnel, his head in the men's room, his legs outside.

"Geez, I gotta pee." A woman in steel-toed boots stumbled over Caine's limp legs and slammed the ladies' room door into his foot. The man didn't even flinch.

Caine's girlfriend materialized at Frank's side. "I couldn't get anyone to carry him out to the car. And even if I did, I wouldn't be able to get him into the house by myself."

Frank commandeered two guys at the bar who found him more persuasive than they had found Caine's girlfriend. Once they got the passed-out man loaded into the patrol car, Frank ducked back inside the Mountainside.

He waved the bartender down to the quieter end of the long horse-shoe bar. "Back when Billy Flynn was in here drinking every night, did he mention any girls he was involved with?"

The bartender delivered a fish-eyed stare. "You have any idea how many guys are in here every night braggin' about who they nailed?" He pointed into his right ear then made a bye-bye wave out his left ear.

Frank knew it was a long-shot that any part of Billy's drunken ramblings had stuck with this jaded guy. "His sister told me he never had trouble picking up girls. Did he ever leave with anyone here?"

Again Frank got the "ya gotta be kiddin' me" glare. "He'd get so drunk, I doubt he was able to get it on with anybody." The bartender stomped away to fill the mugs of desperately waving patrons.

"Billy Flynn?" The question came from a soft-spoken old man sitting alone.

Frank leaned closer to him. "Yeah, you talk to him when he was in here?"

The man nodded. "Talked about war. I was in 'Nam. That was hot and wet. Afghanistan's hot and dry. Both pointless." He took a long slug from his beer.

"Did he ever mention any girls?"

The man nodded. "His girl dumped him when he was over there. Happens all the time. Chicks can't wait."

That was old news. Frank wanted something recent. "Ever mention anyone he was seeing since he came home?"

The old vet studied the pitted surface of the bar. He stayed silent so long, Frank thought he might've dozed off. "Showed me a picture once. Pretty girl. Young."

Frank tried to swallow his excitement. The guy was in his seventies. Probably everyone looked young to him. "How young?"

"Too young to come in here. She had long hair. And..." The man gestured to a spot on his own chest.

Now Frank's heart pounded. "A tattoo?"

"Yeah. Girls didn't used to get tattoos in my day. Now they all do. Things change." The old man swayed on his barstool. "I told him he should spend time with her at home, not waste his time here. But he said that wasn't possible. And then he stopped coming here. Maybe they found a place to be together."

Maybe Billy sent her to that place.

Were they together?

Or had Billy changed his mind?

Chapter 39

"So, what was it like? Creepy?"

Frank tossed a bag with a jelly donut onto Earl's desk on Saturday morning and drew up a chair to listen to the report on the Tabernacle. He hadn't decided yet if he would tell Earl what he'd learned about Billy at the Mountainside.

Earl shook his head as he prepared to take his first bite. "Everyone was super-friendly."

"That's how they win people over. Do you feel brainwashed?" Frank tapped Earl's head with his knuckle. "I see they haven't convinced you to give up donuts."

"No, but I have to admit, the food there was really good. Let me start at the beginning. I met my cousin Sandy in the parking lot of the Tabernacle. She wanted to pick me up from home, but I didn't want to be stuck there with no wheels, so I said I had to do something beforehand, and I'd meet her there. She was pacing around outside when I got there.

"Her face lit up when she saw me pull in, like she'd been worried that I wouldn't come. She was wearing a plain white t-shirt."

"Is that significant?"

Earl nodded and held up a finger to encourage patience. "As soon as we walked in, there was a woman to greet us. And she was wearing an electric blue shirt."

"Like the color Penny noticed them all wearing at the concert on the green."

"Yep. And she acted like she was really glad to see me too. She shook my hand with both of hers and said how happy she was to meet a friend of Sandy's and she hoped I'd feel welcome and have a joyful evening."

Frank pursed his lips. It was a good thing Earl had gone instead of him. He wouldn't have been able to contain his eye rolls.

"Remember how the old Asian Bistro had two separate seating areas?" Earl continued. "Well now, the area on the right is all closed off, and I couldn't see in there from the entrance area. But the dining room that opens out onto the deck is pretty much exactly the same—filled with tables that seat four or six or eight.

"Then another friendly lady came and guided us to a table that already had three other people sitting at it. And she had a blue bow in her hair."

"You couldn't choose where to sit?"

"No, but she didn't make it seem like she was forcing us. She was chatting and walking and we just naturally followed her."

"Did she make you sign in, or collect your phone number and address?"

"Nope. Just got us seated at a table."

"And who were the other people?"

"A married couple from Verona who looked kinda familiar to me and a lady in a yellow shirt who I definitely didn't know. Soon as we sat down, the lady in yellow—her name was Christina—introduced everyone to each other. And then she worked hard to keep everyone talking. She'd ask me a question about myself, and then when I answered, she'd find a way to connect that to something someone else had said. So pretty soon we're all talking and there were none of those awkward pauses where you're stuck not knowing what to say. When I looked around the dining room, I saw that every table had a woman like Christina."

"All in yellow shirts?"

"Yellow scarf, yellow dress, yellow hair clip—something yellow."

"All women?"

"Mostly. One table had a guy."

"Did anyone else notice that was kinda creepy?"

"That's the thing, Frank. It's not creepy because everyone is genuinely having a good time, everyone is talking, everyone is friendly. And it's not like they're wearing some uniform. It's just these subtle little symbols, flags. You wouldn't even notice it unless you're someone who's very observant."

"Like Penny. And you. Did you ask Sandy about the color scheme business?"

"Not there at the table. There was no opportunity. And then the food was served at each table by the people with blue accessories. Really good, too—fried chicken and pork chops and real mashed potatoes and broccoli. There were people back in the old restaurant kitchen doing all the cooking."

Frank stood up and paced to the window. "So the Tabernacle doesn't scrimp on spending money even though they don't appear to be taking any in. Meanwhile, Pastor Bob has a hard time collecting enough cash to cover the coffee and store-brand cookies at Fellowship Hour."

"I tried to find out," Earl said. "But whenever I'd ask Christina a question about herself or the church, she'd give me a really vague answer and turn the conversation back to me or Sandy or the other couple. At first, I thought I was imagining it, but then I really paid attention and I realized she was just that good."

"Did you tell her you were a cop?"

"No way to lie about it with my cousin there. And other people in the room knew me too. But she didn't react much. Just said 'how interesting' and asked me a question about my work."

"How many people were there altogether?"

"Ten or twelve tables, each with six or seven people. Fewer than a hundred."

"And were they all local? Or were some of them on one of these retreats he supposedly holds?"

"I recognized just about everyone. The only people not from around here were the ones in the yellow or blue clothing who were helping to run the show."

"So how long did all the chatting and eating last? What about the praise fest or whatever?"

"They brought around dessert—chocolate cake and cherry pie." Earl grinned. "I thought of you. And by this time, the little kids left the tables and went to one side of the room to play games with a few babysitters."

"Blue or yellow?" Frank asked.

"Blue."

"And what about the teenagers? Did you see any of Laurel's friends?"

"There was a group of teenagers who went off with a blue-shirted guy to play guitars and drums and sing. Not Jenna, but that kid Gordon Brophy and one of the girls whose name was in Laurel's phone because of that school project. It seemed like mostly the straight-arrow kids, not the ones who hang out under the bridge."

Earl tossed his donut bag in the trash and dusted the crumbs off his desk. "And then the woman who first greeted us at the door rang a little bell and told us it was time to move into the tabernacle."

Frank shuddered. "Were you nervous?"

"Kinda."

Chapter 40

"We crossed the entrance hall and walked through the doors that had been closed when we first arrived. This was the area that used to be the rear dining room and the private party room back in the Asian Bistro days. Now the dividing wall has been knocked down and the room is set up like a theater or a college lecture hall with an elevated stage, a high podium, and a big projection screen in the front."

"It just looks like a big classroom?" Frank felt vaguely disappointed. He didn't know what he expected—an altar for live sacrifice.... burning torches.

"The room is totally plain. No pictures. Not even a cross. Just a cloth banner that says "Tabernacle of Living Light.""

"Let me guess: blue and yellow."

"And red. Don't rush me. I followed the crowd and sat down next to my cousin. We didn't get a bulletin, so I wasn't sure how we'd know when to sit and stand and say the Lord's Prayer and stuff. Some of the other people looked a little confused too.

"While we were getting settled, the musicians who played in the park came out and set up on the stage. Then the guitarist faced the crowd and held up his hands. Everyone quieted down, and he said, "Let us begin to offer praise." And the lights dimmed, and the projector came on, and the words to those songs they sang in the park were up on the screen for us to sing along."

"And did everyone sing?"

"Well, most people didn't know the melody and there were no notes projected. But by the second verse, everyone was joining in on the refrain because it's catchy, ya know." Earl sang, a little off-key. "Praise him. Praise him. Give him your faith. Receive his blessing and po-o-w-w-w—ER."

"When the second song came on, I didn't even try to sing. I just studied the lyrics and tried to memorize them." Earl pulled out a sheet of paper. "I wrote down as much as I could when I got home, before I forgot."

He slid the paper over for Frank to read.

In him is the power

The power to conquer darkness
In him is the light
The light to which we all confess

"Notice anything?"

Frank felt like he was back in English class, being put on the spot to find some obscure metaphor in a Wordsworth poem. A cold sweat prickled his neck as his mind went blank.

Earl helped him out. "The song doesn't mention God or Jesus at all. Just *him*."

"Huh. You're right. Just like the refrain to the first one. Were there any Bibles or hymnals in this *tabernacle*?"

"Nope. Finally, after we sang three songs, the projector turned off, the lights stayed dim, and a spotlight focused on the podium. Adam Fortway was standing there. I didn't even notice him walk in."

"How was he dressed?" Frank imagined some glittering cape or maybe a crown.

"He was wearing a bright red shirt. He's not that big of a guy, but he started talking in this booming voice: 'In him there is no darkness at all. If we say that we have fellowship with him, and walk in darkness, we lie, and do not tell the truth. But if we walk in the light, as he is in the light, we have fellowship one with another.'"

"Well, that's from the Bible—Book of John, right?"

"Yeah, but it's not the *whole* verse." Earl produced his battered Sunday school Bible and read aloud from the first Book of John:

"God is light; in him there is no darkness at all. If we claim to have fellowship with him and yet walk in the darkness, we lie and do not live out the truth. But if we walk in the light, as he is in the light, we have fellowship with one another, and the blood of Jesus, his Son, purifies us from all sin."

"So he started after the reference to God and ended before the reference to Jesus. This guy wants his followers to think that this passage in the Bible refers to him? He thinks he's some kind of Messiah, and people from Trout Run sat there and accepted that?"

"It's easy to miss, Frank. Because he doesn't say it directly. After he quoted that passage, he gave this very easy to swallow message about how we should all be working to fan the flames of light and overcome the darkness in this world. And that we can do that by being kind and walking in light hand-in-hand and not giving in to darkness. Blah, blah, blah. And then the people in blue walked down the aisle passing this basket full of candles and everyone took one. And while we were busy with that, Fortway must've slipped backstage. He came back holding this giant lighted torch thing. And he lit the smaller torches of the people dressed in yellow. And they walked down the aisle and lit the candles of the people on the end of each row, and we all lit the candle of the person next to us."

"Sounds like a hazard," Frank grumbled. "I oughta send the fire marshal over there."

"Then the room was totally dark except for our candles and we sang the Bruce Springsteen song, "Blinded by the Light" but with different words. Ours was "Powered by the Light". The projector was off, so only the leaders knew all the words. Everyone else came in on "powered by the light/ set loose by the vision."

"You're shittin' me. That's so cheesy."

"It sounds worse when I'm sitting here in the office saying it out loud. But it kinda worked in the moment. Then there was a moment of silence and the lights came up, and we blew out our candles and everyone hugged everyone else."

"There was no collection?"

"Nope. My wallet never came out of my pocket."

"So he fed everyone a great meal and didn't ask for a penny in return. He's recruiting local people, and the only outsiders are these men and women who apparently work for the Tabernacle. What's this guy playing at?"

Earl leaned his elbows on his desk and propped his head in his hands. "I think it's a big sorting game, and I didn't make the cut. The logo of the Tabernacle—the image that was on the banner and on the projection—was a flame of three colors: blue, yellow and red. Adam Fortway is red. He's the ultimate light. You have to do something to prove your loyalty to move up one level. That's why Sandy wanted me to come so bad ast night."

"She has to recruit people to earn points?"

"It's not that obvious. That Christina woman pulled Sandy aside as we were leaving. She was smiling and hugging Sandy, and Sandy nodded. Then she told her something else and Sandy kinda stiffened up and pulled away a little."

Frank inched forward on his chair. "Did you get it out of Sandy what the woman said to her?"

Earl sat with a sly smile tweaking his lips. He played out his line and let Frank believe he was swimming freely.

"They told your cousin not to bring you back," Frank guessed. "They told her to bring someone different next time."

Earl reeled in his catch. "Yep. Christina said I didn't seem to be fully engaged with the message, so I'd better not come anymore. But Fortway's followers don't understand Davis family loyalty. No one tells one member of our family that another member isn't good enough. Sandy fumed the whole way home. Said Christina and Fortway could shove their church up their asses. Said she'd never go back."

Frank felt a prickle of alarm. "You didn't tell Sandy what I suspect about the church—that it's a tax dodge?"

Earl drew back his shoulders, a gesture Frank had learned meant Earl was insulted. "Of course not. I calmed her down. Told her my feelings weren't hurt too bad. But I left her mad enough that I don't think she'll go back. I don't want my family mixed up with that place."

Frank massaged the bridge of his nose. Of course, Earl wouldn't want his cousin pulled into Fortway's web. But it would have been nice to have someone on the inside. "Did Sandy tell this Christina woman to screw off?"

"Nah, that's not Sandy's way. She was polite to Christina's face, then complained about her to me. That's why I think the Tabernacle targeted Sandy to be a recruiter. She goes along to get along and never argues with anyone. I hate to say it, but my cousin's kinda gullible."

Earl rose from his chair and paced across the office. "I think the whole purpose of the dinners is for the yellow level conversation monitors to look for likely targets."

Frank nodded. "People who are insecure, lonely. If you're too well-adjusted, you don't make the cut."

"Or too firm in your convictions." Earl grinned. "They'd never choose you, Frank."

"I take that as a compliment."

Chapter 41

"Let's take a drive." Frank tossed Earl the patrol car keys. "I want to see these houses that Fortway bought."

Despite Earl's encyclopedic knowledge of every street, road, and lane in his hometown, they drove around for twenty minutes before they found the first house on the list. Only after stopping to consult a man working in his garden were they able to verify that they were indeed on Bill Horton Road. The road sign, the man told them, had been torn down by the snowplow last winter, and the town had still not gotten around to replacing it.

They proceeded down the narrow, twisting road, squinting at the numbers on the mailboxes at the end of each driveway. "It should be the next house," Frank observed.

But the next house had no mailbox, only a raw hole where the mailbox had recently been.

"Looks like they tore out the old mailbox before they had a new one ready to replace it," Earl said.

They peered through a thick screen of trees at a modest ranch house with faded blue paint and a small sapling sprouting out of the front rain gutter. "Needs a little work," Frank observed. "But look at that brand-new steel door. It's just like the one on that house where Charlie supposedly lives."

The next house on the list was equally hard to find. It was on an unnamed, unpaved road full of vacation cottages. A big old tree at the intersection of the paved road had a column of wooden signs painted with the names of all the homes that could be found down the road: Hillier's' Hideaway, The Thorntons, Rick's Roost, Durbin Family. In between the last two signs was an empty space and a nail hole where a sign had been yanked down. "Guess that must be the one Fortway bought," Earl said as he turned down the bumpy lane.

"None of these houses have mailboxes because they're all vacation cottages," Frank said. But "Rick's Roost" and "Hilliers' Hideaway" had jaunty signs marking the houses. And two other houses had brightly painted

185

Adirondack chairs, potted plants, and welcome mats. Only one house looked shabby.

Except for the brand-new steel door.

When they found the third house, they already knew what to expect. Once again, there was only a hole where the mailbox should have been. Once again, a brand-new steel door. "You know, none of these houses have satellite dishes either," Earl said as they stared at the last run-down house. "I could understand that a vacation cottage might not want TV or wi-fi, but if Fortway and his followers are living here full-time, wouldn't they need it?"

"Four things those houses all have in common: mailboxes pulled out, no visible house number, no satellite dish, brand new steel doors," Frank answered. "What does that tell you?"

"Fortway wants to make it hard for anyone to find and communicate with his church members." Earl turned the patrol car back toward town. "And he wants to keep the members away from the news of the outside world."

"When we get back to the office, I want you to research where the Tabernacle of Living Light was located before it came to Trout Run. Find out who owned the church buildings. Why they left. If there was any trouble surrounding the group."

"Got it. What are your plans?"

"I'm going to do what I do with my grandsons."

"Feed goats?"

"Visit by Skype. Jenna Burlingame might be in Chicago, but I'm going to look her in the eye and find out if Charlie Dunleavey is the person who convinced her to go out on the church roof."

AFTER SOME NEGOTIATING with Jenna's mother and aunt, Frank got the Skype connection set up. Jenna's face loomed briefly onto his computer screen, then turned away. "I'm fine, Aunt Renee. You don't need to stay."

Frank heard a murmur of protest, then Jenna's voice replying firmly. "I got this. Seriously."

When the teenager faced the camera again, Frank was amazed by the change in her demeanor. She seemed relaxed and confident—a far cry from the cringing figure he'd rescued from the roof.

"Hi, Jenna. You're looking well. Chicago agrees with you?"

She smiled. "It's great here. So much to do. I'm taking a summer art class at the museum. And my aunt and uncle are really chill."

Frank felt a tingle of optimism. Away from her parents and grandfather, Jenna might be ready to give him the information he needed. "Thanks for talking to me like this, Jenna. I need your help in solving some problems we're having back here in Trout Run. I want to ask you about Charlie Dunleavey. I know you worked with him at the Hungry Loon."

Jenna looked away from the intrusive eye of the camera. "I like Charlie. Is he in trouble?"

"I like Charlie, too. I'm worried about him. He's gone off on another backcountry hike. Last time he did that, he nearly died. I'd like to find him before he gets hurt."

Jenna looked straight into the camera. "Leave him alone! He needs to do that hike. It's so important to him. Don't be the one who ruins it."

"Why is it so important?"

Jenna squirmed in her chair. "Charlie and I spent a lot of time talking during the week we worked together at the Loon. He threw away his phone and his computer, so he wouldn't be ruled by social media and all the expectations people have there."

"When did he get rid of his phone and computer?"

Jenna shrugged. "I never saw him use a phone the whole week we worked together. He was focused on facing his fears and learning to live in the real world. I thought that was so brave. I wished I could do it too."

"The real world is the High Peaks Wilderness?"

"Don't you see? If he can survive there, he can survive anywhere. He wants to prove to himself that he has the guts to do it."

"Okay—that makes sense. So the hike is sort of a symbolic challenge."

Jenna's face brightened. "Yes, exactly. You get it!"

"And going out on the church roof was your symbolic challenge?"

Jenna sat quietly for a moment then stared directly into the camera's eye. "Yes. Yes, it was. It probably seems stupid to you, but the church was like a symbol of me always being such a good girl, always doing what everyone wants me to do. I have to act one way to make my mother happy and another way to make my dad happy and a third way to make kids at school like me."

"So Charlie told you to go out onto the church roof to defy them all?"

"No! He didn't tell me to do anything. He just talked to me about his challenge, and that made me want to do one of my own. My plan was to go out on the roof, take a selfie, and come back. But I got stuck out there."

"You thought that particular challenge up on your own?"

Jenna's eyes darted back and forth. "Ye-e-e-ah."

"Were you inspired by Laurel Caine?" Frank pressed.

"Oh. My. Ga-a-wd!" Jenna rocked back in her chair and stared at the ceiling in aggravation. "Why are you so obsessed with her? I don't even know that girl."

"But the day after you went out on the church roof, you told me you admired Laurel for what she'd done on the bridge."

"I said that?" Jenna chewed on her thumbnail. "I was all messed up that day. I don't remember saying that."

Was she lying? Frank couldn't be sure. He couldn't read subtle tells through the computer screen as well as he could in person.

"Did Charlie know what you were planning to do for your challenge?"

"No, he didn't." Jenna narrowed her eyes. "Are my parents pressuring you to find someone to blame for what I did? Because I'm glad I did it. I'm only sorry I had to be rescued."

Frank held up his hands in denial. "Are you going to tell them what you told me?"

"Yes, I'm writing them a letter. I'll mail it right before I come home. I'm telling them I'm going back to High Peaks High School. And I'm getting another job, so I can pay the church back for the damage I caused. And I'm not going to be a lawyer or a doctor or a financial advisor when I grow up. I'm majoring in art. Maybe architecture."

Frank smiled. "Sounds like a plan, Jenna. Hey, can I ask one more thing?"

She heaved a sigh as if he'd asked her to move a pile of rocks. "What?"

"Did Charlie talk to you about the Tabernacle of Living Light? Is that what inspired him to throw away his phone and take up his wilderness challenge?"

"Yes. That's how he came to be in Trout Run. He joined the Tabernacle when he was in college. The community helped him find the courage to break away from his parents."

"Did the Tabernacle require him to give up his phone? Did they establish this challenge for him?"

"He didn't say that."

"Did he destroy the phone or give it away to someone else?"

Jenna squirmed and glanced around the room. "I don't know. Why does it matter?"

Frank sensed his productive time with Jenna was running out. Time to dive for what he really needed. "Did Charlie know Laurel Caine?"

"He never mentioned her. He hasn't been in Trout Run very long. He doesn't know many people." She squinted at Frank. "Why do you keep coming back to Laurel Caine. I thought you were worried about Charlie."

Frank ignored her question and pressed forward. "Does Charlie know Billy Flynn?"

For the first time in their conversation, Jenna looked uneasy. "Billy Flynn who used to deliver our firewood? I thought he joined the army."

"Marines. He's out and back in Trout Run. You didn't know that?"

Jenna looked puzzled. "No-o-o. Why would I? He's way older than me. And we don't get firewood in the summer."

And yet at the mention of Billy, Jenna's demeanor had changed subtly. Frank wasn't imagining it. Charlie. Billy. Jenna. Laurel. What was the connection? It had to be The Tabernacle.

"Did you ever go to the Tabernacle, Jenna?"

"Your questions are so *random*." She stood up. Frank could no longer see her face; her colorful t-shirt filled the computer screen. "I was invited, but I couldn't go. And now I don't need to go. I'm not afraid of anything."

"Jenna, who—"

"Gotta run. My class starts soon."

The screen went black.

Chapter 42

F rank and Earl sat across from each other comparing notes.
"I found out The Tabernacle of Living Light used to be located in a town called Greenbriar, right outside Glens Falls," Earl reported. "Adam Fortway owned a big old house there, and the church met in a building where he had a short-term lease."

Frank tapped a pencil on his desk. "So why did he move? Any run-ins with local law enforcement?"

"I talked to the police chief in Greenbriar. The neighbors complained about Fortway because there were so many people living in his house. They have an ordinance there that prohibits more than six unrelated adults living in one house. They don't want any boarding houses in their town, or big gangs of college kids living together."

"Were the people living in Fortway's house rowdy or causing trouble?"

"The chief said no, but Fortway was still in violation of the zoning ordinance. The next month, he sold his house, and ended his lease, and moved up here."

"And the house was owned in Fortway's name, not the Tabernacle's?"

"Yep. And the lease on the meeting space was in his name personally too. That's the other thing I found out. The Tabernacle of Living Light has only been classified as a 501c.3 religious organization since it moved here to Trout Run."

"Really? So who decides if you're a church or not?"

"Apparently, you just fill out some paperwork and submit it to the IRS. I looked up the rules. You just have to be organized to promote a religious activity and no single person can benefit from the money you raise. And you can't be involved in politics."

"But what about the Tabernacle's retreats? People pay money to attend."

"From what I read, if the retreats were a totally separate business, the Tabernacle would have to pay unrelated business income tax. But as long as they're run by volunteers from the church and are promoting the religious activity, then it's all considered tax-exempt."

Frank scowled. "You and I are in the wrong line of work. We should establish the Temple of Frank and Earl and charge people to hear us rant on what's wrong with the world."

"The trick is finding people willing to pay. That's where Fortway seems to have a special talent."

Frank tipped his chair back. "Hmm. But does he? He hasn't asked the people of Trout Run for any money. Does he get money from the volunteers you saw running the community dinner? How did he get the money to buy those three houses? Something doesn't add up."

"We need a forensic accountant." Earl grinned as he tapped a cheap calculator on his desk. "Now, what did you find out from Jenna?"

Frank relayed his Skype conversation with the teenager. "We need to find out when and how Charlie got rid of his phone. We know Charlie and Jenna are connected through the Loon. We know Charlie's phone is connected to Laurel, but we can't be positive he's the one who sent the texts. I connected Laurel and Jenna because they both went up to high places. But Jenna claims she just wanted to do something outrageous associated with the Presbyterian Church. So maybe there's no connection between Laurel and Jenna."

"But Charlie has a challenge that he failed at once and seems to be trying again. And Jenna had a challenge that she claims she dreamed up herself. And the text to Laurel said, 'this is your challenge.' They've gotta all be related to the Tabernacle."

"When I asked Jenna if she'd ever been to the Tabernacle, she said 'I've been invited.' Not 'Charlie invited me.' Then she hung up before I could ask her who did."

"There's something else you forgot to ask Jenna," Earl pointed out. "What made her apply for that job at the Hungry Loon?"

Chapter 43

O n Sunday morning, Frank woke up early. He made a big pot of coffee, and after intense lobbying from Yogi, shook some kibble into the cat's bowl.

Frank carried a mug of coffee up to Penny. She slept with one arm flung above her head, and one slender foot poking out from under the covers. He ran his index finger along the delicate arch of her brow.

"Morning, sleepyhead. Time to get up."

She grumbled and rolled away from him.

"I brought you your coffee. We agreed we'd go to church this morning."

"Mmmph."

"I can go alone. I just want to show a little support for Bob."

Penny's eyes flew open. "I'm going!" She sat up and took a gulp of her coffee. "Why did you let me sleep so late?"

"We can arrive after the first hymn. It's not like we won't be able to find a seat."

Penny didn't agonize over her wardrobe selection—worship at Trout Run Presbyterian wasn't a fashion show—and they arrived just as the last verse of "A Mighty Fortress is Our God" thundered from the pipe organ. Frank and Penny slipped into the third pew from the back as the choir—reduced to six sopranos, two altos, and three basses since the death of the only tenor right after Easter—straggled back to their seats. Frank took a rough head count of the congregation—fewer than fifty people, most of them elderly. He told himself the light turn-out was due to the heat wave. The unair-conditioned church felt stuffy despite the efforts of two big fans whirring in the side aisles.

Bob stood behind the pulpit to lead the welcoming prayer. His face looked drawn, but his voice boomed out in familiar reassurance. Frank sat up straight in the pew to make sure Bob noticed his presence.

The service moved along with the small congregation standing, sitting, singing, and responding as they were asked to do. Finally, Bob got to the

Old Testament reading, which happened to be Psalm 130, one of Frank's favorites.

Out of the depths have I cried unto thee, O Lord.

Lord, hear my voice: let thine ears be attentive to the voice of my supplications.

If thou, Lord, shouldest mark iniquities, O Lord, who shall stand?

But there is forgiveness with thee, that thou mayest be feared.

I wait for the Lord, my soul doth wait, and in his word do I hope.

My soul waiteth for the Lord more than they that watch for the morning: I say, more than they that watch for the morning.

Let Israel hope in the LORD: for with the LORD there is mercy, and with him is plenteous redemption.

And he shall redeem Israel from all his iniquities.

He usually found the verse consoling, but today he heard it differently. As a cop, it was his job to mark other people's iniquities, and sometimes that wore him down.

———◉———

THE SERVICE CLOSED with "Great is Thy Faithfulness." Frank belted out the tenor part, figuring the choir needed all the help it could get. By the final verse, he felt quite uplifted. Coming to church today had been a good idea even if Penny had never stopped fanning herself with a folded bulletin.

"Let's get some lemonade," she said, striding down the aisle to the Narthex where the Fellowship Hour refreshments had been set up. Frank let her get ahead of him when he spotted Shannon and Jeff and their two kids exiting a pew.

"Good morning!" Frank beamed the spirit of Christian fellowship, he hoped. "How are you today?"

"Fine. And before you ask, no, I haven't heard from my brother." Shannon took her kids by their hands and beelined for the cookies leaving her husband without a backward glance.

Jeff waited at Frank's side until Shannon was well out of sight before muttering under his breath. "Can I talk to you for a minute?" He glanced over his shoulder as he nudged Frank toward the door to the vestry. "There's stuff going on that I'm worried about, and Shannon doesn't see it the same way I do."

Delighted to find someone in the Flynn extended family willing to talk, Frank followed Jeff into the tiny room. After they were seated on a bench, Jeff's right leg jittered up and down in a nervous staccato. Frank sat waiting, hoping he had perfected his expression of benign concern.

"Shannon's mother has gone missing." Jeff leaned forward and blurted out the statement like he was spitting out a rancid nut. "And Shannon thinks her father is responsible." The leg pumped like a piston. "That he, like, killed her."

Any pretense of disinterest evaporated. Frank lunged forward. "Killed her? Why?" The vision of Gene kissing Nadine Witchel danced in Frank's head. He thought of the dark house no one had returned to.

"Shannon hadn't heard from her mother in a couple of days, so we left the kids with a neighbor, and we drove over to her parents' house. We found Gene sitting on the porch drinking a beer." Jeff leaned back and crossed his arms looking like a prosecuting attorney who'd just delivered the damning evidence to seal his case.

"And....?"

Jeff glanced over his shoulder as if he thought Shannon might come roaring up the aisle and into the vestry. Leaned forward and dropped his voice.

"He said Martha had left...run off. Now if Martha had ever had the nerve to leave Gene, he woulda been furious...calling everyone and driving around tracking her down and dragging her home by the hair. Instead, he's sitting there smiling and drinking a Bud, totally calm. That's what creeped us out. That's when I started thinking Shannon might be right."

Frank raised his eyebrows.

"Gene showed us Martha's drawers—her clothes are all gone. But he could've just thrown them away. And he showed us a note—"

"A note? Was it in Martha's handwriting?"

"Yes, but he could have forced her to write it. It was very basic. Something like, 'I'm leaving. Don't look for me.' I mean, if it had been a real note, she would have written more. If Martha was leaving Gene, she'd definitely have told Shannon. And why wasn't Gene over at our house as soon as he found that note? Why isn't he looking for her?"

"Shannon says Gene isn't looking for her because he knows where she is. Because *he* put her there. He killed her. And buried her somewhere." Jeff shudders. "Shannon thinks he put her through the chipper like in that movie *Fargo*."

"Whoa, Jeff—she's talking about her own father! Does Shannon really believe he's capable of that? Has Gene ever hurt Shannon?"

"Gene used to spank Shannon and Billy both with a paddle he custom made in his woodworking shop. Shannon won't even slap our kids' hands because of that." Jeff looked around the small, shabby room where they sat. A benign clutter of old offering envelopes, serving trays for communion bread, and different color table cloths to mark the changing liturgical seasons surrounded them. "Gene is a maniac, but I don't think he's any crazier this week than he's ever been."

"So you don't think he killed Martha?"

Jeff rolled his eyes. "Gene has always been very 'my way or the highway.' In Gene's mind there's one correct way to do everything from making bean soup to finding world peace. And anyone who suggests there might be another valid approach is a moron or a traitor or a communist. But Martha married the guy, and he's been like that for as long as I've known him, so really, nothing's changed. Why would Gene murder Martha?"

"Any chance that either one of them could be seeing someone on the side?" Frank tossed the question out noncommittally just to see what reaction he got.

"Nah—who else but Martha would put up with Gene? And Martha's so, ya know, mousy-like." Jeff scratched under the baseball cap that he wore even to church. "Still in all, I am kinda worried about Martha."

Frank felt like he was trying to fill in the blank sections of a crossword. "I understand your concern, but why does Shannon think her father killed her mother? That's a pretty big leap."

"I know. But when I try to have a calm conversation about where her mom might be, Shannon goes off on me. It's weird. It's like she knows something that I don't know, and that's why she thinks the worst. But when I said that to her, she started crying and the kids woke up and then they were crying— "Jeff threw his hands up. "I don't know what the hell is going on, but I know it can't be good."

Frank nodded. It sounded like Shannon might suspect the affair, but for some reason hadn't shared that with her husband. "Do you know Nadine Witchel? She runs a flower and Christmas tree farm on the eastern edge of Trout Run."

"Late thirties? Kinda pretty?" Jeff's eyes suddenly widened. "Whoa! No way! Gene and Nadine? What makes you say that?"

"I saw them embrace. He seemed to have spent the night at her place."

Jeff shivered. "You're blowin' my mind, man. Why would she—? When did he—? Geez, Martha will, will...." Jeff stopped stammering and grabbed Frank's arm. "Wait! You think Shannon knows about her dad and Nadine and that's why...?

Frank didn't have the time to explain the intricacies of extra-marital affairs and the effect they had on children to the good-natured Jeff. Something had clicked in his mind. "Tell me Jeff, does Martha ever go hunting with Gene?"

"Huh?" Jeff was still trying to process the sex scandal. "Hunting? Yeah, the whole family would hunt together when Shannon and Billy were kids. They're all good shots. I've seen my wife take down a buck at a hundred yards."

And her mother shoot a poisonous snake through the head?

Had a furious Martha left the snake as a warning for her cheating husband? Frank almost had to admire her guts. But then a darker thought intruded. Maybe Gene had been unconcerned about the snake because he himself had left it as a warning to Martha. *I'll do what I please with any woman I choose. Back off.*

Maybe Shannon understood her father better than Jeff realized.

After Frank assured Jeff that he'd try to track Martha down, the two men made their way back to the narthex to claim their wives. After they shook Bob's hand and exited the church, Penny perked up. "Hey, let's go to the Hungry Loon in Keene and pick up some tarragon chicken salad for lunch.

Frank frowned. "Why do we have to drive all the way to Keene? Can't we buy something at our Hungry Loon?"

Penny restrained Frank from walking across the green and steered him toward their truck. "I really want the tarragon chicken. And I want to enquire at the flagship store about why they're not selling their best product here in Trout Run. Let's take a little drive."

Frank indulged his wife. If they had lunch together now, it would be easier for him to slip away later to put in some inquiries about Martha Flynn. Twenty minutes later they pulled into the parking area of the Hungry Loon's Keene location. At 11:00 on a Sunday, the lunch rush hadn't yet begun, so there were plenty of spots. Two late-start hikers sat at a table on the porch having a muffin under the sign with the goofy cross-eyed loon. Frank and Penny entered through the market, greeted by all the same products that got Edwin so excited at the Trout Run store: shelves full of exotic vinegars and condiments and spices. When they made their way to the café section, this store looked a little different than its sister. The bakery side had the same choice of over-sized brownies and muffins and cookies, but the prepared foods display case brimmed with large bowls of salads and platters of grilled meat and fish. The list of specials on the chalk-board ran to two columns.

"May I help you?" A pretty woman in her twenties peered at them from over the counter.

"There's the tarragon chicken," Penny pointed to a half-empty platter in the case. "We'll take a pound. And some of that curried garbanzo bean salad, too." She continued to squint through the glass like an overwhelmed kid at ToysRUs. "And how about some of that eggplant? We've never had that before."

As the salesclerk packed their order, Penny kept chatting. "Why don't you have the tarragon chicken in your Trout Run store anymore if it's so popular."

The girl gave an exaggerated shrug. "You're, like, the third or fourth person to ask me that. I've never been to the new store. Maybe they— "

A raised female voice from the small kitchen area interrupted her. "And I better not see you hijacking any of my other— "

"Shhh, Jocelyn—there are customers out there," a male voice warned.

"I don't care!"

The door between the kitchen and the store slammed.

"Sorry." The salesclerk rolled her eyes at Frank. "Bad break-up."

Penny took the food and Frank forked over twenty dollars. It seemed to him that tarragon chicken was edible gold. The sooner the Hungry Loon brought it back to Trout Run, the sooner they'd start raking in profits.

Out in the parking lot, Frank helped Penny into the truck and walked around to the driver's side. As he approached the truck door, he felt a finger poking his shoulder. He turned around to face a woman with a mane of curly brown hair.

"You wanna know why the store in Trout Run doesn't have tarragon chicken?"

Frank recognized her agitated voice. It was the woman who'd been arguing in the kitchen. "My wife is curious."

"You tell her it's because that recipe is *my* proprietary trade secret." She poked her thumb into her own chest. "And I did not give *him*," she pointed to the store, "the right to export it all over upstate New York. He bought me out of *this* store. He didn't buy all my creativity to spread around everywhere."

Before an astonished Frank could say a word, she spun around and stalked off to a green Subaru. Frank watched her skid out of the parking lot. Her vanity plates read CHEF J.

Chapter 44

On the way home, Frank discussed the encounter with his wife. "Sounds like the owner and his chef had a falling out right as they were expanding to Trout Run. You may never see that chicken in our town."

"So close, yet so far away," Penny grumbled. "At least we still have the same gourmet market as in Keene. Maybe the domestic drama explains why the Trout Run store opened with so little advance notice. With all the recriminations, the owner must've let the promotion fall through the cracks."

"Mmm." Frank continued to ponder the scene he'd just witnessed. He drove in silence for a couple miles, tapping his index finger on the steering wheel.

"What are you thinking?" Penny placed her hand on his to still the jitter. "I can practically see the wheels turning in your head."

"There's something fishy about that store. No one gossiped in advance about the opening, and yet several people from town had jobs there from day one. How did they know about the opportunities if the jobs weren't advertised? How did Jenna and Charlie both end up there if Charlie moved to town as a member of the Tabernacle and Jenna hadn't actively been searching for a job?"

"I'm sure you'll find out." Penny shifted the bags of food on her lap. "But I hope we can eat some of this food before you set off in search of answers."

BY MID-SUNDAY AFTERNOON, a sultry lethargy had settled over Trout Run. The hazy heat had driven everyone to seek relief in the rushing waters of Stony Brook or the shade of their own screened porches. Frank had shared the carry-out feast with Penny and left his wife dozing over a book. Now he cruised around the empty green, contemplating his options. There was no line at the Hungry Loon; he could go in and ask some questions. He could drive out to Nadine Witchel's flower farm and make some inquiries there.

Or he could take the indirect approach.

Frank parked his truck in front of Malone's diner and strolled to the door. Through the glass he could see an empty counter. A broad figure occupied one stool: Marge Malone herself.

Frank entered, and Marge's head snapped up in irritation. An invoice from a stack spread on the counter fluttered to the floor. Frank rushed to pick it up. "Don't get up for me, Marge. I've already had lunch."

She accepted the paper and studied him suspiciously. "So why're you here?"

"I wanted a little advice. Mind if I pour myself a cup of coffee?" Frank headed behind the counter to the never-empty pot before Marge could object. She returned to entering numbers in a ledger. "Well?"

Subtlety, tact, misdirection—none of that was necessary in a conversation with Marge. "Have you seen Martha Flynn lately? She seems to have run off."

"About time. If I were married to that prick, I'd have run away long ago."

"Any idea where she went?"

"No clue. Those two rarely come in here. Gene's too damn cheap to eat out."

No joy on that inquiry. Frank shifted gears.

"How did the Hungry Loon manage to hire so many local people when they didn't advertise and there was so little notice of the store opening?"

Marge dropped her pen and folded her large, rough hands on the counter. Her droopy eyelids nearly covered her eyes and her head dipped slightly. Frank sat, awaiting enlightenment from the oracle.

Finally, she spoke. "That Tabernacle. People who've been going there for those free dinners, those are the ones where someone in their family got a job at the Loon." Marge extended five fat fingers and counted off connections between Loon employees and Tabernacle attendees.

"You ever ask them about it?" Frank inquired.

"None of my business. I just notice things." She returned to her ledger. "That's why you came to me, right?"

"What about Jenna Burlingame, Marge? She and her parents both say she's never been to the Tabernacle. Yet she got that job. And the kid doesn't even need money."

"Been a lotta bitchin' about that girl. How she needs her ass whupped for causing so much trouble. But Reid and her parents just hustled her outta town. Guess they hope by the time she gets back, all will be forgotten."

"But how did Jenna get the job at the Loon?"

Marge rolled her massive shoulders. "That I couldn't tell ya."

"One more thing. Laurel Caine's mother used to work here. What can you tell me about the girl?"

"Laurel never came in here after her mom died. Too many memories, I guess."

"Any idea why she jumped?"

Marge ran the back of her hand across her nose. "I don't understand suicide. But then, I'm never depressed."

So Marge hadn't heard any rumors about the goading emails sent to Laurel. No one knew about them but him and Earl and the sender. "What was her mother like?"

"She was real smart, a hard worker—she wore the pants in that family. But she was kinda dreamy too. She loved to talk to the tourists. Find out where they were from, other places they'd been. Said it was a way to travel without leaving home. Once a guy offered her some frequent flyer miles after she told him she'd never seen the ocean. But she turned them down. Said she was afraid to fly."

Chapter 45

F rank cruised away from the center of town. The need to talk to Fortway about the Tabernacle gnawed at him, but it was Sunday and the man would probably be surrounded by his followers. Frank wouldn't be able to wring the truth out of him when the man was putting on a show.

But when Frank drove past the Asian Bistro/Tabernacle, the parking lot was empty and the building shuttered. The signboard where the Asian Bistro had once advertised its special dinners now proclaimed a "Light Force Celebration" coming up on Monday.

Of course! He'd forgotten that the Tabernacle moved the Sabbath around. Frank made a U-turn and circled back to the parking lot. Did the inner circle spend time in this building when there were no services open to the public? He walked up the ramp to the double glass door, shaded his eyes with his hands, and peered into the dark interior. As Earl had described, the vestiges of the Asian Bistro were still there, minus the miniature pagodas and calligraphy. He pulled on the door handle, and to his surprise, it opened.

Gingerly, he stepped inside. The place smelled neither like a Chinese restaurant nor like a church. But it did smell vaguely familiar.

Frank inhaled deeply. Burning candles.

The dining room to Frank's left sat dark and empty. He followed his nose down a short hallway and came to a half-open door. Flattening himself against the wall, he peeked around the doorframe. Five people sat in a circle on yoga mats. Candles of various shapes and sizes flickered in the otherwise unlit, windowless room. In the middle of the circle, a much larger candle with a thick white wick burned brightly. The dancing flames cast strange shadows and Frank found it hard to discern the faces of the people in the group.

One of them began to speak. "Only by accepting your challenges and defying fear can you rise up into the light. The light will embrace you and carry you home. Are you ready?"

Frank recognized Fortway's voice, starting out low and rising to a shout.

"Yes! I am ready!" A woman's voice vibrated with emotion.

The other three people responded with a high-pitched hum. One head flung backwards, and that person's hum escalated to a yodel. Frank still couldn't make out the face, but the long hair, slender neck and narrow shoulders convinced him it was a young woman.

One by one, the others also raised their chant to an ecstatic scream. Then the first woman curled into a crouch and bowed to the candle. The others followed her lead. They held the pose for an interminable time.

"Release!" Fortway gave the command and the four followers sprang nimbly to their feet. They must all be young.

Frank ducked back from the doorway. Although he heard footsteps, no one emerged from the room. He edged forward again. The room was empty except for Fortway. There must be a back door he couldn't see.

Frank backed away silently, then started back down the hall coughing and stomping his feet. He rapped on the doorframe. "Anybody here?"

Fortway stuck his head out of the door just as Frank prepared to enter. The two men stood nose-to-nose.

"Good afternoon!" Frank spoke with the hearty cheer he would use to greet whomever was working behind the counter at The Store.

Fortway recoiled. "What are you doing here? How did you get in?"

"The front door was wide open. I figured it was okay to come in. After all, the Presbyterian Church is open during the day for anyone who wants to enter for quiet reflection. I figured the Tabernacle was the same."

Fortway had extinguished all the candles in the room. He stepped into the hall and shut the door behind him. "The Tabernacle is not the same as a mainline Protestant church."

"Tell me, is it Christianity you practice at the Tabernacle?" Frank fell into step with Fortway and followed him down the hall.

Fortway looked pained by such a naïve question. "Christianity, Buddhism, Islam, Hinduism—they are all paths to the light. But they are such twisting, difficult paths. I strive to lead people *directly* to the light."

"No detours."

Fortway beamed. "Exactly."

"And how do you do that?"

The pained look returned. "You would need to attend one of my retreats, Chief Bennett. It's not possible for me to distill my process into a few...catch-phrases."

Right. Glad we cleared that up.

Fortway paused in front of a door labeled office. "You strike me as a pur-pose-driven man, Chief Bennett. I'm sure you came here for a reason. What is it?"

Frank inclined his head to the door. "Let's sit down for a moment."

Fortway hesitated, but then seemed to decide resistance would make his life more difficult than cooperation. He ushered Frank into a very conven-tional office with a metal desk and vinyl covered chairs that must've been left over from the Bistro.

Frank got straight to business. "Tell me what you know about Laurel Caine."

Fortway tilted his head. "Is she that poor young woman who extin-guished her light on the covered bridge?"

One way of looking at it. "Yes. Did she attend services at the Taberna-cle?"

"Not that I'm aware. Of course, many teenagers come to our musical evenings."

"What about Jenna Burlingame? Did she come to the musical evenings?"

Fortway raised his hands palms-up in an exaggerated "who knows?"

"Would the person who runs the youth group know if either girl ever came?"

Fortway took a deep, steadying breath. Frank was reminded of his mid-dle school English teacher trying to explain plural possessives for the umpteenth time before throwing in the towel. "The Tabernacle is an intersec-tional community. No one person is *in charge* of anything. Different mem-bers lead the musical evenings according to their inspiration and their goals."

Frank repressed the urge to lunge across the desk and throttle Fortway. How he longed to be interrogating some low-life punk instead of this slip-pery character. He needed to draw the man out. Let him trip himself up with his own BS.

"Tell me more about these goals, these challenges that your members have. Who establishes them?"

"People arrive in our community burdened by fears, limited by darkness. I work to set them free."

"How? Specifically."

Fortway spread his hands. "Each case is different."

"Let me give you an example." Frank spoke in a helpful tone. "Say a young woman comes to your community upset with her family situation, bored with school, disgusted with her limited options. What challenges might you set for her?"

"There are no hypothetical cases, Chief Bennett. There are only individual human beings struggling with their own inner darkness."

Frank leaned in and locked gazes with Fortway. "Have you or any member of your community ever encouraged someone to do something physically dangerous in order to prove themselves to you?"

"No one has to prove anything to *me*. They must prove inner courage to *themselves*."

Now he was getting somewhere. "By taking risks."

"There can be no growth without risk. Did you not take a risk the first time you kissed the lovely woman who would become your wife?"

Frank froze. Uncanny that Fortway would know how much courage that kiss had required. "I only risked rejection, not death."

Fortway leaned back and crossed his legs. "It appears from these questions that you think I or someone in our community told this young woman, Laurel, to climb up on the covered bridge and jump off. That's preposterous. The Tabernacle is a life-affirming community. What possible purpose would we have in encouraging someone to take her own life?"

What purpose did Jim Jones have in encouraging hundreds of people to drink poisoned Kool-Aid? Power. To say that he could. "People have died in the name of religion since the beginning of time. She might have seen herself as a martyr."

"You're trapped by conventional thinking. The Tabernacle is not a religion that demands sacrifice. It's a spiritual discipline that leads to a higher level of consciousness."

Enough. "Charlie Dunleavey. Do you know him?"

Fortway's expression of otherworldly superiority wavered. Or was Frank imagining that?

"Ye-e-es. He has participated in our retreats."

"And where is he now?"

Now there was no doubting Fortway's nervousness. "I, I'm not sure."

"There's a house on Bill Horton Road. Is that house used for your retreats?"

Fortway cleared his throat and smiled. "You're certainly quite observant, Chief Bennett. Yes, as a matter of fact, we do have retreat participants staying there."

"But the Tabernacle doesn't own that house."

"No, it's owned by a member of our community who has very generously given us access to it."

"What's his name?"

"The owner would prefer to remain anonymous."

"When I went there the other day, a woman named Linnea told me Charlie was off on a hike as part of a challenge he had to face."

Fortway seemed to relax. "Yes, Charlie has felt oppressed by his dependence on 21st century technology. He has been eager to get back in touch with the natural world."

"The first time Charlie hiked in the High Peaks Wilderness he was totally unprepared and had to be rescued by DEC rangers. He was hallucinating from dehydration and exposure."

Fortway shrugged. "He was trying to experience the mountains as the Native Americans once did. He realized he needed to improve his stamina."

"So he went back out again. Has he come back from his second outing?"

Fortway's gaze darted around the office. "I, I don't know. I don't monitor the day-to-day activities of community members."

Was Charlie in trouble again? Was Fortway worried about another rescue, or worse—a body recovery?

"So Charlie is out in the wilderness without a phone. Did you—" Frank chose the next word carefully— "encourage him to get rid of his phone?"

"Charlie came to realize that he needed to relinquish anything that brought darkness into his life."

"I'll take that as a yes. What happened to the phone after Charlie relinquished it?"

"Why does it matter? Surely a person can discard an appliance if he so chooses?"

"Was the phone destroyed? Or did he simply give it up?"

"Sometimes there is a ceremony to help a member let go of an item associated with his fears."

"You're not answering my question. What happens to the object after the ceremony?"

"Members of the community take care of the detritus of a ceremony." Fortway rose from his seat and gestured Frank toward the door. "Really, Chief Bennett—I must leave you now. I have a Light Force service to prepare for." Fortway walked out of the office, giving Frank no choice but to follow.

Frank kept talking as they walked toward the foyer of the building. "One last thing. What's the connection between the Hungry Loon and the Tabernacle?"

Impressive self-control. Frank noticed only a slight stiffening of Fortway's posture. "I don't understand your question. The Tabernacle has no connection to any businesses in Trout Run."

"Charlie works there. And many other people who have jobs there also worship at the Tabernacle." Frank rattled off a few of the names Marge had given him.

Fortway's body relaxed and he smiled. "There's a correlation between releasing one's inner light and embracing new opportunities. I'm delighted that members of our community are finding gainful employment."

Frank felt a wave of frustration rising within him. He'd been onto something, something that made Fortway nervous, when he mentioned the connection between The Loon and the Tabernacle. But somehow, he'd veered off course when he mentioned jobs. He stopped walking and blocked Fortway from moving the last few steps to the foyer. "Is there a financial connection between the store and the church? Is that where you get the money for all you do here?"

Fortway straightened his shoulders and faced Frank. He didn't shout, but his voice got more aggressive. "Why did you come here? Every time I answer one of your questions, you ask me five more. What are you investigating?"

Frank met aggression with aggression. "The death of Laurel Caine. Two young men connected to her have also disappeared. I need to talk to them."

"Charlie hasn't *disappeared*." Fortway spit out the word with a sneer. "He's hiking. What other young man?"

"Billy Flynn. Do you know him?"

Fortway stared at Frank without blinking. "No."

"Really?" Frank felt a flash of inspiration. "Because Billy's a person with a lot of problems...carrying a lot of darkness, as you like to say." Frank didn't conceal his contempt for Fortway's jargon. "Vulnerable, not many friends—seems like he'd be right up your alley." Frank took a step closer to Fortway. With their faces inches apart, he could see the blue vein throbbing in Fortway's temple. "Maybe you've set a challenge for him. A challenge that requires him to put himself, or someone else, in danger."

"You are spiritually bankrupt! You project your own evil onto what I have created!" Fortway placed his hands on Frank's chest and shoved. Slipping past Frank, he darted to the door and held it open. Fortway lowered his voice, but his eyes still glittered. "I will use every force in my power—spiritual, legal, political—to protect The Tabernacle from incursions by the ignorant and the damned."

Chapter 46

On Monday morning, Frank strode into the office without a glance at Doris and any messages she might have collected about broken windows at vacation homes or vandalized road signs.

Sunday night had been a shitstorm.

As soon as he'd gotten home from his encounter with Adam Fortway, his phone started ringing. First Reid Burlingame called demanding to know why Frank was harassing a pillar of the Trout Run community. Frank had to endure an ear-scorching tirade about how he had indulged in needless intimidation while investigating a suicide that no one considered a crime. No sooner had he hung up with Reid than Bill Powers, the Republican who represented Trout Run in the New York State Legislature, called to warn him off any move to restrict religious freedom in the North Country.

And the icing on the cake came when a reporter from the *Adirondack Daily Enterprise* called to get his comment on a story he was writing about how difficult it was for unconventional churches to exercise their Constitutional right to religious freedom. The guy had the nerve to ask if the Trout Run police department was planning a Ruby Ridge-style invasion of the Tabernacle buildings.

Today he would find out once and for all who had sent Laurel those texts.

If the Tabernacle simply offered up a menu of harmless mumbo-jumbo, he'd back off and let Fortway run his show.

But if the Tabernacle was endangering people on his turf, Frank would drive Fortway and his crew right out of town.

On the other hand, if Billy had entered into some romantic suicide pact with Laurel then he would find the man, dead or alive.

Today.

Earl showed up as Frank paced around the office. "Sit down. We need to make a plan. Today's the day we're going to find Billy Flynn and Charlie Dunleavey."

Frank recounted all he had learned on Sunday and the pressure they were under. Then he pulled out a yellow legal pad and began to make a list. "Number one," he spoke aloud as he wrote, "we have to figure out what's going on with the Flynns. Now Martha is missing. I can't figure out the alliances there. All I know is, among the four of them, there's an awful lot of anger. I'm going to talk to Gene's girlfriend, Nadine Witchel."

"Two. We need to figure out if there's a connection between the Hungry Loon and the Tabernacle. Fortway says no, but I sensed he was worried I was onto something. I want to talk to that woman I met at the Hungry Loon in Keene. Her license plate is 'Chef J'. Track her down and get her in here."

Frank continued without waiting for a response. "Three. We have to get the DEC rangers searching for Charlie. Post someone at the trailhead to ask returning hikers if they've seen him. I want to know what happened to his phone after he gave it up."

It didn't take long for Earl to run the CHEF J plates and produce the contact information for Jocelyn Helme, who lived in Keene. She agreed to come to their office after she got off work. Earl said the woman seemed eager for an opportunity to cause trouble for her ex.

Frank left Earl to contact the rangers while he went out to do the morning patrol. Nothing in Trout Run required his attention, so he had plenty of time to stop by Nadine Witchel's flower farm. When he pulled into the driveway, he could see the doors and windows of the house were wide open to catch the faint breeze, while the beds of bright flowers already drooped in the morning sun.

When Frank knocked, a large black dog ran into the hall and jumped up on the screen door. It looked familiar. Gene's dog?

Nadine appeared on the dog's heels and shooed it away. She smiled, as pleasant today as she had been last week when he bought the bouquet.

"Back for more flowers?" She slipped out onto the porch, leaving the eager dog inside.

"Not today. I don't want to spoil my wife." Frank sat in an Adirondack chair overlooking the garden. "Gene around?"

She startled at the question then lowered herself into the other porch chair, extending her long, slender legs before her. "He's cutting wood up near

Peru. Not sure how long he'll be there." She didn't bother denying her relationship with Gene. "Why do you want him?"

Frank noticed her slender hand trembling on the wide arm of the chair. A dark mark showed on the fair skin above her wrist. A smudge of dirt from the garden or a bruise from the tight grasp of her lover's hand?

On gut instinct, he took a risk. "Are you afraid of Gene, Nadine?"

She nodded, looking at him the way a lost child looks at an unfamiliar adult—scared but willing to trust. "I had a bad breakup last year. I really don't want to be seriously involved with anyone. Gene was charming and so helpful to me at the craft market. I figured since he was married, we could just have a little fling with no strings. But he went from casual to crazy possessive in, like, a week." She paused and squinted at Frank. "You didn't come here because you're worried about me."

"I want to find out what happened to Gene's wife. Their daughter is worried that she hasn't heard from her mother. She doesn't think it's...credible...that Martha would leave without telling anyone where she went. Or that Gene would let her go so easily."

Nadine pulled her bare feet up onto the chair and wrapped her arms around her legs. "Gene says they've fought for years. I figured it was the usual 'my wife doesn't understand me' line." She offered Frank a rueful smile. She'd been around the block a few times, this one.

"Gene didn't want a divorce because it would cost him." Nadine rubbed her fingers together.

Frank hung on her every word. Was she about to tell him she too thought Gene had murdered Martha?

She clapped her hands to scare off a rabbit chewing one of her plants. "So that's why he was happy when she ran off and joined that church."

Frank bolted upright. "What? Martha joined the Tabernacle?"

Nadine twisted to face Frank. "She told him Adam Fortway had saved her life. She was going to live in his community. Gene figured if she stayed away long enough it would mean she had abandoned him, and he wouldn't have to split their assets."

"So he was glad she left him and joined the Tabernacle? Why didn't he tell his family where she went?"

"He didn't want his daughter to try to talk her out of her decision. I told him that was harsh—that his daughter deserved to know where her mother was, but Gene said he had to protect Shannon and his grandkids from that church."

"*Gene* is afraid of the Tabernacle?" Frank found it hard to believe a brute like Gene would be intimidated by a scrawny prophet preaching mumbo jumbo.

"The episode of the rattlesnake on the deck kinda freaked him out."

Frank leaned forward. "When I asked Gene about it, he covered up by saying some business rival had put it there. If he knew it was Fortway, why didn't he tell me so I could arrest the man?"

"It wasn't Fortway who did it. It was Martha. And Gene freaked because Martha has always been terrified of snakes. Even garter snakes. She left some kind of crazy note with the snake about how she'd faced her fears and was rising into the light with Fortway. So Gene decided, good riddance."

Nadine gazed out at the mountains beyond her gardens. "But now he's practically moved in here, and he's treating me like he used to treat his wife. I don't like where this is going." She gave a bitter laugh. "Maybe *I* should talk her into going back to him."

Frank pushed himself out of the low-slung chair and offered Nadine a hand up. Her hand was firm and rough in his. Even strong women could fall prey to controlling men. "If you want help getting rid of Gene, I'm happy to escort him out of your home. And you can file for a restraining order to keep him away."

"Thank you. I hope it won't come to that." She squeezed Frank's hand. "But I'm glad to know I can count on you for help."

———◈———

ON THE WAY BACK TO the office, Frank mulled over what he'd learned. If Martha had joined the Tabernacle, maybe Billy was there too. What else could explain his disappearance when he had no resources?

Unless he was shacked up with a woman. Gene's good looks had gotten him a home away from home with Nadine. Billy had plenty to offer in the looks and sex appeal department. Frank had been too hasty in assuming Billy's instability and unemployment made him undesirable. Many women were drawn to bad boys. And lost puppies.

As Frank pulled into the town office parking lot, he told himself that Billy was a bit of both.

Earl was just hanging up the phone when Frank walked into their office. "That was Rusty calling from DEC headquarters. He says there's something on their wildlife cam we need to see."

Frank stared at Earl, too incredulous to speak. With all that was going on, Earl wanted to drive clear to Ray Brook to see some damn beaver flapping its tail so he could cozy up to the cute ranger he had the hots for?

"Rusty says the camera they've been using to spot that bobcat picked up a guy acting strange. He thinks it's the same guy they helped extract from Dix." Earl paused. "Charlie Dunleavey."

Now Earl had his full attention. "Acting strange? What does that mean?"

"The rangers think he could be in trouble. Rusty's sending us the link to the video."

Earl fiddled with his computer then motioned for Frank to join him.

The dim outline of a log filled the screen. Frank squinted at the grainy, gray image until he could make out the flowing stream in the foreground and a patch of ground covered in leaves and pine needles in the background. A grouse skittered past the camera. Then a ghostly figure walked into view.

He was so tall that his head was out of the camera's range.

"How does he know it's Charlie?"

"Wait for it—minute 5:43."

The legs walked back and forth, and the mysterious figure dropped a backpack. He went out of camera range and returned with some sticks. Soon a small campfire glowed in the corner of the screen.

"He said he seemed to be acting out some ritual," Earl said as Frank squirmed, impatient for some action.

The figure's large feet walked around and around the fire.

"What's he doing?" Frank leaned toward the screen just as the man dropped to his knees. Now his face filled the screen.

"That's definitely Charlie." Frank pointed to the screen. "See those bushy eyebrows and that thin face."

Charlie's mouth moved, like he was talking. But the wildlife cam didn't have a microphone, so they couldn't tell what he was saying.

"Is he with someone?" Frank speculated even though Earl didn't know any more than he did.

"He's not looking off screen like he's talking to a person out of camera range." No sooner had Earl spoken than Charlie raised his hands up to the sky. The glow of the fire illuminated his face and torso.

Then he lowered his hands and placed them directly into the flames.

Chapter 47

"**A** ugh!"

Frank and Earl both screamed and recoiled from the screen. "Jesus! What did he do that for?"

They watched in fascinated horror. Charlie held his hands in the flames for what seemed an eternity. The clock on the camera ticked away twenty seconds—plenty of time to cause third degree burns. Frank fought the urge to reach into the computer to pull the kid from danger. Finally, Charlie rocked back on his heels and held his damaged hands before him. His face contorted in pain and his mouth formed a perfect O.

Earl twisted in sympathy. "Geez, I can practically hear him screaming even though there's no sound."

Charlie stumbled to his feet and lurched away. The screen went black.

"That's it?" Frank asked.

"Tess just sent the clip with Charlie in it. They've already got rangers on the way up to where the camera is."

"Let's go. We'll meet them there."

On the short drive, they discussed what they'd seen.

"Jenna, Laurel, and Charlie—all doing crazy, life-threatening things." Frank thumped the passenger side door as Earl drove. "These episodes have to be related to each other. And I don't care what Fortway says, I know they're related to the Tabernacle."

"And Billy's missing. For all we know, he's off doing something terrible too."

Unless he's the one urging the others along. Frank held the thought to himself. This was no time to pick a fight with his assistant. "Adam Fortway is always prattling away about reaching for the light, overcoming challenges, blah-blah. Laurel died reaching to the full moon. Charlie put his hands in fire. Both of those are sources of light."

Earl careened around a bend in the road. "Yeah, but no one has reported seeing Charlie or Laurel or Jenna at the Tabernacle services."

"Not at the *public* services that anyone from town can go to. What about these private retreats? What about those three houses with the new steel doors? No one knows what goes on there."

When Frank and Earl arrived at the trailhead, a swarm of DEC vehicles and the Rescue Squad ambulance awaited them. "We found the campfire," Rusty said. "Luckily, it had gone out on its own. And his backpack was still there."

"He can't have gone far. He's probably passed out from the pain."

"You better find him soon," the EMT warned. "Burn victims are very susceptible to infection. How many hours since he got hurt?"

"According to the timer on the camera, he lit the fire just before dawn. We didn't watch the video until nine." Rusty checked his watch. "It's after eleven now. We've been searching for an hour and a half."

The EMT shook his head. "Five hours is a long time to be wandering around in the forest with third degree burns."

Frank paced anxiously. He should have listened to Mrs. Dunleavey. He shouldn't have undervalued her motherly instinct. Was he going to have to call the woman and tell her her son was dead? Dead because some crackpot led a vulnerable kid astray?

A dirty Toyota pulled into the trailhead parking area, and a middle-aged man stuck his head out the window. "Hi—is the trail closed? My wife and I are getting a late start, but we were hoping to hike Phelps."

"We have a seriously injured hiker lost on this trail sir," Rusty explained. "I can suggest several other hikes near here that would be just as nice."

The man exchanged a glance with his wife then looked back to Rusty. "You're still looking for him?"

Isn't that what lost meant? Frank had no patience for dim-witted tourists this morning.

Luckily, Rusty was much nicer. "Yes, sir. A hiker was burned at his campsite, and we're concerned that he may have collapsed."

The tourist scratched his head. "Oh...but we saw a guy." He gestured in the direction from which he'd driven in. "My wife and I are staying in a cabin on a road about a half-mile back. We saw a young man come out of the woods. He was staggering. And then a truck came along in the other direction and picked him up."

The wife leaned across her husband and called out some additional information. "Looked like he had tee-shirts wrapped around his hands."

Chapter 48

"Let's get over to the Tabernacle." Earl pulled the patrol car keys from his pocket. "Fortway's followers must've taken Charlie."

Frank put a hand on his assistant's shoulder. "They could have him hidden in any of those three houses. We'll need a search warrant. Charlie's clearly a danger to himself, but we can't prove anyone from the Tabernacle has committed a crime. We can't even prove that he's currently with anyone from the Tabernacle. The judge will never give us permission to search three homes and a church on a fishing expedition. You know how he feels about private property rights. And I'm already in hot water for violating Fortway's freedom of speech and religion."

"You're just going to let Charlie be taken by those people?" Earl's eyes widened in dismay.

"No. I'm going to root this cancer out of our town." Frank kicked the tire of the patrol car. "But to do it right, we need incontrovertible evidence of illegal activity. Mind control is impossible to prove. Charlie was all alone when he put his hands in that fire. No one pushed Laurel off the bridge or shoved Jenna onto the roof."

"So what are we going to prove?"

"Follow the money. Someone is financing Fortway, and I'm more and more convinced it's not grateful churchgoers. There's something bigger going on. And we have to put someone inside the Tabernacle to figure it out."

Earl warmed to the idea. "We need someone to spy like I did, but get further in. Who can we get who'd be convincing as a potential follower? It has to be someone who can get past the first level, yet not get taken in by these people."

"Someone who could seem vulnerable, but who's actually strong."

"I'll do it." Tess had been standing on the periphery of the circle. Close enough to hear but far enough for Earl not to be aware of her.

Frank's eyes lit up. "You're into acting, right?"

"Yes, I've played all kinds of different roles—ingenues, crazy girls, rebels."

Earl spun around. "No—we're not talking about a class play here. This could be dangerous. I don't want you taking that risk."

"Excuse me?" Tess glared at him. "Since when are my choices up to you?"

"I didn't mean it that way. It's just—" Earl ran his fingers through his hair. "This guy is crazy. We can't guarantee your safety."

"I don't need a guarantee. This is an important mission, and I want to be part of it."

Tess's confident words had no effect on Earl. He looked green with anxiety. But Frank was impressed by her gumption.

"There's a service at the Tabernacle tonight—six o'clock," Frank told Tess. "Go by yourself. See if you can get selected for extra attention. I think the key is to tell them you've got some problems, some fears, that are holding you back in life."

Tess squinted at the horizon. "I could say that I'm afraid to swim in water over my head. That I'm afraid my boss and partners will find out and it will hold me back in my career."

Rusty chuckled. "That'll take some acting. Tess is a tri-athlete. She swam across Mirror Lake."

By now, everyone was gathered around Tess, offering advice and high-fives.

Earl stood with his hands jammed in his uniform pockets.

"This won't be a one-shot deal." Frank laid a hand on the young ranger's shoulder. "You'll probably have to go a few times."

"A few times!" Earl glared at Frank. "Every time she goes there she's putting herself in harm's way."

"The only people who've gotten hurt are the people who fall for this charlatan's line of voo-doo. Fortway isn't going to convince Tess to jump off anything or burn herself up." Frank smiled at Tess. "She's too smart for that."

———⊙———

WITH A STRATEGY SET for that evening, Frank returned to the office to initiate his own game plan to follow the money flowing into the Tabernacle. Step one was talking to Jocelyn Helme.

He found the young woman waiting for him when he got in. Frank barely had to ask a question to unleash an avalanche of words.

"Troy and I met working at the Gilded Morel in Brooklyn. I was the sous
chef and he was the pastry chef. We learned a lot working in a Michelin-rat-
ed restaurant, but the hours were long, the pressure was insane, and the pay
sucked. One weekend we took a vacation to the Adirondacks, and we saw
this building for rent right in the middle of Keene. We started fantasizing
about opening a gourmet café and market because there was nothing edible
for miles around."

Frank let that assessment pass. He happened to think the Trail's End in
Trout Run and the Noonmark Diner in Keene Valley offered plenty of edible
meals.

"So we scraped together our savings and borrowed from our families and
we opened the Hungry Loon. It was an immediate success. Everything was
great—we were making money cooking the kind of food we loved to eat. Our
customers were wonderful people. I was happier than I'd ever been in my
life." Jocelyn's eyes welled with tears. "But Troy couldn't keep his damn pants
zipped. He started screwing the counter help. He denied it and acted like I
was some crazy jealous bitch until the day I caught them going at it in the
supply closet." Jocelyn's hands trembled with rage at the memory.

"After that, it was impossible to work together. I couldn't even look at
him. I wanted to sell the Hungry Loon, split the money and move far away
to start over. Troy wanted to keep the Loon open. He offered to buy me out
over time with installment payments. I told him to stuff that offer up his—.
Sorry. I turned down the offer because I needed the money—all the money—I had sunk into the Loon in order to start my new restaurant in Long
Lake. We argued about it endlessly. Then one day, out of the clear blue, here
comes Troy with a check for twenty-five thousand dollars. I asked him where
he got the money and he wouldn't tell me. I thought it was suspicious, but
I took it because I needed to get going on my new venture. Then one of my
old customers told me about this branch of the Hungry Loon that opened
in Trout Run, and that they were serving *my* grilled eggplant dip and *my* tarragon chicken."

"How could Troy afford to pay you for your share of the original Loon
and open a new branch at the same time?" Frank asked.

"You better believe I wanted to know exactly that. I went over there at closing time two weeks ago, and I refused to leave until he told me where the money came from. Took me an hour to pry it outta him."

Jocelyn leaned forward and tapped the blotter on Frank's desk. Despite her petite build, she had the strong, rough hands of a woman who worked hard every day. "Troy has nothing to do with the Trout Run store. Some investor dude strolled into the Keene store in June and offered Troy forty grand for the rights to the Hungry Loon name." She leaned back with a smile of satisfaction at the shock she'd produced on Frank's face.

"Sketchy, right?" Jocelyn flipped an unruly strand of curls behind her ear. "At first Troy thought they were paying for his expertise, but they just asked for a few recipes and some questions about where to order supplies and told him they didn't need him anymore."

"And what happened when you demanded they stop serving your proprietary recipes?"

Jocelyn's eyes widened. "That's what's even crazier. Troy was afraid there would be a lot of trouble when he asked them to stop serving those dishes. But the guy he made the deal with said, "no problem," and pulled them just like that." She snapped her fingers.

Frank scratched his eyebrow. "If someone wanted to open a fancy market in Trout Run, why would they feel the need to buy the Hungry Loon name? Couldn't they just call it the Starving Pheasant or the Gourmet Grouse? We would all shop there anyway."

"Right," Jocelyn said. "And why would they agree so easily to stop selling some of their most popular products?"

Frank pulled his pen and notebook closer. "So what's the name of this mysterious investor who flings money around so generously?"

"Troy said the guy who made him the offer was called John Harris. He gave him a Gmail address as his only contact. The check was written on a company account—Luna Associates, LLC in Delaware."

Frank felt a prickle of excitement. Delaware again. How could there be three different Delaware-based businesses operating in Trout Run?

Jocelyn rose. "The check Troy wrote to me on his account has cleared the bank. I've put down a deposit to rent a store in Long Lake. You and your wife should come and visit me there in a couple of months." She grinned. "Maybe I'll call it the Gourmet Grouse."

Frank watched through the window as Jocelyn sashayed out to her car and drove away.

Hell hath no fury like a woman scorned.

Chapter 49

While Frank had been talking to Jocelyn, Earl had been on the phone to various doctors and the Adirondack Medical Center to see if anyone had come in for burn treatment.

"Nothing," he reported. "They haven't brought him in for care. And the doctor at the Cascade Clinic says with burns like I described, Charlie will have an infection raging through his body by now." Earl put his palms on the desk and leaned toward Frank. "Charlie doesn't have much time, Frank. We can't wait for Tess's undercover operation to turn up evidence. We have to find him today."

Frank gazed up at the water stain on the ceiling. That ever-changing shape—today it looked like Texas with a little bit of Oklahoma attached—had focused his thinking on many occasions. Earl was right. They needed a route to infiltrate the Tabernacle right now. A route that didn't require threats or search warrants. A route provided by a member of the Tabernacle community.

Through the open window, he heard a faint boom.

"What was that sound?"

Earl scowled at the irrelevant question. "I dunno. A load of logs dropping at Stevenson's maybe. Listen, maybe if we go to those houses—"

Frank held up his hand for silence and listened. The boom sounded again, three times in a row. "That's gunfire. Hunters' guns firing." The sound was the background to their daily routine in October and November. But not now.

Earl cocked his head. "But nothing's in season in July."

"Exactly. So who's shooting?"

Earl walked to the window and listened intently. "A firing range. Guys taking target practice on private property. Sounds like it's coming from the direction of Verona." Earl got a funny look on his face.

"What?" Frank asked.

"Remember I mentioned that group of guys at the Mountainside who invited Billy to go to this camp near Verona to drink beer and shoot, but he said no."

"So maybe they're shooting today."

Earl shook his head. "They all work during the week. They invited him to go on the weekend."

"But Billy knows where the place is?"

"Yeah, Billy and all those guys have been going there since high school."

Frank could see where this was heading.

"The Tabernacle requires everyone to face challenges, challenges that test their deepest fears," Frank said.

"And Billy's is loud noises," Earl replied immediately. "Gun fire."

"If Billy is performing his challenge for the Tabernacle, maybe we can use him to get in and find Charlie." Frank jumped up. "So where is this camp?"

Earl picked up the phone. "I'll find out."

Within minutes, Frank and Earl were racing to a piece of property owned by the great uncle of a friend of a friend of the guy at the Mountainside located in the unincorporated area between Trout Run and Verona. The sound of gunfire continued to echo around them, growing louder as they drove closer to the camp.

"I don't like this." Frank's hands gripped the steering wheel. "Billy hasn't had any counseling, and now the Tabernacle is forcing him into prolonged exposure to gunfire. We have to approach very cautiously." He shot Earl a stern look. "You have to think of Billy as an unstable, armed perpetrator, not as your personal friend."

Earl heard the warning but didn't respond. He perched on the edge of the passenger seat keeping an eye out for the vague landmarks Billy's friends had provided.

"There," he shouted as Frank steered the patrol car over the ruts in an old dirt logging road. "Make a right after that maple sugar shack."

Frank turned onto an even narrower dirt track. Branches scraped the side of their patrol vehicle, but the 4-wheel drive kept them moving slowly up the hill. The forest enveloped them silently.

"The gunfire has stopped." Earl craned his neck to look for people or another vehicle, but the dense trees revealed nothing.

"This road is the only way in, so whoever was shooting hasn't driven out." Frank's heartrate kicked up a notch. He didn't know what they were heading into. They might find a group of kids fooling around, or they might be driving right into an ambush. "Let's turn our car around in case we have to make a quick exit. We'll leave it here and go the rest of the way on foot."

With the patrol vehicle blocking the narrow road, they proceeded uphill, using the trees for cover.

At the top of the ridge, the land flattened out. Frank gestured Earl into a crouch and they both crept forward. Positioned behind a large rock, they peered out at the shooting range. Someone had cut the trees and cleared the brush to provide a wide alley. At the end stood four big bales of hay with targets attached. More targets were nailed to trees deeper in the woods. A bunch of buckshot-riddled beer cans lay scattered around the targets.

Earl had fighter-pilot vision. "Those cans are blue and yellow. Pabst. That's Billy's brand. And there's a can of Skoal. That's what he chews."

Frank scanned the scene. Where was Billy? Had he heard their vehicle approaching and ended his target practice? That seemed unlikely. The sound of shooting had stopped when they were still far down the trail.

Then, as if intermission was over and the second act of a play had begun, a slender woman walked into the clearing. She wore hunters' camo and carried a rifle on her shoulder. Her hair was shoved up under an olive drab baseball cap.

"Is that Martha?" Frank whispered.

Earl nodded, his gaze transfixed by Billy's mother.

Martha began to sing in a soft vibrato:

In him is the power
The power to conquer darkness
In him is the light
The light to which we all confess

Then she raised the rifle and sighted the target. She fired four times in quick succession. Four new holes appeared near the bullseye.

Martha lowered the gun and threw back her shoulders. "Get out here."

Frank held his breath. Nothing moved.

"Billy! I said get out here!"

From the thick stand of trees directly across from Frank and Earl, Billy's face appeared.

Martha slapped her thigh. "Now!"

Well trained Marine that he was, Billy crawled forward on his elbows and knees as if he was dodging enemy fire. He too was dressed all in camo. Above him, a warbler let out a long trill.

Frank and Earl exchanged a puzzled glance.

When Billy finally reached his mother, he was breathing heavily through his mouth and wiped sweat from his eyes with the back of his sleeve.

Martha waved him up and extended the gun toward him.

But Billy cowered at her feet. He curled in a ball with his hands over his head and swayed from side to side.

She stamped her foot. "This is your challenge. You must accept it."

Billy drew his head further into his clasped arms.

"You told me you were ready, ready to embrace the light. What will the master say if I fail in my task to bring you into the light? I cannot fail a second time. Rise! Rise, you coward!"

A cold shiver passed through Frank's core. Martha's words echoed the text that had sent Laurel to her death. Had Fortway persuaded Martha that if Laurel's faith was stronger, she could have survived a plunge onto the rocks? And that Laurel's lack of faith was Martha's fault?

"Rise!" Martha's screech was tinged with panic.

What did Martha want her son to do?

Slowly, Billy lifted his head and stumbled to his feet. Earl lurched forward, but Frank held him back. He drew his own service weapon and waited.

Billy accepted the rifle with trembling hands.

"Aim!"

Billy lifted the rifle and squeezed the trigger. No hole appeared in the target, but a spray of hay flew up from the bottom of the bale. Was Billy's challenge simply to be able to tolerate gunfire again?

Martha stood in front of her son and turned his face with both her hands. "You must release your darkness and embrace the light. This is your salvation. If you trust in him, he will guide you as he has guided me."

Billy's head bobbed in agreement, but his expression was dazed and vacant.

Martha released him and trotted toward the targets. She stood in front of the closest one and bent over.

She straightened with something in her hand.

She placed a beer can on her head, squared her shoulders, and commanded her son.

"Fire!"

Chapter 50

F rank and Earl raced toward Billy. Earl ran faster and brought his friend down with a sliding tackle.

The gun discharged a split second later.

The three of them thrashed on the ground for a moment as Earl removed the gun from Billy's trembling hands. Only then could Frank lift his head to see if Martha was still standing.

No one was in front of the target.

Frank leapt to his feet and ran toward the cluster of hay bales.

In three steps he stopped.

No Martha, crumpled in a bleeding heap.

No Martha anywhere.

Frank scanned from left to right. Where was she?

A bullet whizzed by his ear and he hit the ground.

"Frank!"

Frank raised his hand to let Earl know he hadn't been hit. The shot had come from the spot in the woods where Martha and Billy had emerged after Frank and Earl first arrived. They must have a cache of weapons and ammo there.

Earl had pulled Billy back behind the rock where they'd been hiding. Martha was somewhere amid the flickering shadows in the woods. But Frank was wide out in the open.

Frank tensed for the next bullet. If Martha wanted to kill him, she would. Eternity passed in the next three seconds.

Still the shot didn't come.

Frank risked using his voice. "Martha, let's talk. We don't want anyone to get hurt."

She slipped out of the shadows carrying a revolver aimed at Frank's head. "Get out. You have no right to be here. This is a sacred space."

"Okay, okay. We're going to leave." Frank had his gun in his hand, but he didn't think he could aim and fire faster than Martha. The woman was a damn good shot. Keep her talking. That was his best option. "Tell me about Billy's challenge. Why does he have to shoot the can off your head?"

Martha walked steadily towards him. "He must relinquish his fears and embrace the light. He must have faith in the light. The light will lift him up."

Martha was close enough for Frank to see the deranged glint in her eye. This wasn't the timid wife and obsequious saleswoman he'd encountered previously. This was a whole new Martha.

A fanatic.

"I think Billy's a little worried he's not as good a marksman as he used to be. He's scared he'll hurt you. And if he does, he'll go to prison. You wouldn't want that."

Martha's eyes grew huge in her thin face. "He must relinquish fear!" she roared. The gun trembled in her hand. "The light will guide him. The light will protect me."

"Did the light guide Laurel?" Frank spoke with a neutral voice as if he were asking directions to Lake Placid.

Martha's face hardened. "Her faith wasn't strong enough. That is why the light didn't sustain her. She did not deserve to be a follower of the master."

Or maybe Martha had established a challenge that conveniently got rid of a beautiful rival.

"What about Charlie? Did he pass his challenge this time?"

Martha smiled, her eyes dreamy. "Charlie is living the master's word. He has fully embraced the light. This is what I want for my Billy."

Whatever happened to wanting your kid to grow up to be a doctor? "Where is Charlie now, Martha? Have you seen him since he returned from his challenge?"

"He's at Moon Haven. The acolytes are tending him." The snap of a stick made Martha pivot toward the rock. "Get out here, Billy. We must resume your challenge."

The split-second distraction was all Frank needed. He lunged for Martha and knocked the weapon from her hand, then kicked it far away. He struggled to pin her, but she was lithe and wiry.

As he and Martha rolled on the ground, Frank could hear footsteps running toward him.

Earl coming to help? Or Billy ready to defend his mother?

Frank twisted to see, and that instant of inattention gave Martha the opportunity she needed.

She wriggled from his grasp and sprinted toward her cache in the woods. Frank stood as Earl and a bewildered Billy reached his side.

"Let's get out of here," Frank said. "We're not prepared for a gun battle with a lunatic. Keep Billy between us and run for the car."

They ran down the hill, Earl keeping a firm grip on his friend's arm. Billy didn't resist, even when Martha's shriek reverberated through the trees, "Bi-l-l-e-e-e, embrace the li-i-i-ght!"

Chapter 51

They piled into the car.
Jolting down the narrow track, Frank heard the ricochet of bullets—Martha trying to blow out their tires. But they had too good a start on her, and she soon gave up.

Earl called for back-up, and by the time they got to the main road, the Trout Run EMS had arrived ready to transfer Billy to the Adirondack Medical Center for psychiatric observation. A few minutes later, a state police patrol car rolled up, miraculously in the right vicinity at the right time. Frank talked to the trooper about assembling a search party to arrest Martha, telling him about the three Tabernacle houses that she might try to make her way back to.

Meanwhile, Earl talked to Billy. He sat beside his friend and gripped the ex-Marine's hand. "What house have you been staying in, Billy?"

"Sun Haven," he whispered.

"And is that house blue or brown?" Frank joined Earl but let him handle the questions.

"Brown."

"Big front porch or small?"

"Big."

"Have you ever been to the other houses? The blue one or the brown one with the small porch?"

Billy shifted restlessly. "Does your mom stay at Sun Haven too?" Earl pressed.

"No, Star...." Billy's voice grew fainter and his eyes darted back and forth."

"So your mom stays at Star Haven," Earl confirmed. "Is that the blue house?"

Billy nodded. "Blue. White stars. Blue sky."

Earl squeezed his friend's hand. "Okay, Billy. You helped a lot. I'll see you tomorrow, bro."

Earl watched the ambulance roll off. "We've narrowed it down. If Billy can be trusted, Charlie's in the brown house with the small porch. Does that help when we can't get a search warrant?"

"Ah, Earl—there's a bright side to almost getting killed. Someone who freely admits she was performing a ritual for the Tabernacle has assaulted two police officers. I think the warrant just came within reach."

Earl's kind eyes searched Frank's face. "What the hell's wrong with Billy's mother? How could go from being a normal mom to such a freak in a couple weeks?"

"We don't know how long she's been involved with Fortway. Remember, he was here in Trout Run remodeling the Asian Bistro long before we were aware of him. Martha must have been his first recruit. Who knows how they connected?"

Earl looked up at the western sky, where the sun cast beams between glowing clouds. He patted his pockets for his phone. "What time is it?"

Frank was old enough to still rely on a watch. "Six-thirty. Time flies when you're under attack."

Earl's lips pressed into a thin line. "Tess is at the Tabernacle right now."

"That's right." Frank tensed with excitement. "The Celebration of Light service has begun. Fortway and most of his followers will be at the Tabernacle. This is the perfect time to get Charlie out of Moon Haven." He pulled out his phone and called the magistrate, explaining all that had happened.

In a few minutes, Frank hung up with a satisfied smile. "We got the warrant. Let's pick it up and head straight to Moon Haven."

"How are we going to get Charlie to the hospital?" Earl asked. "We just sent the Trout Run EMS off with Billy."

"We'll have to get back-up from Wilmington or Keene—see who can meet us there."

"We should get more back-up from the state police." Earl shifted his weight from one leg to the other. "If we raid the house during the service and word gets back to Fortway, that could put Tess in danger."

Frank turned away. "We're pretty sure none of them has a phone—Fortway makes his followers give them up. Besides, we've already got the available troopers searching for Martha. It would take hours to assemble more to go into the house. You and I can do this." Frank clapped Earl on the shoulder.

"Fortway hasn't connected Tess to us. We're not going to let that girl get hurt."

Chapter 52

Half an hour later, Frank and Earl approached the small brown house known as Moon Haven. The Wilmington EMS crew were standing by half a mile away on the main road.

"Let's circle the house to see if we can establish how many people are inside." Frank gestured Earl to follow him as they crept around the bushes and trees that grew close to the house. The large, weedy backyard ended in a stand of woods that ran behind all the houses on the road. They saw no vehicles, heard no sounds but tree frogs. Only one window one the side of the house showed a sliver of light from behind a drawn curtain.

Frank silently approached the window, motioning Earl to stay back and cover him. Peering through the slit in the curtain, he saw one section of a small parlor. A young woman sat in a chair, her eyes focused on something out of Frank's sight.

Charlie?

If this girl was the only acolyte standing guard, they had nothing to worry about. He returned to Earl's side and whispered instructions. "I'm going in through the front door. You watch this window and the back yard. If anyone runs out, just let them go. We're only concerned with getting Charlie out, and he's likely too sick to run."

Earl nodded and took his place under the illuminated window. Frank marched up to the sturdy steel front door and pounded on it. "Trout Run police! Open up."

Frank heard heavy footsteps and a shout inside. "Is the girl moving?" he called out to Earl.

"No, but she looks scared."

So someone else was in there. "I have a warrant. Open up or I'll break the window."

A high-pitched scream and a shout from within. "They're going out the back," Earl warned.

Frank used his nightstick to break the front window. He ripped down the curtains and shined his flashlight into an empty dining room. Climbing through the window with his weapon drawn, he crossed the dining room and headed deeper into the house to the room where the girl had been sitting.

Inside, the house was hot and stuffy, and a horrible smell engulfed him. Frank twisted the handle of the door to the parlor. Locked. But the hollow core door gave way under two forceful kicks.

He stepped forward and something hard and heavy hit him from above. Staggering back, Frank saw the door had been booby-trapped with a concrete block. His right shoulder had taken the brunt of the hit, and the radiating pain made his hand numb. He raised his weapon unsteadily; however, the girl he'd seen through the window had disappeared.

But Frank wasn't alone. The sound of ragged breathing emanated from a blanket-shrouded form on a saggy sofa. The disgusting smell churned Frank's stomach. A familiar tousle of auburn hair lay against a dirty pillow.

Frank pulled the blanket back.

The pale, wizened face before him was barely recognizable as Charlie Dunleavy. Only his bushy brows confirmed his identity. Frank didn't have to touch the young man's forehead to feel the fever heat radiating from him. His hands, inexpertly wound with gauze, oozed blood and pus. The stench of decay knocked Frank back a step.

How could anyone have let Charlie suffer like this? You didn't need medical training to see Charlie wouldn't win this battle against infection if left untreated for another day.

Earl appeared at Frank's side. "Two people ran out the back door, a guy and a girl. But when I came in through the kitchen, I noticed three mugs in the sink."

"Good observation. Let's search the house before the ambulance gets here. I don't want any nasty surprises."

They crossed the hall and checked the larger living room. Finding it empty, Frank and Earl climbed the stairs to the second floor. On the landing, four closed doors greeted them. Methodically, Earl pressed his ear against each one and listened. Years of sitting in tree stands waiting for deer to reveal themselves with one snapped twig had given him a finely tuned sense of hearing. At the third door he tensed and made eye contact with Frank. Together they kicked in the door then jumped back to avoid another booby trap.

When nothing fell from above, Frank edged closer. Again, his nose wrinkled at a strong smell, but a different one than what permeated the downstairs.

Sweat. Piss. Vomit.

A young woman sat in a hardbacked wooden chair. Her headed drooped, and her hands appeared to be resting on the chair's arms. One step closer and Frank could see she was tied to the chair. She raised her head as he approached.

"I have repented," she whispered.

"I bet you have," Frank muttered as he untied the girl, who looked to be in her early twenties.

As they helped her downstairs, the EMS crew arrived, and Frank guided them to their patient, leaving the listless girl with Earl in the front hall.

When they wheeled Charlie out, the girl showed the first signs of life. From her perch on the stairs, she extended her hand toward the gurney. "Charlie," she whispered.

Outside, the EMS crew struggled to move the gurney across the sloped gravel driveway. Frank and Earl rushed to help. Then they returned to get the girl.

The stairs were empty.

Frank swore loud enough to wake a hibernating bear. Earl dashed back to the kitchen, shouting as he ran. "She can't have gone far."

But the backyard was fully dark now. The girl had melted into the trees.

Charlie's condition demanded an immediate departure by the ambulance, so Frank sent them off. "We'll find the girl in the morning. We have enough evidence of criminal behavior now that we can search all the Tabernacle's houses. Let's head back to the office."

Earl lifted his head. "Listen!"

Now that Frank's heart wasn't pounding with anger and anxiety, he could hear sounds outside his own body. In the still night air, the mournful howl of a siren rose and fell and rose again.

The siren summoning the volunteer firemen to the station to go out on a call.

"Where's the fire? We had our radios turned off. We missed it." Earl radioed in as soon as they reached the car, and Frank watched as his partner's eyes widened. "Let's go. The Tabernacle's on fire!"

Frank raced toward the Tabernacle knowing that he and Earl would arrive before the fire crew. In Trout Run, by the time all the volunteers assembled and got their gear on, most fires would have destroyed the building and the firemen would be needed only to put out the embers and knock down the charred shell.

What would they find at the Tabernacle? A small grease fire in the kitchen that could be put out with an extinguisher? Or a whole church full of people engulfed in flames?

As they drew closer, the acrid smell of melted plastic seeped into the closed car. Earl opened the windows and the smoke carried by the breeze made Frank's eyes water.

This was no grease fire.

They crested the hill and below them the valley glowed orange and red. Flames towered over the low-slung building. The old Asian Bistro sign stood like a glowing torch.

"Jesus! Tess!"

Earl had been dialing the young ranger incessantly as Frank drove, but she didn't answer. Frank told Earl she must have her phone turned off because she hadn't wanted it to ring during the service.

He prayed the phone wasn't burned up in her pocket.

They got within fifty yards of the building before intense heat forced Frank to park the car. Melted vinyl siding dripped off the building. Windows exploded rhythmically in showers of splintering glass. All through the Tabernacle parking lot, frantic people darted back and forth like schools of disturbed minnows as they searched for the friends and family they'd come with.

Earl charged into the crowd. "Tess? Tess!" He grabbed a man to ask if he'd seen her, then grabbed another passing teenager. But no one knew who Earl was talking about. And they were too preoccupied with their own friends' safety to care about this stranger.

Frank waded after Earl trying to move the people who were gawping at the spectacle out of the way. He recognized a man who worked at Stevenson's

Lumberyard shepherding his wife and daughter away from the fire. "What happened? How many people were in the building?"

The man shuddered. "It all went down so fast. The candles they use during the service...I guess one dropped and the curtain on the stage went up like a dry Christmas tree. Every seat was full. There was a stampede for the door. I got separated from my daughter." He choked back tears and pulled the girl tight against him. "We gotta get out of here."

While Frank was talking, Earl had gotten ahead of him, fighting the fleeing crowd to get closer to the burning building. Frank ran after him and snared him by the back of his shirt. "You can't go in there. You'll be overcome by smoke right away."

Earl spun around and shoved Frank with both hands. "Don't tell me what to do! You got her into this mess. I'm getting her out."

Frank trotted by Earl's side, tears streaming down his face from the thick smoke. "You don't even know if she's inside." He jumped in front of Earl to block his progress. "Killing yourself won't save her."

Earl reared back and threw a roundhouse punch that sent Frank flat onto his ass. When the exploding stars in Frank's eyes cleared, Earl had disappeared.

Chapter 53

Trout Run's two fire trucks finally arrived on the scene. While four of the men sprayed the building, Frank found a firefighter equipped with breathing apparatus and sent him into the building through the door Earl had been closest to when Frank had last seen him. Swallowing his fear, he focused on the only thing he could do—clear people away from the crumbling building. Frank dragged up an older person who had fallen into a coughing heap. He grabbed a little girl wandering aimlessly and got another family to take charge of her.

Nowhere in the crowd did he see Adam Fortway. Had the pastor run for his life, or had he stayed in the building to help his congregation?

Frank continued around the perimeter, finally arriving at the back side of the Tabernacle. The parking lot dissolved into gravel and scrubby weeds here, and a large metal Dumpster stood where a patch of birch and maples marked the end of the Tabernacle property. With all the smoke, someone could have become disoriented and wound up back here. He shined the beam of his flashlight around and something metallic twinkled back at him.

"Hello? Is someone there?"

Something fell behind Frank, and he spun around. He couldn't see anyone through the smoke, but a moment later an arm linked with his and he felt something against his neck.

Something cold and sharp.

"Don't move," a voice whispered in his ear.

Frank stood still and looked down. A woman's hand held the handle of a ten-inch hunting knife.

The point pressed against his throat.

Frank had seen that hand before. Wiry. Strong. Nails cut short.

She stood behind him, her left arm linked with his. The woman's breath felt hot on his ear. He could feel her heart thumping against his back.

"Our leader is ready to rise into the light." She spoke again, her voice low, urgent. "Only a few may accompany him through the purifying fire. You should not have interfered."

Frank knew he'd heard that voice before. He looked at the hand again. Not Martha, whose hands showed the veins and freckles of age.

This woman was young.

Tess.

He relaxed a bit. She must be acting, putting on a show for someone watching from behind that Dumpster. Martha? Some other follower?

Fortway himself?

He would have to play along with the charade. Frank hoped he could be as convincing as Tess was.

"Yes, I can see now that interfering was a mistake." Frank's voice came out scratchy and raw. He didn't think Tess needed to press that knife quite so close to his jugular. "What can I do to make things right?"

She snorted. "The chosen one is always feared and persecuted. His most loyal followers will start again. This was not a fertile ground for our effort."

He had to hand it Tess—she was quite an improviser. Really had their line of BS mastered.

"So you're leaving town? That's a good choice. We'll all just go our separate ways, okay?" Frank glanced toward the Dumpster to see if their audience would react.

Tess twisted his left arm harder. Geez, the woman didn't know her own strength! Frank's shoulder ached from the falling concrete block. His jaw throbbed from Earl's punch. His eyes burned from the smoke. He wanted to bring this to an end.

"We found Charlie," he offered. "He's at the hosp—"

Footsteps pounded toward them coming from the front of the building. Earl emerged through a haze of smoke.

"Tess! There you are! My God, I was so—" Earl's face contracted in confusion as he took in the scene.

Relief that Earl wasn't dead surged through Frank. Just as quickly, he panicked that his partner would draw fire from whomever lurked behind that Dumpster. "Earl, get down! There's someone—"

The tip of Tess's knife broke his skin. "Augh, watch—" Instinctively,

Frank twisted away from the knife.

He turned just as Tess lifted the weapon high above her head, ready to plunge it into his chest.

Earl launched himself into the middle of their bizarre dance. Tess lost her balance, and the knife sliced Frank's hand.

"What the hell?"

Her muscular arm rose above her head, the knife tight in her grasp.

The truth dawned on him. This was no act.

Tess was trying to kill them both.

Earl rolled against Tess's legs and brought her down. Frank grabbed her right hand and twisted until the knife dropped from her grasp.

She emitted an unholy shriek. "Master! Don't rise without me!"

As if in response, the Tabernacle itself moaned. The roof collapsed in a tremendous roar of smoke and flying embers.

Chapter 54

A wave of intense heat enveloped them. Frank looked over his shoulder and saw the rear wall of the Tabernacle swaying as it tried to decide which way to fall.

"Run!"

He and Earl and Tess bolted away from the imploding building. Frank couldn't see where he was heading, he just knew he had to keep the Tabernacle behind him. For what seemed like hours, he dodged trees and tripped through ditches trying to find his way to the safety of the road. "Earl!" he called, but his throat was so raw from smoke that he could barely hear himself. The sound of other footsteps crashing through the brush reassured him that Earl was nearby.

Unless it was Tess.

His back tingled with the imagined sensation of her knife between his ribs. How could both he and Earl have misjudged her so completely?

At last he saw the ghostly outline of headlights and ran toward them. Seconds later, Earl arrived panting at his side. They stood together on the road and surveyed the chaos around them.

Volunteer fire departments and rescue squads from every town in Essex County had responded to the blaze. The collapse of the building had turned the tide, and the teams fighting the fire seemed to be bringing it under control. A group of EMS volunteers and nurses performed triage to get the most seriously injured people to the hospital. Half the population of Trout Run had showed up to offer help, and cops from Lake Placid had arrived to manage the flow of cars ferrying victims home. Frank scanned the crowd: no sign of Tess.

One person at the medical tent had been put in charge of keeping a list of those sent to the hospital. No Fortway. No Tess. Everyone who had been searching for the friends and family they had arrived with had been reunited. As far as anyone could tell in the confusion, no one from Trout Run seemed to be missing.

Finally, Frank connected with the state police. But they too had nothing to report. Martha Flynn hadn't been apprehended. They had checked all three of the Tabernacle's houses and found each one empty—abandoned with clothes in the closets, food in the fridges. No one they had questioned at the scene of the fire had seen Adam Fortway after the first panicked minutes of the fire.

Earl kept staring at Frank, then glancing away when Frank met his gaze. He knew the kid was embarrassed about the punch he'd thrown. Frank clapped Earl on the back. "Let's both get some rest. Billy and Charlie are safe. Tomorrow morning we'll go to the hospital and interview everyone able to talk. I suspect Fortway, Martha and Tess are together. If we find one, we'll find them all."

So Frank and Earl parted ways, but there was one more person Frank wanted to talk to before morning: Rusty McGill, Tess's boss.

Frank called Rusty and relayed the story of his encounter with Tess. At the conclusion of the crazy tale he said, "I assume you had no idea she was involved with the Tabernacle. But did you ever notice anything strange about her?"

The silence on the other end of the line extended so long, Frank thought their call had been dropped. "Rusty?"

"I can't believe she did that. I'm stunned, and yet..."

"You're not."

"Tess came to us highly recommended. She was a tireless worker. Volunteered for any project, no matter how exhausting or unpleasant it might be."

"Did the other rangers like working with her?"

Rusty hesitated. "That was the one issue. Tess was a stickler for following every rule. If another ranger cut a corner or didn't follow procedure to the letter, she'd complain. She ruffled some feathers. But I figured she was young and dedicated and didn't realize she sometimes rubbed people the wrong way. I talked to her about it. Told her to relax."

"How did that go over?"

Again the long silence. "She didn't argue with me. After all, I'm her boss. But I got the sense she disapproved of my attitude."

"Any idea where she might run to? Where's her family?"

"Her father was—is still—in the military. I got the sense she had no home base. Wasn't close to her siblings."

"And what DEC office did she work in before she came here?"

"Warrensburg."

"That's close to Glens Falls. Close to where the Tabernacle was located before it moved here."

WHEN FRANK FINALLY made it home, Penny flew into Florence Nightingale mode. As she bathed his red eyes with saline solution and held an ice pack to his swollen jaw, Frank told her his theory about Fortway's followers.

"They're all people who are used to having an authoritarian figure in their life, but that figure abandoned them. Gene left Martha for another woman. Billy came home from the Marines, and his father rejected him because he couldn't work alongside him anymore. Tess also came from a military family, but she couldn't follow her father around to his postings once she was grown. She must've sought that feeling of security and regimentation when she joined the DEC."

Penny cocked her head. "Every ranger I know is pretty mellow."

"Yes, I think Tess must've been disappointed that the DEC didn't give her the authority figure she was seeking."

"And that's when she found Fortway." Penny dabbed ointment onto Frank's cut hand. "What about Laurel? Her father certainly isn't authoritarian. The man's a wreck."

"In Laurel's case, it was her mother who provided structure. Marge said she wore the pants in the family. She had big dreams for Laurel. When she died, Laurel looked for someone else who could take her beyond the boundaries of life in Trout Run."

Frank stretched out on their bed, his aching body longing to slip into a deep sleep, but his brain still spinning with ideas. "And finally, there's Charlie. His mother is overprotective, his father seems irritated and disapproving. Charlie seems dreamy, trying to find a place for himself in the world." Frank kneaded his eyes. "I dread calling the hospital tomorrow. I hope Charlie gets a second chance to find his way."

Chapter 55

The morning spent at the Adirondack Medical Center had been more frustrating than illuminating. Overwhelmed by the influx of patients the night before, the small hospital had transferred the most seriously injured, like Charlie, to Plattsburgh. The staff psychiatrist said Billy wasn't stable enough to be questioned. But dozens of patients remained for treatment of smoke inhalation. Frank and Earl interviewed them all but came back with precious little useful information.

Everyone agreed that the fire had started when the stage curtain had ignited during the service.

No one offered the same account of how that had happened. Some said a large candle had tipped over. Some said they hadn't noticed anything at all before the curtain ignited. They'd been singing, caught up in the music.

But one or two claimed to have seen the person who lit the candles with a torch apply that tool to the curtain.

And who was that torch-bearer?

No one knew. Because all the people who'd been hospitalized lived in Trout Run. And the person who'd lit the candles was someone who'd followed Fortway here from his old church. The locals admitted there was a division between them and Fortway's inner circle. Those others were friendly, but distant. They went by their first names only. Three of them had played the music for the service last night.

And none of those followers had sought medical attention.

Had they needed it but been afraid to ask for help?

Or had they all known about the fire in advance? Known to have an escape route planned?

Or would the county fire investigators now combing through the wreckage find the bodies of some of those acolytes?

Frank and Earl sat in the hospital cafeteria comparing notes. They had leapt into work without a word of commentary on what had happened between them the night before. "How many people are we talking about?" Earl counted on his fingers. "Fortway, Martha, Tess, the three people in the house with Charlie, the candle lighter, and three musicians that everyone remembers at the service. That's nine people! They can't have vanished into thin air."

"We know that Tess and Charlie's guards weren't inside the Tabernacle, and it's unlikely that Martha made it back there either. But some of the others might have died in the fire."

Earl shivered. "You mean, they might not have even tried to escape? Because no one we talked to said that Fortway's followers heroically stayed behind to help them get out. It sounded like a mass stampede for the exits."

"We should know by the end of the day if they find any human remains at the Tabernacle. I got a message earlier—there are no vehicles registered in Fortway's name or in the name of the Tabernacle. Yet we know he had a vehicle to get around town." Frank massaged his temples. "I wish I could remember what he was driving that night he came to dinner at the Inn. Edwin thinks it might be an SUV, but he's not sure."

Earl methodically gathered up the stirrers and torn sugar packets and stuffed them in their empty coffee cups. "Tess drives a green Jeep Wrangler."

"I know. The state police have an APB out on it."

Earl kept his gaze focused on the cup, as if it were filled with gold not trash. "I'm so sorry for what I did, Frank. I thought Tess was making a sacrifice to help us. I never imagined...I shouldn't have let myself get so infatuated..."

"Forget about it. How could you have known? I thought she was acting when she first grabbed me...putting on a show for whoever was behind that Dumpster watching us." Frank grabbed the cups and jumped up, eager to end this awkward interlude. "Let's get back to the office."

On the long ride back to Trout Run, Earl gazed out the window, uncharacteristically silent. Frank let him stew. He had too much on his own mind to offer advice to his partner. After watching Martha at the shooting range yesterday, Frank was confident she had sent those goading texts to Laurel. It made sense that she would have access to Charlie's relinquished phone if she were one of Fortway's key lieutenants. And she must have used her handsome son as a way to lure the girl into her grasp. But he would never get solid evidence a prosecutor could use. He would have to satisfy himself with finding Fortway's followers and charging Martha and Tess with assaulting a police officer. They'd get a few years in prison for that. Maybe it would be enough to break the grip of their fanaticism.

Or maybe jail time would simply strengthen their resolve.

Unless he could charge Fortway with a serious crime, the charlatan would start up his cult somewhere else and be there waiting when his followers were released.

Did he care, as long as the somewhere wasn't on his turf? Frank gripped the steering wheel. He wanted Fortway behind bars where he couldn't prey on any more vulnerable people.

Anywhere.

Ever.

Chapter 56

Back at the office, Earl soon lost himself in follow-up work with the state police, who had been combing the three Tabernacle houses looking for evidence and clues to the whereabouts of the missing church members. Frank offered up thanks for Earl's patience and tenacity with this detail work. He knew he'd be snapping with irritation if he had to be their liaison.

Restless, Frank set off for the Rock Slide to talk to Martha Flynn's boss. Maybe now that he knew the right questions to ask, he could glean some useful information from a person who'd spent many hours a day with Martha.

Like how she'd first met Fortway.

Frank found the store empty of customers and the owner on his knees amidst a stack of shoe boxes.

"Unpacking some new stock?" Frank inquired.

"Trying to get ready for the weekend rush. I really miss Martha. I can't believe she quit without a word after all our years together."

"Brace yourself." Frank sat down on the bench customers used to try on shoes. "I'm here to tell you more stories you'll have a hard time believing."

After Frank filled him in, he asked a question. "The first time I met Adam Fortway, he was wearing a brand-new pair of hiking boots. Did he buy them here?"

The owner got up and headed for his office. "If he bought them with a credit card, I can tell you." A few computer keystrokes later, Frank had his answer. "Yes, Adam Fortway bought a pair of Merrell hiking boots on May 19. Martha made the sale. Then there's another charge for some clothing a couple days later. Martha again."

"That must be when he got his hook into her. Were you aware Martha was unhappy in her marriage?"

The owner nodded. "She didn't confide in me, but I overheard her phone conversations. A lot of tension there. I guess I can see Martha going off with this guy, Fortway. She's not a person with strong opinions of her own."

Frank was about to leave when another thought occurred to him. "Jenna Burlingame, Reid's granddaughter—you know her?"

"Sure, she shops here all the time." The owner grinned. "She can afford all the latest North Face gear that's so popular with the kids."

"So Jenna knew Martha?"

"Yes. As a matter of fact, the last time Jenna was in here, I remember Martha having a long conversation with her. We weren't busy, so I didn't care, but they did seem oddly intense. Is that important?"

Frank waved his thanks. "Just another little detail."

On the way back to the office, Frank spotted a large black Mercedes with New Jersey plates pulling onto Route 86. Could that be Patrick Dunleavey's car? He and Maeve might have come to upstate New York to be with Charlie, but why come to Trout Run if their son was hospitalized in Plattsburgh? As he stared at the car, he had more doubts. Would the Dunleaveys even be aware that Charlie had been hospitalized last night? When Frank had checked on him this morning, hoping he might be able to talk to the kid, the doctor said Charlie was in ICU under heavy sedation. Somehow Frank doubted that after all the "relinquishing" Charlie had done at the Tabernacle, the kid would have his insurance card with next of kin in his pocket.

So maybe this was some other luxury car-driving-New Jerseyan. Frank called Earl and asked him to run the plates. In the meantime, he kept a few car lengths between his truck and the car and followed. In half a mile, the car turned left and headed toward the Tabernacle. Was it just a coincidence?

When the Mercedes reached the ruins of the Tabernacle, it slowed to a crawl. Frank pulled into the driveway of the small engine repair shop across the road and watched. While Frank waited, Earl called back and confirmed the car was Dunleavey's.

Now Frank was keenly interested. Why was Dunleavey looking at the ruins of the church that had nearly taken his son's life? How did he know? Had Charlie been in contact with his family after the last time Frank had talked to him? Had he told his parents about his membership in the Tabernacle?

The scene crawled with fire inspectors, cadaver dogs, and state police. Dunleavey didn't attempt to ask any questions, and none of the workers took any notice of the Mercedes inching past. No doubt rubberneckers had been cruising by all day.

Now Dunleavey sped up and headed toward the center of town. Frank tailed him at a discreet distance. Once he got to the Green, Dunleavey pulled up in front of the Hungry Loon. Frank watched as the man trotted up the steps and entered the market. He seemed pretty chipper for a guy whose son was going to need major reconstructive surgery on his hands.

Frank was about to leave his truck to stroll into the market and stage a casual encounter with Dunleavey when the man came flying out of the Hungry Loon. He held a bright yellow piece of paper in his hand and looked around as if trying to get his bearings. Then he loped across the Green toward the library.

Why was he going there? Frank drove around two sides of the Green, arriving at the library just a few moments after Dunleavey. He still planned a casual encounter, using a visit with his wife as his excuse. But when Frank entered the library, he heard Penny's voice raised in outrage.

"Excuse me—why are you shouting at me? I've been taking care of this cat for weeks ever since he showed up lost on my back deck."

"That looks like Bruiser, my daughter Mandy's cat. What's he doing here?" Dunleavey leaned across the front circulation desk to scream, drops of spittle flying from his mouth. Meanwhile, Yogi stood on the credenza behind the desk with his back arched and his tail fluffed to twice its normal size.

"I need to get a closer look at him. Bruiser has a nick in his ear." Dunleavey grabbed for the cat, who hissed and bared his claws in defense.

"Stop! You're scaring him!" Penny jumped up from her desk and caught sight of Frank. "This man claims Yogi is his, but look how he's treating our cat! I'm not giving Yogi back to someone like this."

Frank came up behind Dunleavey and grabbed his shoulder. "Take it easy, Mr. Dunleavey. What's the problem?"

Dunleavey spun around and jerked out of Frank's grasp. "Why do you have my daughter's cat? How did you get him?"

Why was the man so angry about the cat, but not asking a thing about the fire? "As my wife just said, we found him on our back deck crying late at night. We took him in, and Penny put up signs hoping to find his owner."

"That's impossible! My daughter's never been to this two-bit town. Mandy's in Italy right now on a summer study abroad program." Dunleavey spoke feverishly as if he were trying to convince himself. "Bruiser is with her college housemates back in Saratoga Springs."

At the name "Bruiser", Yogi's ears pricked up and he meowed. Penny scooped him into her arms. Frank saw her check the cat's ears and her face fell. "He does have a nick in his left ear. I never noticed it before."

"Well, someone brought him here. The cat didn't walk from Saratoga to Trout Run," Frank said.

"I'll get to the bottom of this." Dunleavey pulled out his phone and stabbed a key. Then he barked into the phone without uttering a greeting. "Find the lease I signed for my daughter's house in Saratoga. Text me the names and numbers of the other girls." He clicked off and directed his attention to Frank. "My secretary will have the information we need."

Frank stifled a stab of envy that anyone could have such an efficient assistant. "So while we're waiting, what brings you to Trout Run?"

Dunleavey clasped his hands behind his back and thrust out his chest. "I came to check on my son. His mother is on a trip with her lady friends. I thought we could have some man-to-man time. I went to that store where he has a job, but he's not working today. That's where I saw this sign." He showed Frank the yellow "Found Cat" flyer, then narrowed his eyes. "Why is the police chief in the library in the middle of the day?"

Again, Dunleavey didn't mention the Tabernacle despite having cruised by to look at it. And he seemed not to know his son was seriously injured in the hospital. Frank nodded in Penny's direction. "The librarian is my wife. Are you aware your son is in the hospital?"

A strange expression passed over Dunleavey's face. Frank couldn't interpret it, but it sure didn't look like concern. Before the man could answer, his phone trilled the arrival of a text. He dialed one of the numbers the secretary had sent him and began talking, again without a hello. "This is Mandy's father. I'm calling to check on her cat. Why isn't it there at the house?"

As he listened to the housemate's answer, his eyes widened. "That's impossible. She's in Italy. I put her on the plane myself."

The girl responded something Frank couldn't hear, and Dunleavey's hand dropped to his side. Right before Frank's eyes, the man changed from hard-charging businessman to trembling sufferer. "She says Mandy came and got the cat. She says Mandy canceled her study abroad trip with the school."

Dunleavey's eyes darted back and forth as he attempted to make sense of this information.

"And you had no idea she wasn't in Italy?" Penny asked.

Dunleavey pawed at the library carpet like a panicked horse. "I can't believe she did this. Mandy sent me emails with pictures of the sights of Rome." He searched his phone and squinted at the screen. "She's not in the picture. I thought that meant she was taking it."

Frank looked over the father's shoulder at a shot of three co-eds in front of the Trevi Fountain. "She must have pulled this from her friends' social media."

Dunleavey found an earlier picture. "Here she is waving goodbye to us at Kennedy airport. She must have turned around as soon as her mother and I left the terminal."

Frank gazed at the picture and his heart quickened. The smiling, waving girl looked like a happier, healthier version of the tied-up girl who'd run away from the house where he and Earl had found Charlie.

"Why would your daughter deceive you like that?" Penny's question interrupted Frank's thoughts.

Dunleavey's Adam's apple danced in his neck. The color left his ruddy cheeks. "Mandy must be with her brother." He grabbed Frank's arm. "Where is she? You've gotta help me find her."

Frank thought Dunleavey's behavior was awfully strange. Why would he be so panicked that his daughter was with his son unless he knew his son was a member of a cult? Frank put his hand on the small of Dunleavey's back and guided him toward the door of the library. "Come with me, Mr. Dunleavey. We have a lot to talk about."

Chapter 57

"How long have you known that Charlie was a member of the Tabernacle of Living Light?"

Dunleavey paced the police department office, his agitated turns making papers fly from Frank's desk. "What Tabernacle? You told me Charlie's in the hospital. If he's in Plattsburgh, where's Mandy? Is she with him? Tell me what you know."

"I'm asking the questions here, Mr. Dunleavey."

"I'm calling my lawyer!" Dunleavey started pounding his ever-present phone. Frank began to understand why Charlie wanted to give up his own device. "Go right ahead and lawyer up, Mr. Dunleavey. It'll be hours before your lawyer gets here, if he's even willing to drop everything and come this far. We'll just put the search for your daughter on hold until he arrives."

Dunleavey killed the call. He pointed at Frank and narrowed his eyes. "You know something about Mandy. You've seen her, haven't you?"

"I have. That means I have information you want, and you have information I want. So we're going to make a deal."

"That's outrageous! Your job is to protect an innocent girl. Go out and rescue her right now!"

"My job is to protect the world from an evil charlatan named Adam Fortway. He's responsible for seriously injuring your son. I suspect your daughter is with Fortway and his remaining followers right now. But I don't know where that is. To find them, I need to know more about Fortway. So let's start with when you first met him."

Frank's assumption hit its mark. Dunleavey recoiled and started stammering. "I never...I didn't say I..."

"You came to Trout Run for a reason—to check up on the Tabernacle, not to have a heart-to-heart with Charlie. I saw you gawking at the scene of the fire an hour ago. You must've left home very early, right after Fortway let you know the building had burned. You're able to get in touch with him by phone, correct?"

Frank was speculating, but every guess hit Dunleavey like an arrow to the heart. Unlike a drug dealer or a gangbanger, he had no experience with keeping a poker face while being interrogated by the police. He really should have waited for his lawyer, but he was desperate to find his daughter.

But not his son.

Why?

Dunleavey's shoulders shook. Frank realized the man was crying.

He rubbed at his face and faced Frank. "Mandy loved that cat," he gasped. "She never had a pet growing up because Maeve is allergic. She must've brought the cat to Trout Run because she was intending to stay here with, with...him."

"Her brother?"

"And Fortway."

Frank dug out the "found cat" poster with the handwritten message that had been delivered to the library. He handed it to Dunleavey. "Could this be your daughter's handwriting?"

"Yes, it does look like her writing." Dunleavey read the words aloud, "*Thank you for this news. He was right.* What does that mean? Where did you get this?"

"Someone took down one of my wife's posters and wrote this note on it. Then she...or he... slid it under the library door after hours. It sounded to us like the writer was the owner of the cat and was relieved to hear he was okay. We were puzzled by the 'he was right' but now— "

Dunleavey's gaze met Frank's. "Fortway forced her to give up the cat."

"Kinda looks that way."

Dunleavey jumped up and grabbed Frank's arm. "If this man could persuade her to get rid of Bruiser, he must have tremendous power over her. We've got to find Mandy. We've got to get her out of there."

Mandy. Not Charlie.

Frank studied Dunleavey's face. He had thinning hair that he kept buzzed to avoid a comb-over. His eyes were gray, his brows so pale they were nearly colorless. Mrs. Dunleavey, as Frank recalled, had fine, wispy hair and thin brows. Charlie was tall and thin, like his mother, but where had he gotten that head of thick, auburn hair and those distinctive, bushy eyebrows?

"Charlie's not your biological son, is he?"

Dunleavey wavered as if he was going to object. Then he ran his hands over his bald head and started talking.

"When I met Maeve twenty years ago, she was a struggling young mother with an infant son. She'd been living with a guy, a rock musician—" Dunleavey rolled his eyes— "and when she got pregnant, he said they'd get married. Then he got an offer to tour the country with some band. He took off and left Maeve to manage her pregnancy on her own. And then a week after Charlie was born, the scumbag died when the band's bus crashed."

"That's rough. Charlie knows you're not his birth father?"

"Yes. I married Maeve when Charlie was a year old, and I adopted him, so he'd have my name. Two years later, Maeve and I had Mandy. But we never lied to Charlie. He knew about his birth father, but he always called me Dad."

Called him Dad, maybe. But did Charlie think of Patrick Dunleavey as his father? More importantly, did Patrick consider Charlie his son?

"But you and Charlie aren't close? Not as close as you and Mandy?"

"Mandy was such an easy child. Sunny. Athletic. A good student. Lots of friends. Charlie struggled in school. Couldn't follow directions. Couldn't stick with anything. He's musical, like his father, but he wouldn't practice. Piano, guitar, flute, marimba—he can pick out a tune on them all, but he's not good at any of them. Same with sports. We have a garage full of equipment he used once or twice. Maeve and I argued about what to do. I wanted to send him to military school, but of course she wouldn't hear of that.

"Charlie's high school grades were terrible, but he managed to get into a small, over-priced liberal arts college near Glens Falls." Dunleavy kept talking, lost in his own memories.

Glens Falls. The original home of the Tabernacle of Living Light.

"He changed majors every year, nearly flunked out a couple times, but they wanted my tuition payments, so they kept him. And then senior year, his grades suddenly improved. Maeve saw it as evidence that Charlie had finally come into his own, found his passion. He was a philosophy major. Whatever." Dunleavey waved this notion aside like a sticky cobweb. "I figured he was probably getting laid and the girl was having a good influence on him."

But you were both wrong.

"By this time Mandy had started college at Skidmore. Maeve missed both kids terribly, but she was glad they were only a half an hour from each other. She figured Mandy would be a good support for Charlie."

"Not the other way around?"

"We didn't worry about Mandy. She never gave us any trouble."

"Last Thanksgiving, Maeve was already getting wound up for Christmas. She always goes overboard on gifts for the kids. Charlie said he only wanted one thing—to be able to go on a retreat at the Tabernacle of Living Light to the tune of two thousand dollars. Of course, Maeve had her checkbook out right away. I wanted to know more about it."

Dunleavey stopped talking and massaged his temples.

"So you went to the Tabernacle in Glens Falls and met Fortway?"

"Yes." Dunleavey whispered his answer, unable to make eye contact with Frank.

Silence hung between them. Frank threw Dunleavey a lifeline. "And were you impressed with Fortway? Did you think his retreat would help Charlie?"

Dunleavey shook his head. "I could see the man was a shyster, but I was tired of arguing with Charlie...arguing with Maeve...always being the bad guy. I let him have his way. How was I to know Charlie would get sucked into a cult and drag his sister along with him?"

Frank leaned back in his chair and studied Dunleavey. Nothing about his behavior—today or the last time Frank had met him—suggested a man who capitulated to avoid conflict. No, he had paid two thousand dollars to let his son go on a retreat for a reason.

A self-interested reason.

"Tell me about your work, Mr. Dunleavey."

"Huh? What's my work got to do with anything?"

"Charlie told me you move money around to help the rich get richer. What did he mean by that?"

Dunleavey rolled his eyes and snorted. "Charlie disapproves of the way I earn a living, but he's always been happy to live off the profits of my work."

"Which is...?"

Dunleavey straightened up in his chair. "I'm an asset manager for high net worth individuals."

Frank thought Charlie had summed it up fairly accurately. "And do any of those high net worth individuals happen to own shell corporations based in Delaware?"

Dunleavey reared back as if Frank had slapped him. "Who told you that?"

"I'm not the country bumpkin you take me for, Mr. Dunleavey. I've always thought the source of Fortway's funding was suspicious. I bet when you met the man you saw an opportunity to launder your clients' money through a nonprofit religious institution. You gave Fortway a source of revenue in exchange for access to his accounts, so you could process your clients' money through them as donations."

Frank improvised as he spoke. He didn't truly understand the high-level financial shenanigans Dunleavey had cooked up, but he could see he'd hit close enough to the mark to scare the man.

"This can't get out. I'll be ruined." Dunleavey licked his dry lips and tugged at his shirt collar. "When I first met Fortway, I didn't think he really believed all the things he preached. I thought he was like an actor who never broke character. I offered him legal help to set up the Tabernacle as a 501c3, and get the money he needed to sustain his operation. I thought I was making a simple business transaction. But recently..." Dunleavey shuddered. "I think he's come unhinged. He seems to believe he actually possesses special powers, that he can lead people to some higher level of truth. He talks about his acolytes. Sometimes he won't answer the phone, and I have to talk to this woman named Martha, who sounds even crazier than he is. Fortway creeps me out, honestly."

"So you do have a way to get in touch with him?"

"Yes, I can call him. But half the time, he doesn't listen to me. He goes on these rants. He—"

Frank interrupted. "The fire wasn't an accident, correct?"

Dunleavey took a deep breath and gave his head a quick shake. "I told him I needed a way to incur a big expense that we could write off as a loss, an even bigger loss than it really was. I promised him ten grand if he could pull it off. He started ranting about fire being the purest form of light. Cleansing the spirit through the crucible of flame, blah, blah."

Frank scowled. "Surely you could read between the lines and see what he had planned."

"I thought he'd just damage the building while it was empty." Dunleavey leaned across Frank's desk. "I told him nothing dangerous, I didn't want anyone to get hurt. Is that fire why Charlie's in the hospital?"

"Not the fire at the Tabernacle. Watch this." Frank cued up the video of Charlie on the wildlife cam and watched as Dunleavey's expression changed from idle curiosity to abject horror.

Frank clicked the video off and stared into Dunleavey's eyes. "That's what Fortway is capable of making people do. You never cared that Fortway had Charlie in his grasp. But you want your daughter back. To make that happen, you have to work with me to lay a trap for the man."

Dunleavey dropped his head into his hands. "All right. Tell me what I have to do."

Chapter 58

F rank spoke in front of his assembled troops: Earl, Pastor Bob, Dunleavey, and Rusty McGill.

"What are some of the common threads in Fortway's stunts?"

"Fire," Earl said.

"Wilderness," Rusty added. "The hikes."

"Yes," Dunleavey agreed. "He wanted to leave Glens Falls to get further away from civilization. He liked this location because it was so remote, so wild."

"Music—all those songs at the Tabernacle and at the park before Laurel jumped," Pastor Bob said.

Earl nodded in agreement. "Yeah, and remember Martha sang during her challenge with Billy, and Charlie's lips were moving on the video like he might've been singing."

"Heights," Bob continued. "Laurel jumped off a bridge. Jenna went up on the church roof."

"So what can we offer Fortway that would incorporate some of those elements? Something that would induce him to bring all his followers together for his big finale?"

Dunleavey slammed his ever-present phone onto Frank's desk. "Why can't I just offer him the money I promised, and when he comes to get it, you arrest him and make him tell you where my daughter is?" Dunleavey looked at them all as if they were overlooking the obvious. "I told you I'd testify against him about the money laundering. Isn't that enough?"

Frank spun to face Dunleavey. "You always think you're the smartest person in the room, don't you? Fortway took your daughter to gain power over you, man. He's not going to give her up for one cash payment. We have to use his own narcissism, his need to control others, to bring them all in together."

The men sat in silence staring at Frank. But he didn't have the answer. He'd called them together to help him brainstorm, get inside the head of a fanatic.

Bob spoke first. He had a faraway look on his face. "Something in the mountains...close to whatever force he thinks he's channeling."

"And the fire element—how can we incorporate that?" Frank prodded. Bob understood religious symbolism, rituals. He could imagine how to twist that into something appealing to Fortway.

"You're not starting a fire in the state forest," Rusty protested.

"Not a fire." Bob jumped up. "A fire tower. The highest spot on a mountain, where you go to watch for flames."

"There's a fire tower on Hurricane and a lesser known one on Waverly." Rusty picked up Bob's enthusiasm. "And Tess would know how to lead him there."

"You could tell him that Billy and Charlie are both out of the hospital and want to be reunited with him. That they want to rise up the embrace the light with him." Earl quoted the words Martha had used. "Tell him those two are already at the Waverly fire tower waiting for him and Martha and Mandy. Tell him Charlie has the money."

Dunleavey looked at the faces surrounding him. "This is crazy. How do we know this will work?"

"We don't know." Frank slid Dunleavey's phone across his desk. "But it's our best hope."

Chapter 59

People hear what they want to hear.

Dunleavey called Fortway and delivered the script Pastor Bob and Earl had prepared for him, full of references to rising up to embrace the light while letting the flames burn away their darkness.

The phone call hadn't sounded all that convincing to Frank's cynical ears.

But Martha longed to be reunited with Billy. And Fortway wanted to regain Charlie, his most impassioned follower.

And they all wanted to be closer to the sun to watch the promised flames erupt below them.

So the glittering lure had done its job.

—————◆—————

BEFORE DAWN, FRANK, Earl, Rusty, and several state troopers hiked up to the Waverly fire tower. They made some preparations to set up their trap then took their places. Earl, carefully concealed in the tower; Frank and Rusty behind boulders; and three troopers below outcroppings of rock.

As the sun peeked above the mountaintop, a red knit cap showed through the sparse alpine vegetation at the summit of Waverly.

Rusty spotted it first and silently alerted the others.

Tess stepped into the clearing and scanned the area. A forest ranger has a keen eye for disruptions in the natural environment. Would she spot them?

Frank held his breath, and her gaze passed over him. Tess waved her hand, and a smaller woman in a red tee shirt appeared.

Martha. With a hunting rifle slung over her shoulder.

Where were Fortway and Mandy?

Frank prayed this crazy charade wasn't going to blow up in his face.

"Charlie, Billy—where are you?" Martha shouted. "Reveal yourselves!"

"I'm up here," a hoarse voice answered from the top of the tower. Earl, with the most youthful voice and plenty of exposure to Fortway's line of patter, played his part.

"Charlie?" Martha headed toward the open wooden stairs that led up the outside of the tower. But Rusty and Frank had pulled off the four lowest steps. Martha stood at the bottom, perplexed. "How did you get up there?"

Frank and Rusty exchanged a glance. Martha was falling for their ruse. She believed Earl was Charlie.

"I ascended," the hoarse voice replied. "You can ascend with the master's help. Call him forward."

Frank tensed. Would she go for this?

"Master, come! Help us to rise!"

Hook, line and sinker.

A scramble of footsteps sounded from the trail leading to the summit. Fortway emerged, dressed entirely in red. Behind him, through the trees, Frank could see the movement of people dressed in yellow and blue.

"Where is my sister?" the voice in the tower shouted.

Fortway extended his right hand behind him, and Mandy Dunleavey stepped forward and took it. Together they approached the fire tower.

Everyone they wanted to apprehend stood just yards away.

The tricky part: taking them into custody without anyone getting killed.

"I have passed through the fire and been purified," the voice in the tower called out.

Oh, Earl was good!

Fortway's face lit up with joy. "Yes! Yes, my dear one! You have shown the others the one, true path. Now, they must pass through the flames as you have."

Mandy's eyes grew wide with terror. "No! No, Charlie! Please, don't make me do that. I can't." She yanked her hand out of Fortway's and darted into the woods.

Perfect. Frank pulled out his weapon and steadied it on the rock in front of him. "Drop the gun, Martha," he shouted.

She spun at the sound of his voice but didn't see him.

Tess was more alert. She spotted Frank's weapon and ran straight at him.

"Frank, look out!" Earl called to him in his own voice, horrified by his bird's eye view of the scene below him.

Fortway's head jerked up. "Charlie?"

"The forces of darkness are among us!" Martha swung her rifle around and aimed it at Frank.

A shot rang out from the rocks below the tower.

Martha crumpled to the ground.

"Hold your fire!" Earl shouted to the troopers.

His plea came too late. Tess fell at Frank's feet.

The prophet stood under the steps to the top of the tower.

As the sun burned away the morning mist, and the blue outlines of the Sentinel Range gave way to the circular outline of Lake Placid, Adam Fortway raised his arms to the heavens. Golden beams illuminated his ecstatic face.

"I am rising into the light! I ascend! I ascend!"

Frank yanked his arms down and slapped on the handcuffs.

Chapter 60

"**A**ny more news about how Adam Fortway is surviving in jail?" Penny passed a bowl of black bean salad to Frank and accepted the platter of chicken coming around the dinner table at the Iron Eagle Inn. Lucy and Edwin had invited them to an Indian Summer party before the fall foliage season kicked into high gear. They had all been so busy during the late summer that they hadn't seen one another much.

"The man still hasn't accepted that the plea deal he made let him off easy. He seems surprised he wasn't able to levitate right off that fire tower," Frank said. "They moved him into a protective housing unit after a bunch of inmates beat the crap out of him for preaching his BS nonstop."

"Couldn't happen to a nicer guy," Pastor Bob muttered.

"That's not very Christian." Edwin scolded his friend with a wink as he carried in yet another dish from the kitchen.

"The sentence Fortway is serving for tax fraud isn't anywhere near harsh enough for all the pain and suffering he's caused. We pray for Laurel Caine's father every Sunday." Bob stroked the brilliant red petals of the asters in Lucy's centerpiece. "God works to bring good out of evil. Attendance at church has doubled since the Tabernacle burned. Jeff and Shannon have agreed to take over the youth program. Jeff says they want to give back to the community after all the support they've gotten for Billy. His job at Jackie's goat farm is a good first step for him."

"I guess Gene is happy to be a widower," Penny said. "He'll probably have no problem finding another woman to take Martha's place, but thank goodness it won't be Nadine. She sent him packing."

"And how's Earl?" Lucy asked. "Is he nursing a broken heart over Tess?"

"No," Frank took a big swig of wine to wash down the strange mushroom he'd bitten into. "He had an awkward visit with her while she was recovering from her gunshot wound. She's very focused on the physical therapy she needs to rehab her leg. The psychological therapy—not so much. But Earl and I agreed not to press charges on what happened behind the Tabernacle during the fire."

Edwin frowned over his meal. "I hope Earl doesn't think it's his job to save her."

"Even Earl's kindness has a limit. I think he's sworn off romance for a while."

Frank dove into the food on his loaded plate. "But I couldn't resist following up on Charlie Dunleavey. Unfortunately, he has so much nerve damage to his left hand, he'll never be able to play a musical instrument again. But he's enjoying his job at the Adirondack Museum in Blue Mountain Lake. I think he's turned his life around. He's stopped looking for a father figure."

"And his sister?" Bob asked.

Frank shook his head. "The girl's still in a private psych hospital getting deprogrammed. And her father's struggling to pay for it after dealing with all his legal bills and his alimony."

Lucy refilled Frank's wine glass. "I guess that means Bruiser is going to stay Yogi forever, eh?"

Penny smiled at her husband. "Frank's grown quite fond of him. They discuss the problems of the world every morning over coffee and kibble."

"That cat always agrees with me. What's not to like?" Frank paused in his chewing and studied the morsel of meat on his fork. "Is this marinated tarragon chicken salad?"

Edwin beamed. "I learned to make it myself. That woman, Jocelyn, who used to be a co-owner of the Hungry Loon in Keene, shared her recipe with me. Now that she got her new restaurant going over in Long Lake and our branch of the Hungry Loon has closed, she didn't mind being generous."

Penny sighed. "I'm really sad that our Hungry Loon has closed, but I guess we all should have known Trout Run couldn't support a gourmet market."

"Marge has added curried carrot ginger soup to the rotation at the diner, and the Store has started carrying balsamic vinegar." Edwin clinked his wine glass with Lucy's. "That's our consolation prize from their brush with high-end competition."

The dinner party wound down with more town gossip. After dessert and coffee, Bob announced he needed to get home to put the finishing touches on his sermon. Frank and Penny followed on his heels. Out on the Inn's front porch, Penny gazed up at the sky. "Look at that full moon, risen so early!"

It hung low and golden on the horizon. "The Harvest Moon," Frank said. "It's supposed to illuminate the fields, so the farmers can keep bringing in the late crops."

Penny took her husband's hand. "So this one's a friendly, helpful moon."

"I'm not superstitious."

She rested her head on his shoulder. "I want to believe the insanity that swept through our town is behind us."

Frank gave her a reassuring hug and led her to the car. Once Penny was inside, Frank looked over his shoulder at the glowing orb.

"Don't you ever mess with me again."

<hr/>

THANK YOU FOR READING *Tailspinner*. To help other readers discover this book, please post a brief review on Amazon or Goodreads. I appreciate your support!

Receive a FREE short story when you join my mailing list. You'll get an email whenever I release a new book. No spam, I promise!

Like my Facebook page for funny updates on my writing, my travels, and my dog. Follow me on BookBub for news of sales. Meet me on Twitter and Goodreads, too.

Read these mysteries by S.W. Hubbard

F rank Bennett Adirondack Mountain Mystery Series
The Lure
Blood Knot
Dead Drift
False Cast
Tailspinner

Palmyrton Estate Sale Mystery Series
Another Man's Treasure
Treasure of Darkness
This Bitter Treasure
Treasure Borrowed and Blue
Treasure in Exile

About the Author

S.W. Hubbard writes the kinds of mysteries she loves to read: twisty, believable, full of complex characters, and highlighted with sly humor. She is the author of the *Palmyrton Estate Sale Mystery Series* and the *Frank Bennett Adirondack Mountain Mystery Series*. Her short stories have also appeared in *Alfred Hitchcock's Mystery Magazine* and the anthologies *Crimes by Moonlight, Adirondack Mysteries,* and *The Mystery Box*. She lives in Morristown, NJ, where she teaches creative writing to enthusiastic teens and adults, and expository writing to reluctant college freshmen. She LOVES book groups and would be happy to visit yours in person (in NJ) or via Skype. To contact her or read the first chapter of any of her books, visit: http://www.swhubbard.net.

Made in the USA
Columbia, SC
14 April 2023